The Case of the Flying Corpse

By

James Michael Walker

A Sherlock Holmes Mystery

Library of Congress and Printing information.

First Printing July, 2016
Second Printing December, 2016
Third Printing June, 2017

Printed in the United States of America

ISBN 978-0-9981121-0-7

Prologue

Of the multitude of people I have encountered in my thirty years as a producer of theatrical productions across America and abroad, most I have ignored, some I have befriended, and a few I have loved with all my heart.

I have born witness too many incredible acts, performed by William Hooker Gillette both on stage and off. Through our years working and traveling together, and enjoying life's bounty, we have found ourselves in the midst of an several enigmas in need of unraveling. Always, he has acquitted himself with clarity and panache', and never sought accolades for his brilliant and complex solutions to crimes.

I have recorded many of these accounts, though they still, to this day, remain fallow in my personal cache. They were written by my hand for my amusement alone.

Yet, today as I put pen to paper, I do so with the hope that this narrative may one day come to light. What I am about to describe could have been one of this country's greatest disasters, if not for the deductive crime solving talents of my dearest friend. In this case, my prose is treason to our government which would have severe penalties to our young nation if uncovered. I feel compelled to record this most recent event, and that it be kept secret for one hundred years.

To William Gillette's Friendship

Charles Frohman 5/26/1915

Summons

The day started like any other. I woke, threw on a robe and made my way down to the small dining room for my breakfast and paper.

The house was abuzz with its usual morning weekday activities. My children were running amok, gathering their school papers and each one talking at the top of their collective lungs. Our maids chased them about, dispersing hats, coats, and lunches while my wife orchestrated the entire waltz.

My place was to sit at the table with an open paper and receive my morning greetings from each of them. With the youngest, it was accompanied by a kiss on the cheek and from the older, more often than not, a request for a boon, whether it is for money or permission.

Once they are out the door, the servants go into their routines and I usually spend a few more minutes over my tea and toast, chatting with my wife, Denise, about anything from the household to world events. It was our time to be ourselves, as we were so many years ago.

"So, what stick have you got up your bum this morning?" she asked, raising the tea cup to hide her smile. She couldn't hide the twinkle in her eyes.

"Oh nice talk!" I replied, "From the President of the St. Francis Hospital Auxiliary!"

She laughed, "Don't you try to divert me, and I know when you're sulking. What's bothering you?"

"Brood," I corrected her. "Children and Jewish girls sulk. Men brood."

She just looked at me. After thirty years she knew better

than to let me off on a tangent. "Oh, I don't know!" I raised my arms and waved my hands around, "I'm just feeling all this sameness our lives has become! Remember the day when I had to get out of bed. Had to go to work? Hustling day to day just to make ends meet?"

Denise reached over and patted my hand. "Is it really all that bad, dear? We live in a beautiful home and our children and family are well provided for. We want for nothing and have enough to last us the rest of our lives with plenty to leave behind! Isn't that what you worked hard for all these years?"

"Well, sure," I grunted. "But now what?"

She had no answer but to smile and let out a little laugh. "You're just bored, dear. You always get moody in the off season. Just keep yourself busy until your trip to London. You'll feel better once you're back on the water."

She knows me so well.

"Alright then," I smiled, "I guess I'll 'put on my togs and gussy up', as Pop would say. Might as well go to the office and see why I spend a fortune in payroll."

"That's the spirit, you old shark! Now, will you need the carriage? I was hoping Leon could take me to a committee meeting."

And so I found myself riding the New York City trolley that morning. Not that I minded, it was at least a small change in my routine and I actually enjoyed it. It was a two block walk after I got off, but one of those blocks belonged to me.

I bowed at the front door, crossed the lobby, accepting and bestowing greetings on my staff like I was royalty, and then took a private elevator to the top floor. Once there, I just sat at my clean topped desk, slowly coming to the realization that I had little or nothing to do this day. After ten minutes or so, I began to brood again.

It occurred to me that success was twofold. At times, it was a golden cape one flaunted for the world, and other times, it was an iron shackle, no different from the one that held a slave to a galley's oar in ancient times.

Perhaps it was my middle age. The sands of time slowly wearing the sparkle off my spirit, like the ocean and tides that make sea glass. I found myself longing for the days when I lived in a three story walk up, penning my scripts, then dogging them up and down the theater district, desperate for a chance.

Now, I pay people to write scripts. In fact, I pay people to find the people who write them. Then I pay more people to find directors and production people to stage them and more staff to find and woo the actors. I even pay people to hire the people who hire them!

As much as I try to keep my hands in, I really just write the checks and nod at the business meetings, especially around this time of year. The season was winding down and most of us were looking for a respite before the summer stock began.

I was thinking all this as I sat in my corner office, looking out floor to ceiling windows on either side with a view on a dreary spring day. The air was thick with moisture, a heavy mist trying to be a drizzle, and it was still cool enough to seem raw.

The dampness did nothing to improve the mounds of grime and debris left over from the heavy snows of winter. I sat there, just thinking how ugly New York looked on such a gray morning, with the only bright spot being the view of Central Park from the window at my right. Though the trees were bare and what little snow remained huddled beneath them, it was far cleaner and emptier than the busy streets below me. Perhaps I mused; I just needed to get out of the city for a while.

I had inherited my great grandmother's house in

Amagansett when she passed away last fall and was planning on using it for a family summer home, even though most of my family was there already. I'm still hesitant about having a second home for vacationing where the rest of my family made their living.

I had half a plan for the weekend when there was a sharp rap on my office door and my personal assistant let herself in, spitting drivel at me as soon as she was in range of my hearing. She used to just be my secretary until she gave herself a raise and the title to go with it. Not that I should complain, she runs the office like a well-oiled machine and handles most of the day to day fiddle-faddle.

Only lately, whenever she puts on her glasses to read my itinerary, it's like she put on my ring! 'Personal nag' was a more fitting title for her.

I was saved from having to hear her out when a small lad past her hips and did a quick step to get past her hand that was about to snare his collar. The blur solidified in front of my desk and, suddenly, I had a more interesting visitor, a uniformed street urchin, scruffy around the edges, about eight or nine years old, wearing a shiny messenger service vest and breathing hard. He held out a telegraph to me, stiff armed, without a word. His face held the perfect combination of trepidation and determination that only a young boy can achieve.

The nag stepped forward about to collar him with one long fingered hand, most likely wringing his neck in the process, when I shot her a look and held up one finger. She froze as I held up the rest of my hand and she straightened and backed up a step.

I turned my attention back to the kid. I had a feeling his telegram was going to be the highlight of my day. Shaking my head in mock dismay, I plucked it from his hands and said to the lad, half joking, "You know, I paid a lot of money for that contraption," I gestured to the new candlestick shaped telephone on my desk. "And I'm still getting these!" as I waved the telegraph paper.

The kid, who looked quite worldly in his mannerisms, shrugged. "Ain't puttin nutin wit dat electricity next to my head!" He seemed surprised he answered and quickly added, "Sir!"

When I saw who and where it was sent from, I knew my hunch was right. I sat back and took a cigarette from the box on my desk. Used to be a cigar box but I had to put them away for the time being. Doc said the harsh smoke was burning out my mouth and he steered me towards the cigarettes. I noticed the lad's eyes following my every movement, so I turned the box around and offered him one.

"Thanks, Sir!" he said with real appreciation and then tucked the smoke behind his ear and waited patiently for me to read the note.

I was impressed by his manners, "Go ahead, young man, take another, join me for one while you wait for a reply."

Eyes gleaming, he took another and had a match popped before I could shut the lid. He took a long drag then offered me the light. We both puffed away in contentment for a moment. It did my heart good to see the lad take to it so. Everyone knows smoking cures an array of discomforts and the sooner they start the better they'll live.

The telegraph read:
The Seven Sisters are ready to accommodate. STOP.
Need a man of your experiences urgently. STOP.
Can you be in New London by four pm.? STOP.
I will meet you at station. STOP. WHG"

I scribbled a hasty acceptance and handed it to the messenger, along with a fiver. His eyes nearly bulged out of his head. Stammering his thanks and beaming ear to ear, he took off at a dead run.

Despite the protests of my assistant, I wasn't far behind him. I would need every minute of the morning if I were to make New London by four o'clock. While one of my secretaries made arrangements for my rail ticket, I telephoned my wife and told her where I was going. She wasn't thrilled, but she was used to my sudden departures and absences, so I collected a kiss over the wire and she sent my dearest friend her regards.

I keep an apartment in the building, for when I'm stuck late, or need to rest or refresh between meetings and shows. I packed a bag with a few changes and some essential toiletries and had just enough time for a brief stop at the Drake hotel to get a survival kit from my favorite bartender, Donnie.

In short order, I found myself heading out of New York City and up the Connecticut coastline in a private compartment on the 12:42 train.

Fixing myself a martini from my traveling larder, I sat back to watch the urban landscape change to rural. By the time I finished the first one, I felt the hustle and bustle of the Big Apple slowly drain from my system. On one side, Long Island Sound sparkled in the bright spring air and on the other, stone walls and fields stretched as far as the eyes could see. I started to realize why my friend had chosen such a quiet, barren wilderness in which to build his home, though I wish that he was closer to the city.

I took out his telegraph and read it again chuckling to myself. Only old friends and long married couples know how to manipulate each other with such precision. William would only make a request on such short notice if he needed my help – what has he got himself into I thought. My friend knew exactly how to word his telegraph that would pique my interest. I had just folded the telegraph and put it back inside my pocket when suddenly the door

11

to my private compartment popped open.

Standing there, one hand on the doorknob, was the most adorable little girl I had seen in quite a while, at least since my daughter was the same age. She was seven or eight years old wearing a paisley printed dress white stockings and white buckle shoes. Her reddish brown hair cascaded in curls down across her shoulders and back, and her gap toothed smile lit up the compartment.

"Well, hello my dear and what can I do for you?"

She did not answer me, but simply stepped inside the compartment, closed the door behind her softly, and hopped up on the seat across from me. She smoothed her dress out, folded her hands in her lap, and beamed at me again. "Good morning, Sir. My name is Isabella."

"That is a very pretty name, and what brings you to my private compartment?"

She shrugged, and smiled at me again, "It was the only door that wasn't locked."

That tickled my fancy, but as a parent, I knew it wasn't a good idea to encourage that type of behavior. I tried to look stern, yet kindly, and admonished her, "Well, it is nice of you to drop in for a visit, but young ladies should not intrude into private cars. It might not be safe. There are a lot of bad people out there in the world. Where is your Mommy?"

"Oh, she's taking a nap with my baby brother. I got bored so I decided to go exploring. Who are you?"

I sat back in my seat. 'Now, there was a question', I thought to myself. The son of a fisherman, I grew up in the small village of Amagansett, located on the south fork of Long Island. My family had been fishermen and bay men for generations. Except for three months out of the year, fishing was too cold, boring most of the time, too wet, and smelly all of the time.

I was always more of a dreamer, thinking of myself as a

young American Dickens, and I knew that I would never get to show my stuff in a backwater burg like the Hamptons. So shortly after I finished school I headed to the big city with dreams of becoming a writer. Working various jobs, I was a dishwasher, a boiler man, a watchman, and a few occupations I'm not proud to admit. I managed to worm my way into backstage jobs at theater and lived to survive while I learned the ropes enough to squeak out a few mediocre screenplays. I even had a few acting parts in productions. I was a regular jack-of-all-trades of the theater.

But I soon realized my true calling was theater organization. I could talk a seagull off a fishing boat and soon I was making money with young theater talent -a natural for falling into the role of a producer.

After a few successes, my reputation grew and I formed a syndicate along the east coast. Soon, we pretty much controlled the theater business from the Carolinas to Boston and branched out overseas to London. I would love to say it was hard work and perseverance that brought me so much wealth and success, but the truth is, I owed it mostly to one man. The man I was going to visit.

"My name is Charles Frohman," I answered.

"Well Mr. Charles Frohman, we are going for a visit to my Aunt Lucy's in Rhode Island," Isabella stated. "Why are you on the train?"

"I am going to visit a very old friend of mine. He has built a new home in a town called Haddam." And before she could ask me, I added, "His name is William Gillette."

The little cherub tilted her head sideways and asked, "Who's that?"

I chuckled. Only a child or a hermit would ask that question!

William Hooker Gillette was undoubtedly the greatest actor of our time, a household name. Not only has he starred in thousands of productions, he has written many successful plays, and single-handedly brought the phenomenon of the great Sherlock Holmes to the America public.

Actor, writer, and a stage manager of unbelievable talent and you could also add inventor to his resume. Many features of today's modern lighting and sound effects were of his device. Watching one of his plays was as close to actually being there as possible.

We met at my wedding, when I married his late wife's second cousin. At the time, I was just starting out as a producer and William offered me a chance to produce one of his plays, the now famous production, "Secret Service".

It was a huge success and our partnership has held firm ever since. In fact, a lot of the influence that I used to form the syndicate came from my relationship with William. But, crazy as it may sound, what I really missed was watching him work.

It was absolutely amazing to watch him transform into whatever character he was portraying. I have seen thousands of actors in my day, some great, many mediocre, and some not worth the rotten tomato to throw at, but none could match William's single minded focus as he played the role of Sherlock Holmes.

I introduced Arthur Conan Doyle to William in 1885, when I first brought my syndicate to Europe. Doyle was the brilliant creator of the Sherlock Holmes character and mysteries. Doyle's writing was complex and only for the most literate and William was brilliant and loved to read Doyle's works. They have been friends ever since and I was there when Doyle gave William carte blanch with the character, for he knew William would continue to craft the character of Sherlock Holmes.

William took full advantage of the offer and really brought Holmes from Strand Magazine's printed pages to a vibrant stage presence.

Look at any rendition of a drawing of Sherlock Holmes in the last five years and you'll see they all look like William Gillette. It was he who donned the deerstalker cap and cape and coined the phrase "Elementary, my dear Watson," symbols he made synonymous with the famous detective.

William Gillette's writing, directing, and acting in so many productions, with me in the producer's seat, made us both wealthy men. Over the many years of our association, our mutual respect grew into a lifelong friendship that is stronger than blood.

William had decided to 'retire' again and high tailed it up the coast to build himself a permanent home. This was William's first in thirty years, as he generally rented or lived aboard his yacht.

My mind continued to wander until I heard a polite little cough across from me. It was then I noticed my glass was nearly empty and the child was still there.

"He's a very famous actor." I kept it short.

"Does he have any children?" she asked sweetly.

"No, he doesn't." And he probably won't I thought to myself, as I poured another drink and mused on.

The love of his life, his wife, Helen, passed away years ago, and in an ugly way. Since then, William has shown no interest in a lasting relationship. Both my wife and I always thought it a shame they never had children before she fell sick.

He had always been something of a loner but it became more pronounced after Helen left us. Though he has many admirers, and legions of associates, I am fairly certain that I am his only steady friendship outside of his household, male or female. If there has been any dalliance with the fairer sex, and I'm more than sure there have been, I was not privy to the details. He is an extremely private person and the very definition of discretion.

I will attest he was always wonderful to my children, lavishing them with gifts on birthdays and Christmas. Ironically, he had a deep, genuine love of children and would have been an excellent parent, though I think the role of "favorite uncle" was all he wished for at this stage of his life. Over the years, I've come to believe that Ozaki and whatever employees he had on his personal payroll was enough family for him.

Suddenly, I was uncomfortable, as I realized that the young girl just sat across from me silently the entire time as I sipped and daydreamed. My embarrassment was cut short by a cry I heard out in the hallway over the clacking of the train tracks. A woman was calling for Isabella. The little girl hopped off the seat and opened the door.

"I'm in here, Mama," then she came back inside and sat down again.

A matronly looking woman holding a young baby against her breasts popped her head inside. "Isabella," she barked crossly, "what are you doing in here?"

"Not to worry, Madam," I cut in, not wanting Isabella to get in Dutch with her mother, "Your daughter has been delightful company."

"I am so sorry she disturbed you, sir. The baby fell asleep and then I dozed off. When I awoke, she was gone. This one needs a leash," she gestured to her daughter, "Come along Isabella, and let's leave the nice gentleman alone."

So we bid each other farewell and her mother took Isabella firmly in tow back to their seats. I went back to my martini and my relaxation and moved over to let the morning sun warm me. I must have slipped into a nap somewhere shortly after New Haven, for I awoke as I felt the train slow and heard the conductor cry out, "New London!" and rapped on my door.

16

Port of Call

I was slow coming around and didn't get my focus until the porter rapped harder on my door and repeated our stop again. My little catnap had turned into a full blown siesta. I woke a bit disoriented and muddled from the martinis. You would think I'd know better than to drink mid day on an empty stomach. I was half wondering if I had dreamed of the little girl.

I also started getting more than a little nervous about the transportation William would provide from the station to his new home, which, if I remembered right, was nearly twenty miles away. I groused to myself as I gathered my things.

I knew damn well it wouldn't be a nice carriage with good springs and a strong team to pull it!

It would be some motorized new contraption that had four wheels. I was damned if I was in any condition to take an hour long death ride.

So, I was pleasantly satisfied when I stepped off the train to find myself face to face with my escort and no steel ponies in sight.

Trim, ram rod straight with his head slightly bowed, he was spotless from spats to bowler and just as Asian as I remembered him.

"Ozaki! Where the hell have you been?" I roared, just to trip him up a little. He was the most 'Johnny-on-the-spot' servant the western hemisphere has ever hosted. Not only had he discovered what door I would exit the train from, he already had retrieved my luggage and had it piled onto a small cart behind him. Japs were clever that way. An Irishman would still be trying to read the arrivals board

17

inside the station.

"Ah. Mr. Frohman. It is very good to see you; I hope your journey was present?"

I knew what he meant. Ozaki and I went back a long way. I was with William when he took Ozaki on as his personal valet many years ago. As a point in fact, Ozaki wasn't really his name at all.

When he first came to this country, and his English was rudimentary at best, he misunderstood the question; "What is your name?" for "Where are you from?" He was from a town called Ozaki, so the name stuck. Even William used it now. It was easier to pronounce us ugly Americans.

William wasn't there to greet me. Wherever he went, he was mobbed by crowds of adoring fans. I assumed he had a carriage waiting for us, but to my surprise, Ozaki led me away on foot, toward the docks. I knew what that meant and I was delighted by the prospect.

New London was a thriving seaport and the docks and piers were bustling with activity. I was amazed at the level of activity. There wasn't an empty berth as far as I could see in both directions. Two berths being taken by navy frigates, one with sails and one a coal fired steamer.

Drunken sailors, streetwalkers, merchants and dockworkers all wove an orchestrated dance of commerce. There were ships of every type from barges to whaling ships, the latter which gave off an odor that threatened to bring up the gin I drank on the train.

Ozaki skillfully threaded his way through the crowd but it didn't prevent an obviously inebriated sailor clutching a barfly in a one armed bear hug from stepping directly in front of him. Ozaki nearly knocked the floozy off her feet.

The sailor, a rather large specimen and even more imposing in his uniform, quickly stood upright then whirled on Ozaki.

"Ya stupid clumsy yellow monkey! What the hell do you

think you're doing?" He balled his fists and went up on his toes.

I could see every muscle in Ozaki's neck tense and I knew his temperament well. He was more than capable of giving this swab the rough side of his tongue when he had his dander up.

I stepped in front of Ozaki to defuse the situation. I tipped my hat to the woman and made a slight bow, "Our pardon, Miss. Please accept our apologies," I said in my most charming manner. She giggled and nodded.

The sailor wasn't ready to let it go. He leaned in closer, not a foot from my face and growled. "What's it to you, Toff? Is this monkey yours?"

I placed the tip of my cane between my feet and stared back at him, unafraid. Though I was older and slower than my brawling days, I had experience on my side and a twenty-five caliber - two shot derringer disguised as the handle of my cane. I always took it when I traveled. In one motion I could draw it, cocked automatically, before he could pull his arm back to throw a punch.

His eyes were a bit wild with drink but he was sober enough to be a bit uncertain at my calmness. Keeping my right hand on the cane, I took a bill from my pocket with my left and held it out to him.

"Be off with you, lad. Go buy your lady a drink."

He must have been low on funds, because he just snatched the bill and his girl, in that order, and grinned.

"Thanks, Mister!" he stammered as he rushed off, the skirt in tow.

Ozaki looked up at me, shaking his head with a serious expression.

"There was no need to pay him, Mr. Frohman. He was drunk and I would not have hurt him if I could avoid it."

I just wanted to burst out laughing, but couldn't for the seriousness of Ozaki's manner. The last thing I wanted to

19

do was offend him at the beginning of my trip.

"I couldn't take the chance," I said with a solemn face.

"You should have more faith in me," he muttered as he set off again.

Luckily, just past the whaler was a three masted trader sloop, and then the Aunt *Polly*, William's yacht, though the term 'yacht' doesn't really describe her correctly. She looked more like a floating hotel, with two stories and a large open deck above. A glassed in wheel house graced the front of her, giving her bow a snub look.

Not designed for deep water, it was essentially a long house with a small bow and an open deck at the stern. She was built for comfort, rather than the high seas, a one hundred forty foot houseboat, that looked like she'd turn turtle with a sneeze, yet she had logged a lot of miles in style.

Ozaki plowed on through the small crowd that had gathered along the pier, slowly strolling the length of the *Aunt Polly*, trying to peek in the windows while not seeming rude. I slowed my pace as a wave of nostalgia hit me, thinking of all the good times and trips William and I had taken on her. It had been a few years since I had been aboard.

The old girl looked great. Freshly painted, her brass sparkling in the afternoon sun and every piece of glass gleaming, she looked as good or better with age. Standing loosely at attention, on the railing at the end of the boarding plank was one of the reasons why, I surmised.

He had to be one of the two men that William had hired to take care of the *Aunt Polly*.

Initially, I was surprised when William had written and explained that he had taken on a crew. He and Ozaki had always kept the ship in spades since he bought it years ago. But he went on in great lengths in his letters that he and Ozaki had enough to do just building the new estate, never mind keeping up the *Aunt Polly,* building her dock and moorings.

I further assumed that he was the mate. He was a youngish man, middle to late twenties, handsome and fit, if a bit small in stature, with an unruly mop of jet black hair. His apparel was not quite a uniform, white pants and shirt with a canvas belt, but his black shoes shined so I surmised it wasn't his regular work clothes.

I thought him a bit of a pipsqueak when I got closer, and I wondered how he fared with some of the heavier tasks a crewman must perform. That is, until Ozaki, stormed up the plank and onto the deck, snarling instructions at the lad and rudely gesturing for him to get my bags.

The boy gave Ozaki an insolent look as he passed by. With the barest of nods and no eye contact, he easily hoisted all three of my bags off the cart and began to stroll slowly back up the gangway past Ozaki again. The lad didn't look at Ozaki but everything about his casual saunter, even under the weight of my baggage, said "Fiddle dee dee!"

'That's my boy!', I chuckled to myself.

It was just like Ozaki to be harsh with Will's employees. After so many years together, he was overprotective of Will to a fault. He was jealous of anyone who got close to Will. It took us a long time to get used to each other. Worse than a best friend's wife in that regard.

I stepped across the plank, but stopped before I set foot on the deck. This was a ritual me and Ozaki played out, except once, when I snuck on board, many years ago.

"Permission to come aboard?" I asked formally.

Ozaki smiled and gave me a low bow, then straightened. "Now and forever, Charles Frohman," he replied. Then he abruptly headed off along the gangway to get drinks and a snack for me. I was left to find my friend. I sauntered across the small deck and let myself through the double

21

french doors that led into the salon. There he sat, lounging in a chair with one of the ever present cats in his lap.

He rose gracefully, fluidly extending his long, lanky frame until all 6 foot something of him was standing. He automatically posed, back straight, head high and one foot pointed slightly off to one side. His every movement was slightly exaggerated though graceful. He was the personification of what Shakespeare meant when he wrote "All the world's a stage." William's eyes brightened with happiness and we embraced.

"Charlie! It's good to see you, my oldest friend. How was your trip? I hope Denise isn't too cross with me for luring you away on short notice." He always loved to tease me about being henpecked.

"Never think it Will!" I countered, "I doubt the old girl would realize I'm not around for a least a week. We have plenty of time to drink and wench before she sends out the dogs." William neither drank nor chased women. As a rich, wealthy and handsome celebrity, he had no need to chase anything.

He laughed, "The drink I can help you with," he said, gesturing at the cabinet where Ozaki was already pulling out a bottle, "But I'm afraid you'll find the wenching to be slim pickings where we're going."

"Not to worry, my boy! At our age, it's quality we're looking for, not quantity." I felt the big diesel engines rumble to life under my feet as Ozaki handed me a Sherry. Dock lines were cast off and the Aunt Polly gracefully eased away from the docks as onlookers strained for a peek.

Will was eager to take me on the nickel tour of the *Aunt Polly*. "The old girl's had been refitted since you were last on her," he explained. Our first stop was the wheelhouse where I was introduced to the new crew.

Captain John Roy was a tall, lanky fellow, whose frame

suggested a powerful quickness about him. He was sporting a full beard, with an unruly patch of sandy colored hair spilling out from under a Greek fisherman's hat. His dark blue pants were crisply creased and a Captain's jacket fit perfectly over a clean starched shirt and tie showing he took pride in his appearance. He looked the consummate yachtsman. Captain Roy even had a tiny anchor hung from his tie clasp.

"Welcome aboard matie...ah...er...Mr. Frohman," he bellowed, and took my hand in his enormous paws. "Tis a pleasure having you aboard! Mister Gillette tells me you are no stranger to the *Aunt Polly*. I be thinking ye'll be amazed at the work we've dun to her. She's ship shape in Bristol fashion."

"As long as you get me to Will's house with dry feet, I'll be satisfied, Captain Roy."

"Har!" he barked, "Have no fear, Mister Frohman. In five of the Seven Seas and all the oceans, I haven't had a ship go out from under me!"

I just smiled and turned my attention to the younger man I had seen on the deck that was standing off to one side. "Charles Frohman," I said to him, holding out my hand.

The lad yanked his cap from his head and clutched it to his chest with his left hand while shaking with his right.

"Nickolas Ivanovich. I am the first mate," he said in acceptable eastern European accented English.

"Har, the first of one!" The captain barked and then laughed loudly, never taking his eyes off the harbor water as we made the river's mouth.

Nickolas's face flushed with an embarrassed anger, but I quickly brought his attention back,

"Well, you're doing a fine job. I've never seen her look so clean and polished," I assured him to take the sting out of the Captain's remark. He grinned ear to ear and almost seemed to blush at the compliment.

Unfortunately, from the wince on Will's face, I knew I made a major faux pas, but didn't realize what it might have been until I looked over my shoulder. Ozaki had slipped onto the bridge and was standing right behind me.

That innocent comment was like a slap to Ozaki's face, who was the primary caretaker of the *Aunt Polly* before these two were hired. His work was his honor and I had just rated it inferior. Something like that could turn him into one of those demon warriors his society produced.

His eyes were like the slits of a snake and his nostrils flared. Having left my cane in the salon, I was ready to jump overboard, but thankfully, Will saved the moment.

"Ozaki, would you be so kind as to fix us a light lunch? We'll have it in the salon as soon as we finish our tour."

Ozaki shot the crew a venomous look, gave me a haughty sniff and nodded to William before he walked, stiff backed, out of the wheel house.

"Be this the first time ye been in these waters?" Roy asked cordially over his shoulder, "Mister Frohman, Sir?"

I almost laughed out loud at his mannerism, but kept a straight face. "In these waters? No. But I have passed through this area on my way to Norwich. One of my production companies did a season there a few years ago. My longer sailing trips," I added with a smile, "are usually in that direction." I pointed out towards the horizon in what I hoped was the general direction of Europe.

"Well, we have a good port. Quiet most times, though you just missed some big doings by a few watches." Captain Roy seemed eager to tell me the news, perhaps one of the reasons I was summon from New York city on such short notice.

"Which I will fill you in on after our lunch," William cut in smoothly. "So, we had better finish our tour before Ozaki finishes preparing it."

"Yeah, I suppose we should." I answered with a sigh. "I

guess his feathers are ruffled enough. Even for an old buzzard like him."

Nickolas giggled like a school girl at how William cut off the Captains chit-chat.

We went through the door and down a few steps into what William always called the hold. When the noise of the engines could mask our voices, Will asked me, "What do you think of the crew?"

"Your captain needs a parrot and a peg leg and somewhere in Russia there's a cow still waiting to be milked." I replied.

Will laughed, "Oh, How I've missed your humor. But you're right. Roy can over do the sea dog bit, but he's competent and works hard, or at least keeps Nicky working hard at keeping the *Aunt Polly* going. And Nicky isn't the rube you may think he is. The few conversations I had with him tells me he's educated."

"Will, so he made it to sixth grade." I teased, "He was blushing for Pete's sake and he seems shy around the captain. A rube! Or rather an Americanized Russian."

He shook his head and sighed, "It's good to see your perceptions are still keeping pace with your mind set."

"Harsh but true, Will." I admitted with a laugh. "Well, you always were a sucker for stray characters."

"Now, I'll admit they are a couple of characters, but they've done a bang up job so far. Aside for some wasteful spending, Captain Roy has exceeded my hopes for the docks. Wait until you see the mooring rope system they constructed! Roy and Nicholas are in the process of refurbishing a launch for me."

"Really, you bought a second boat? I can't believe it! Planning on downsizing? What is she? "

I guess I should have let him answer one question at a time, but he just laughed and replied,

"Yes, of course, not!...and a twenty-four foot runabout,

but that's all I really know about it right now."

When I cocked an eyebrow at him he explained, "Roy told me that Nicky wanted to surprise me when it was finished, so I haven't seen her refit yet."

He shrugged, "I will need something smaller and more maneuverable to use on the river," he explained, "The *Aunt Polly* is too big to go back and forth to town. Truth is Charlie, since we moved into my home, we haven't spent much time on the old girl. In fact, last summer I gave Roy the use of the stateroom full time and Nicky is in Ozaki's old room. I feel better with someone living on board rather than letting the old girl sit and rot."

"And it saves you the money you had to put out for their lodgings every month," I teased him.

He snorted, "That too! But, truth be told, this is the longest trip I made in over a year. The house has taken all my attention which is a pity with all the improvements they've made. Seriously, take a look at these engines. You won't recognize them."

I didn't and I was impressed. Many a time William, Ozaki, and I had to monkey with the motors when one thing or another went wrong, but this was far beyond our tinkering. The engine was two feet longer than it was and the new drive shafts were two inches thick. I raised an eyebrow at him.

"I think you'd see it right away" Will said as he lifted back the housing cover, "She's got eighteen inch props now and 40 more horsepower. She'll do nearly twenty knots on flat water."

"Planning on bringing back the slave trade or smuggling?" The copper tubing and brass fittings gleamed in the soft glow of the lamps. The cylinders had been bored out making room for pistons that were an inch bigger that the old ones. This was beyond an overhaul. It was a total engine refit, "Seems like a lot of expense for such an old boat. Why not just buy a new one?" I teased him.

He looked at me like I had three heads. "Sell *Aunt Polly*? Have you gone mad, sir? I'd sooner send Ozaki back to Japan!"

"I'm just pulling your leg." Then my eyes caught sight of a new contraption tucked in just under the aft decking. I walked over to get a closer look. Three cylindrical tanks sat upright in a row, connected by various pipes, each seemed to have a valve and a dial that measured PSI. I recognized this type of machinery from my boilermaker days, but I didn't understand why it was here.

"Why the air compressors?" I asked.

"Ah! That's a new design for the bilge system. Roy claims it's his own design, but I have always thought Nickolas was behind it, as he did most of the installing. The idea is, after making the inner hull and bilge airtight, the compressed air can be pumped into the bilges to force the water out and hopefully keep the ship afloat until it can be beached or the breech repaired.

"That's a novel idea. One heck of a bilge system. Are you going to patent it? This could be a moneymaker if the design really works." I said to Will.

I was surprised to see how high some of the gauges read, though they were all dormant at the moment. But I also knew, you'd have to pump a lot of air to keep the *Aunt Polly* afloat for long.

"I know, I said the same thing to Roy. He said it passed all the tests. He swears by it."

"Tests?" I questioned, "How would you go about testing it. Run over a rock? Hit an iceberg? Even if you open the seacocks, it's a measured flow in!"

"Believe me, I asked the same question, I mean, if it's only theoretical, what's the necessity of it? And the cost! It wasn't cheap, I can tell you. But do you know what he said to me?"

I shrugged.

Will scrunched up his face and replied in a great imitation of Roy, "When you be out on the open waters and the seas be a-comin' in faster than it agoin' out, that's when your problems get bad! Ye'll be a thankin' ole captain John then for his foresight!"

I laughed, "Makes sense, if you look at it that way," then something caught my eye. For such a big lump of machinery, there was only a small hose that handled the outflow through a hole in the hull. "But doesn't that hose look kind of small. I remember the other outflow was twice the size on the old pump."

"Ah, that's the other twist. Apparently, excess air can be bled out through a special valve in the hull. Thus, you can adjust the pressure from the bridge. If the old girl was heavy on one side or listing for any reason, she could turn turtle in a flash! A good safety measure. The Captain and Nicky said it worked fine when they tested it, though I'm not sure I'm convinced."

"The meal is ready!" Ozaki cut him off from the port hatch that lead up to roughly the middle of the ship. His tone had just the right mix of annoyance at having to prepare it and he couldn't give a fat rat's ass if we ate it.

I took out my watch, subtracted six hours and, indeed it was four in the afternoon already.

Then he muttered in a voice just loud enough for us to hear, "I can but hope my cooking skills have not diminished, as my boat keeping has!" He finished with a heaving sigh and shuffled off like he was one hundred and four years old all of a sudden.

Will shook his head and gave me a look of reproach. "I wish you'd be more careful what you say around him."

"I know. I know," I replied, "I'll fawn over the lunch.

28

That usually works."

"You're a good man, Charles Frohman." he said, patting me on the shoulder.

'Damn!', I thought to myself as I followed him up the short stairs, 'Probably going to try and feed me that raw fish again.'

Happily, I was mistaken.

Lunch

Ozaki brought us platters, heaped with local scallops, a rice noodle dish he made from scratch, artisan breads, and various fruits and cheeses. All foods I loved. William and I had a great time catching up, chit chatting about the business sprinkled with a little gossip about others we knew from the theater.

William commented, "I often miss the orchestrated chaos of our business. Things move at a much slower pace out here in the country. I do enjoy it, but it can be a bit too slow."

"You mean frustrating - to get everyone to move at your pace," I teased him.

He started to protest but I cut him off, "William! Face it. You and I know that you're building this home like you'd put on a production. Now tell me I'm lying!"

He laughed and gave in, "I suppose you're right." He gave me a sly smile, "It did take quite a while for the local tradesmen to get on the same page with me."

He hesitated for a moment and his face grew a bit long, the smile slowly fading away. Whatever he was thinking was troubling him.

"It has been difficult making adjustments and settling in these parts. But we can talk of that later, over brandies after dinner."

I knew something was bothering him deep down, and my years in his company told me that it was part of the reason he summoned me here this weekend. He'd tell me when he was ready. It's like I told my children: true friendship isn't about camaraderie, or honesty, it's about respect.

30

Respecting the other person's wishes and timing.

"Well, what was Captain Roy trying to tell me, back in the wheelhouse when we first met, without breaking into a sea chantey? Something about "big doin's a few watches ago?"

"Oh Yes," he brightened visibly, "That slack jawed buffoon nearly let the cat out of the bag!" As if on cue, one of Will's cats jumped up into his lap. William began to stroke its head slowly and went on,

"After all these years of mundane, something particularly intriguing has happened."

"So what was the big surprise?" I asked, goading him on as he seemed to rise out of his funk.

"Not a surprise, Charlie. A genuine mystery! One of robbery, murder and mutilation! Thus the real reason I summoned you on such short notice. I have been thinking about it nonstop since I first heard word of it yesterday morning and, as of now, unsolved." As he looked up from petting the cat, I saw his face change. It seemed to grow longer, with sterner features, with a concentration cast to the eyes that danced beneath raised eyebrows. He looked different. Like another type of William Gillette. I had a sick feeling I knew then where this was going.

I was pole-axed. I didn't know what to say, but I never know when to shut up so I had to ask, "What are you talking about?"

Will gently put the cat to the floor and half stood up, I assume to mark our position. He nodded with satisfaction then settled back into the sofa.

"There should be enough time, at least for a synopsis. I'll tell you what little I know from what I gleaned from my sources."

"Wait. What sources? Why do you have sources?" I wasn't trying to be rude, but his intensity merited some extra details.

William laughed, "Just a fancy term for my cook and house keeper. They keep me apprised of all the local gossip."

"Really?" I asked, "It's not like you to get so worked up on gossip. You usually shun it."

"Yes, well, though I still feel it's repulsive, I have been forced over the past year to pay more attention to gossipy details. Besides," he amended with a wink, "my housekeeper's uncle is a sergeant on the Chester police force and she overheard the whole story when he told it to his brother."

"AH! Straight from the horse's mouth!" I put my drink down and folded my hands in my lap.

He leaned back, crossed his legs, and steepled his hands at his waist.

"The night before last, Wednesday, the Chester-Had Lyme Ferry, which we will pass our way shortly, was chartered for a special run at dusk, about seven o'clock. As it was a simple run, the captain had just two of his crew manning the ferry along with himself.

The special trip was for one carriage, pulled by a team of six horses. There were only two people with the carriage. A driver and one occupant, who was not seen until he was found later."

"Found where?"

"Found dead!"

"Damn! Go on!"

"As I was saying, the start of the trip was uneventful. The captain and one mate stayed in the wheel house, the captain to run the boat, and the mate to watch out for obstacles in the water. The other mate drew engine duty and he was stationed in the aft section, stoking the boiler. The driver stayed with the carriage and tended the horses. Suddenly, over the steady groan of the engines, the crewman stationed in the back heard the horses jump and snort loudly in agitation. Wanting to see what the commotion was, he left his post, but as he stepped onto the main deck, he stopped dead in his tracks, panic seizing his breath away. For all he saw of the driver was a pair of legs, sticking out from under the horse's flailing hooves!"

It always kind of irked me whenever he took a story and turned it into a dame novel, but he had a full head of steam, so I bit my tongue, and played the straight man.

"Ouch! Was he the one they found dead?"

"No Charlie" he replied raising his fingers to his lips. "The quick actions of the crewman saved him. He threw his buckets down and sprinted over to drag the man out from under the horses. The captain and mate witnessed the commotion from the wheelhouse and the captain sent the mate out to help, while he put the engines in neutral, then he joined them. After a few moments, the driver came around and immediately asked for the man inside the cab, who had still not made an appearance. When calling out and pounding on the side of the carriage, he still did not elicit a response. The driver took out a key and opened the cab."

William paused in his narrative to slowly sip some water, though I was wise to his dramatics.

"And he was dead," I said, just to steal a little of his thunder.

"Not just dead, old friend. Dead and mutilated! Not only was his throat cut, but is right arm ended in a bloody stump with the severed hand lying on the floor of the cab!"

"Damn!" I exclaimed. I didn't see that coming. "Must have been some kind of vendetta!"

William perked up, "Why would you think that, Charlie?"

I shrugged, "I don't know. If you've already slit a man's throat, why bother to take the time to cut off his hand unless there was motive. Like revenge or to send a message. Hell, gangs in the city do that sort of thing. They'll cut off more than your hand if you cross them hard enough! And usually stuff it down your throat to boot!"

Will winced but plowed on, "Be that as it may, after a quick search of the cab, the driver pulled a revolver and forced the captain and crew to accompany him as they searched every square inch of the ferry. Not satisfied at the results, the driver held the crew at gun point and forced them to finish the trip. When they reached the dock, there was already a police escort waiting. They searched the boat again and even sent crafts out onto the river searching for whomever or whatever.

They found nothing and no one. All they could do was take the captain and his crew into custody, where they are still being held. However, I heard rumor, just before we left to retrieve you that they were going to be released soon."

"But you said there was no one else on the boat! Or on the river! It would seem to me, if one man is knocked out and another murdered on a ferry in the middle of the night, there would be a short list of suspects!"

"Ah, Frohman but you are overlooking a key fact in my narrative."

I got a little nervous when he used my last name, but I let it go for the moment as I was completely caught up in the tale. "And that would be?"

William looked at me, eyes wide with anticipation with my reaction, "The driver had to use a key to open the cab!"

It took me a moment to process the fact, but I was stunned, "Good Lord! It's like a locked room murder mystery, but inside a boat floating across a river in the middle of nowhere! This is a real Houdini!"

"Who were these guys? Why were the flatfoots waiting for them?"

"I don't have that information yet, Charlie. The police

are keeping a tight lid on this one, though I'm hoping we can change that tomorrow."

"We?"

I knew I didn't like the sound of that. William could be a bit eccentric when he got the detective bug, and I had no desire to mix myself up with murder. I wasn't all that bored with my life just yet. Still, he was so animated about it and I had really missed him these last few years, only seeing him occasionally when he came to the city. So, in my stupidity, I humored him.

"And what conclusions have you come to?" I asked. "And don't tell me you haven't thought about it." I was baiting him, not sure why I wanted to throw another log on the fire.

"I have several, Charlie. The foremost being that the occupant of the cab was dead and mutilated before the carriage got on the ferry and the driver is the killer or knows who did it."

I was stunned. I'd have never thought of that. "Will! That's brilliant! That would explain everything!"

"No, Charlie. It's all useless supposition without the proper data to back it up."

"One needs proper data to make logical deductions, Frohman" he pronounced in his stage voice. Then added in a normal tone, "and as I said before, the authorities are as tight lipped as clams. I couldn't get a glimmer of details from the young inspector who came to interview me yesterday morning."

"Ah! So you're a suspect, huh?"

He laughed. "Hardly, Charles. The lad was just asking anyone in the area if they witnessed anything the previous night. He used a quaint term. He said he was canvassing the area. I had never heard that before.

In any case, there was no 'quid pro quo' to our conversation."

"Are you sure you're just not slipping in your old age? Or is retirement dulling your 'powers of observation?'" I needled him, partly because he called me by my last name again.

I'm not sure why I kept goading him. Perhaps I just missed his performances, or maybe I was wondering if he could still draw upon his stage persona, as he did from time to time at parties, to the delight of his guests. Yet again, I knew just how acute his deductions were from personal experience.

He smirked at me, in that smug manner that he so often enacted on stage, and looked me over, up and down. Tenting his fingers in front of his face, he spoke in one long sentence.

"I know that you did take the trolley to work this morning, instead of your horse and carriage. I see that you came to me directly from your office, without a trip home, but a small detour to the Drake most likely to get your 'survival kit' from Donnie. You sat on the train, on the left side, and you faced forward for most of the ride. You have switched to cigarettes from the cigars and you are planning on traveling to London within the week."

Stunned, I was in awe at his little displays. I racked my brain in silence for a moment and quickly gave up. I made a 'give me' gesture and said, "Alright then, let's have it. How did you know all that?"

"Simple observation, my good fellow." The corners of his mouth twitching in a near smile, "You have dirt on the back of your collar, which you inevitably collected while sitting with your back to the open windows on the trolley. There is a coffee stain on your tie that had to have been from your office, for I know Denise only serves tea at breakfast. And had you gone home, I know that Denise would have at least made you change your tie." Will shrugged and gave me a sly look, "The survival kit, well, that was a given, I'll admit!"

"Not bad," I admitted grudgingly, with a laugh. "The rest is true too. I gave up on the cigars, both my Doctor and Denise could not abide the smell and I'm leaving for London in six days. Now that I think about it, you were even right about the train ride, though I can't fathom how you guessed."

He sighed, "I guessed at nothing! Observation and reason, Frohman, it is just observation and reason. Your position on the trip up here was simplicity itself. Your left ear is noticeably a shade darker than your right ear. Thus, you must have had a left side window seat to get that much of the morning sun. The cigarettes were simpler to deduce. You no longer wear a trimmer on your watch fob, yet there is a noticeable yellowing between your fore and middle finger - the telltale mark of a steady smoker. Also, the square lump in your breast pocket is too small for a cigar case."

That sat me down. I had forgotten I took the trimmer off when I gave up the cigars and those ugly yellow stains had begun to creep up my digits. I had thought my suit was better tailored than to show a lump at all!

"Right again. But how did you know I was going overseas? You must have heard it from someone!"

He arched his eyebrows at me, "What time is it?"

I started to pull my pocket watch out and he added, "In London."

Ah! I thought to myself, he must have seen the time when I checked earlier and he knows that about a week before I traveled overseas, I would set my watch to the time of my destination and simply subtract or add the time difference from Eastern Standard Time. In this case, London was six hours ahead of us, so I was subtracting six hours. It amused me to 'catch up' with my pocket watch when I arrive in London.

"That's pretty amazing Will," I said.

When I said his name, he immediately sat up straight and picked up a cat at his feet. "Not really, Charlie. It's all easy stuff and I know you well, old friend." He winked, "It is all how you present it." He laughed then sat back, stroking the cat, which leaped up on his lap, "Tomorrow, we'll have a challenge."

I felt the boat slow as we turned into the Connecticut River. I could tell by the tree line that filled the view from the windows behind William, as it also did in the windows behind me.

I noticed a launch veer off in our direction. I assumed it was just another gawker, William's boat was easy to spot, easily the largest on the river. As it neared, I saw that I was right. Two men out of the four on the boat had a pair of binoculars to their faces. Only these men wore uniforms.

They slowed and took a good look before putting on more steam and peeling away. I didn't think much of it; people were always trying to get a glimpse of the "Great William Gillette"!

I was trying to find a way to diplomatically tell William that I wasn't about to get mixed up in one of his crazy jaunts, but the ship's whistle blew three times and William jumped to his feet.

"And now for the moment of truth, Charlie," he said with a flourish and a bow, "let us step out onto the deck."

When we stepped outside, it was dank and chilly with a steady rain beginning to fall, though we were sheltered by the deck above us.

"Damn this weather," Will said exasperated, "It's rained the last two Fridays."

I stepped over to the railing and begin to scan the shoreline. We were abreast of the ferry landing that was in the process of loading lumber to frame a new modest home further upriver. I saw no other houses in the immediate vicinity. I turned to my friend, a confused look on my face.

He laughed, "Up, Charlie look up."

And as I raised my eyes, my jaw dropped so low I could have trolled for flat fish on the river bottom.

The Castle

"Holy Mother of God!" I croaked, when my mind finally caught up to my eyes. I didn't know whether to laugh or cry for my friend.

I mean, I know I had some preconceived notions. I knew it would be big and grand, yet I was thinking more along the lines of those new places they were building up in Newport, Rhode Island. Something ostentatious, yet with Will's touch. What sat upon that hill was something out of a fairy tale.

A huge stone castle, straight out of the Scottish landscape, sat majestically at the apex of a steep terrain that rose from the river. Complete with battlements and towers. It was completely out of place along these shores, yet it looked like it had been there forever.

Will's new home looked like stone boxes tastily stacked on top of each other, though it jutted out in many places to break up the squarish look. Where it sat, it seemed as big as a city block rising amongst the trees dwarfed only by the majestically tall trees that grew in the forest surrounding it. In the rain and mist it looked mysterious and foreboding. In fact, my first impression was that it looked like a great dragon's head, with the side towers for horns and the upper windows for eyes. The open front, facing the river under a long balcony, seemed like a gaping maw.

I was flabbergasted. I didn't know what to say, so I joked, "And did you lock the Seven Sisters in the tower before you left?"

He laughed, "No, Charlie. The Seven Sisters is the name of the property after what the locals call this series of hilltops," he pointed out the seven hills that made the chain his castle sat on.

I shook my head in disbelief, "I knew you'd build something special Will, but I didn't think you were starting your own kingdom, complete with a cas..."

"Stop right there, Charlie," he cut me off, hand in air, "It is NOT a castle!"

"No? Then what would you call it?" I asked. "Certainly you don't intend to call it the Had Lyme Stone Heap like you wrote to me in the past? And if you didn't want a castle why did you build it?"

"It is simply my home, Charlie, NOT a castle. I swear, I just drew up plans with the architect, and I was surprised as anyone when it ended up looking like it does!"

"If you say so, but it looks a little wobbly," I said with a jest intended, but really, on closer study, it did look a bit haphazard to me. The stones were not squared off and they jutted out at odd angles everywhere.

"I'd hate to be inside that if it fell down."

William gave a theatrical sigh. "You'll be a safe as a babe in a mother's arms." He gave me a sideways look, "As long as you watch what you say around Ozaki."

The rain had tapered off as we approached the dock, though we stayed under the awning over the stern deck. Having practically grown up on boats, I couldn't take my eyes off all the pylons, pulleys and ropes that dangled from them. There seemed to be miles of line, some stretching from post to post while others hung loose and some went straight into the water. I was still trying to discern the need for all that hemp as Captain Roy quickly brought us alongside the pylons and Nickolas and Ozaki each grabbed ropes in preparation for docking.

The docking itself was quite a process. The captain brought the *Aunt Polly* alongside a set of huge timbers that were spaced three to a side of the dock. Ropes and pulleys stretched between the pylons. As we idled, the first mate hooked lines on the bow and the stern and together with Ozaki, began to pull us towards the pier as the captain shut down the engines. It was no small feat for a boat this grand, but the pulley system made it look easy.

"Wow," I remarked. "This is elaborate. Whatever happened to just pulling up to the dock and tossing out a line?"

Will smiled, "That's alright for temporary stays, Charlie, but I needed something more flexible for a permanent berth. I need to tie the boat off away from the dock when there is a storm or strong tides. The captain and Nickolas put it all together. Quite ingenious. The six lines to the boat keep the old girl settled nice and securely, without having to worry about her bouncing off the pier."

Ozaki suddenly appeared with our coats and hats, gathered my bags and we disembarked.

I looked around but I still didn't see one of Will's infernal motorcars, which I fully expected to ride up to the castle. To our left, there was only a stack of building material next to a rickety lift of some sort that went up the side of the cliff and a rather large shed that sat up from the docks on our right. I assumed the machine was stored there so I headed in that direction.

"Where are you going, Charlie?" Will asked. "That's the boat shed.

We'll go directly to the house."

I looked around but didn't see a horse carriage or any other mode of conveyance.

"And how are we to do that, Will? Do we climb up?" The castle looked like it sat at the top of the mountain from here.

42

"No, no, my friend," he answered as he started to stride toward the base of the hill, "You're in for a real treat!" With that he turned and started towards the building materials. A short walk brought us to the wooden contraption built into the side of the cliff that led straight up to Will's Castle. A large wooden platform, suspended by ropes and pulleys, was slowly jerking its way down to us.

"Are you pulling my leg? What in God's name do you call that?" I stopped and looked at my friend, who wore a smirk on his face.

"It's an aerial tramway. We use it to bring material and laborers from the barges to my home."

I wasn't impressed. "Stop fooling around, William, Where's your whatchamacallit? Your automobile?"

He barked a short laugh, "What Automobile? Why do you think I have one here?"

"Cause I know you have one! You always have the latest contraption, at least if it rolls or floats!"

"Well, in fact I do own several automobiles."

"Hah! I knew it!"

"But the garage isn't ready yet, so they are in storage. I'm afraid you'll just have to try my latest "contraption". I'm trying to add flying to my rolling and floating addictions."

I'd need a couple more slugs before I could even think about riding that thing up the cliff. I found myself trying to stall. "It looks a little shaky to me. Are you sure it will take the three of us up safely? And my Luggage? Maybe we should send that up first." I looked at the mechanism and saw thick jagged strands sticking out of the cables that lifted and lowered it and a suspicious looking end popping out of a weld.

"It looks like it's starting to unravel," I protested.

"Don't be so fainthearted Charlie. I designed this

tramway myself and those cables are nearly two inches thick. It's carried ten times the weight of us and your luggage every day. You'll be safe as a babe..."

"In its mother's arms," I finished for him.

"Excuse me, Mr. Frohman." We turned to see Ozaki smiling at us. "If you would feel safer warking, Mr. Frohman, the path that reads up your accommodations is only a half mirel or so that way," he said pointing to the north, "It is only a rittle more than a half-mile to Mr. Girrette's home from there." He looked at me dead seriously, "Though rather a steep grade for taking by foot."

I gave him the evil eye.

He pretended not to notice, and while William did his best not to laugh, Ozaki droned on. "By the time you arrive, I could have dinner prepared, and make sure your room is ready, and get a nice fire going, and..."

"Alright, alright!" I steeled my nerves. "If I'm going to fall to my death, we might as well get started. Tell me the truth," I added, as we walked, "Did you ever have any mishaps with this thing?"

"Nothing permanent," he deadpanned as he took my arm and stepped us onto the wooden platform. "And never repeated!"

The ride was not as harrowing as I feared, but it was no carriage ride either. The platform swayed to an alarming degree as the ropes jerked us upwards inch by inch. He explained the mechanism in detail, how he designed it and had it built to his specifications. I hardly heard a word as he pointed out various landmarks, standing like the captain of a ship in stormy weather. Every gust of wind seized my heart and it was all I could do to not scream like a little girl whenever the floor beneath us lurched. A bell suddenly pealed loudly, not more than a few feet away, and we lurched to a stop.

"What the hell was that?" I asked, looking around for the source of the noise, "Who did that?" For I had not seen William or Ozaki move.

"Settle down Charlie," Will said with a sigh, "It rings whenever we reach the top. That piece you pointed out below strikes it. I thought it was rather clever, actually it's just an alert..." I heard that word and jumped off the tram to good old terra firma. Will rolled his eyes and sighed, "...to let the operator know whether the platform is fully up." He waited for Ozaki to step off with my bags and joined me on solid ground.

Now that I was finally on the same level of the castle, I stood rooted to the spot, amazed at William's home that rose before me. You had to crane your head around to take it all in.

The side that faced the river really didn't look like any design I had seen in a castle. It was four stories high as far as I could tell by the window placements, but it was by no means symmetrical. Each window had a stone overhang to shed the rain and sun. The sections were square for the most part, but they seemed stacked in an odd way. The natural stone, not cut or set squarely also threw off the eye. Both the balconies, on the top level and second were lined with stone railings that were wavy, almost lacking a solid look to the construction. I could imagine pulling out a lower stone and the whole thing would crumble.

In the mist, it looked down right sinister. Like a demon smiling down on its next meal of souls. I would never say that to William who stood next to me beaming like a proud parent.

"It's fourteen thousand square feet of rock and mortar. Five feet thick at the base and tapering to two feet at the top." Will informed me.

"Where did you get all that stone?" I asked

incredulously. "Did you import it?"

He laughed, "Hardly, Charlie. Connecticut is ninety percent rock! Most came from a quarry a few towns over and the rest was floated down the river and hoisted up. Twenty two stone masons have been working on the place for nearly five years now."

"Zounds! Has it been that long?"

"Time flies when you're ruling the theater world," William teased me. "You should come down off your lofty mount once and a while."

"Ha!" I snorted, "I've had to work twice as hard since you fell off the face of the earth!"

The wind was a bit chillier up here and as the rain was picking up again, I started looking for a doorway, but dead ahead of us was a solid rock wall, about fifteen feet tall or so. I could only see a set of windows and what I thought were french doors over the top of the wall, but no door openings in sight. To our left was a humongous pile of flat cut stone and what I assumed was mortar under secured tarps.

"So, do we scale that wall now?" I joked, "Or do you have a secret entrance nearby?"

Will laughed, "No, Charlie, that's going to be the courtyard off the great room. At least it will be when the masons get here to lay the stones."

"That's a high wall for a courtyard, my friend," I said, "Isn't being the only dwelling within miles enough privacy for you?"

"Oh no, Charlie. That's all been filled in to make it level with the main floor. The actual wall will only be a little over three feet tall, from inside the courtyard," he explained. The property is not level. My workshop is below the main level, the sleeping rooms on the second and third, and my library and art gallery will be on the fourth."

"What about the very top level, with the balcony?" I asked, pointing up.

He waggled his eyebrows at me and grinned, "That secret will be revealed only after you have had a chance to freshen up. Let's get out of the rain, like sensible men. We'll have to walk up to the front door."

He turned to his left and led the way. I noticed that Ozaki had already disappeared, though I wasn't surprised. Most likely he had my things unpacked in my room by now.

We passed a side door, but William ignored it, I'm sure so he could make a grand entrance into his new home. As I was probably the first guest he had invited to stay, I figured it was only right to give him slack and let him run. I was sure to be impressed.

We walked down a few steps into a covered portico. At the bottom step, a massive wooden door, at least six feet by ten feet, loomed before us.

"Gads, William," I exclaimed, "Do you drive your wagons into the house?"

He laughed, "Impressive, isn't it?"

"Make a Viking quail." Big as the door was, it swung smoothly on the hinges with a little push from William and we entered the large living room. William called it a sitting room, but it was a bit more like a scaled down great hall from the castles of legend. Great wooden stairs rose from my left that led to the second story where a walkway connected various openings in the stone above which I assumed were rooms. All had doors, but some looked empty and unfinished.

And the doors! Each one was uniquely carved from New England white oak. William told me they each had a different latch and locks, like a puzzle that must be solved prior to entry. All designed by William himself!

Strange too were the light switches. Not satisfied with simple buttons or pegs, each was about six inches wide

47

and four or five inches tall, also made from carved white oak also. No chance of missing them in the dark!

The ceiling rose nineteen feet above us where it blended into the shadows. The walls were all of stone, with beautiful woodwork built into them that gleamed like burnished gold in the low light.

To my right the wall was dominated by a huge fire place. eight feet or so wide at the base and ran floor to ceiling, where it tapered off to five feet. Made of field stone, I could see the sides were designed so that someone could climb up and water the exotic plants William had. The fire place had plenty of nooks and crannies for plants, knickknacks and mementos. I had to smile when I saw the deerstalker hat his stage persona sported, hanging from a peg, and what looked like an old sock sticking out to the left of the mantle.

The interior looked smaller than one would expect from the monstrous outer wall, but the inside was sectioned off and laid out in a way that made it seem more like a residence than a seat of government. What really amazed me was that even though so much had been built, there was evidence everywhere that there was much more to come. Ladders were stacked against the walls in dim corners, bags of mortar and stacks of wood piled just outside the doors.

Three men, in working togs came from around the corner. They stopped as a group to doff their hats to William and bid him a good night. The oldest came over, as the other two slipped out a door, when William gestured to him to join us.

He nodded to me and I put out my hand, "Charles Frohman." He gave me a quick shake and mumbled a 'how do?"

"Ollie here is my lead man. He's been overseeing the interior wood working and doing an amazing job."

Ollie smirked and said to me, "Don't you believe him, sir. I just do what Mr. Gillette tells me to. He was born to raise this roof."

"Well," Will returned, "let's see if I'm not dead before I can finish it. Is the courtyard ready for the masons tomorrow?"

"Tamped her down today, Sir, just a hair under level with a slight pitch to the drains and smooth as a baby's butt."

"Good! I certainly do not want an encore of their last performance." He looked at me, "The last job they did, the walkways, I said the pitch was wrong, and they left. I did not see the smoke of their wagons for a month!"

"Smoke?" I asked in surprise.

"Yes, from their wagons. They come in great big buckboards, cook wagons and live on the grounds until they finish. They should be camped out for a week or so while they do the courtyard."

Remembering that Ollie was still waiting, William dismissed him, "Though I suspect they'll be traveling by new trucks as soon as they are through scalping me."

I laughed. The idea of anyone scalping William was pure folly. He was a swamp Yankee to the core. He wasn't a stingy man but he had a great head for business.

"What are you grousing about? This place certainly was not built on a budget." As the words left my mouth, they sparked a realization. William had invested far more into this location than any of his other passing fancies. The thought sobered me. "Looks to me like you're setting some deep roots, my friend."

He gave me a small, sad smile, "How about I try to make you feel at home."

Biscuits

Our first stop was the kitchen, where I made the acquaintance of Mrs. Woods, William's cook and housekeeper. She was a handsome woman, tall and solid but by no means stout. I fell hopelessly in love when she opened the oven and the smell of warm biscuits wafted out to engulf us. I wasn't hungry, but the aroma made me famished for one. I eagerly took the first biscuit with some soft butter and wolfed it down.

Watching me inhale her offering, she raised an eyebrow to William, "I think I'll bump up the portions tonight, sir."

"Good woman," I commented as I snatched another biscuit before she took them away.

A young woman came bustling into the room, her arms full of cleaning materials.

"Ah," William said, "And here is our young Catherine. She assists Mrs. Woods and provides the small comforts we enjoy amidst all the chaos."

She was a pretty thing, ample bosom and slim hipped. She stored her supplies in a cupboard and returned to us, "Mister Gillette means I give him clean sheets and try to keep the construction dust off the furniture," she said with Yankee bluntness and a coy smile. "Pleased to meet you, Mister Frohman" she said with a half curtsy.

"You know who I am?" I asked, pleased to be recognized. It was usually just the stars who got public recognition. "Most folks outside the theater wouldn't know me from Adam."

She gave me a confused look, "Ozaki-san told me to lay a fire in Mister Frohman's room in case it got cold

50

tonight."

Will turned red trying not to laugh at me, so I went for another biscuit, but stopped short when Mrs. Woods's eyes frowned. Instead, I thanked her again and told them both I was pleased to meet them.

William pulled me out of there quick. "Ne pas faire le Cuisine!" he whispered in my ear.

We walked past a narrow alcove with beautiful woodwork. There were bench seats and three sides and an enormous table dominating the space. I couldn't understand why it was laid out this way when William told me it was the dining room. I couldn't see how knowing his preference for entertaining, how it could seat more than six people before you had to climb over others to get a seat. But Will just smirked and told me I had to wait for dinner.

On the other side of the sitting area, facing south was the conservatory, which William assured me was complete. I could hear water running but workmen blocked the entrance with scaffolding and tarps as they had to finish pointing the stones around the wood of the archway. Yet, William assured me we would have coffee there in the morning.

Our next leg of the tour took us to the upper portion of the castle, where William had a modest room tucked away from the rest of the bedrooms. Our next stop was the guest room I was in, which had a comfortable feel. The fireplace, with Catty's laid wood pyramid, gave it the makings of a cozy retreat. William showed me how to work the crazy latching system that opened and closed the windows, his design, of course. He tells me that almost each window that opened had its own unique latch. Again, each one created by William. I'm not sure how practical they were, but I knew my friend and I would wager that each one worked, and in style. The view was serenity itself. I could see nothing but tree tops in the mist, until they too dissolved into the grayness of the day.

Ozaki's room was on the same level. Will explained that Ozaki would live in the house until his was completed. It turned out that it was the unfinished house I saw by the ferry landing.

There was also a lavatory. A big tub, toilet and vanity, it was clean and comfortable. I was grateful for this leg of the tour and I had to shoo him out, for my bladder was bursting.

William then took me up some more stairs to another half finished room that he identified as the future library. It held just one table, piled with mechanical journals, manuals, and all kinds of publications about inventions. No doubt this is where he got many ideas for his ingenious fixtures throughout the place. The library room was bare otherwise, the few finished shelves were empty and I was wondering why we were dwelling so long here, when he led me to a cleverly hidden passage.

A few steps up and suddenly we were stepping into an open sided room that led to the outside deck with a large balcony - the highest point of the house. William did a quick shuffle and bow, gesturing towards the panoramic views. He spoke softly but emphatically, "I give you... The Tower Room!"

I was going to make a bad joke about Rapunzel, but the view made my jaw drop for the second time this day.

Below us, the stonework stretched out like giant steps to an immense white half circle where the courtyard was to be laid tomorrow. Just past the wall, the level ground ended. Beyond that, was a glorious fusion of water and forest where the Connecticut River cut through the countryside. In the mist, I could clearly see the town across the river and the ferry landings on both sides. To the left, I could guess that on a clear day, one could see all the way to the mouth of the river and into Long Island Sound beyond. To the right was a scene of up river and the magnificent forest that bordered her.

Dead to the west, the sun had begun it's decent into the horizon. The sunset was intensified by the low clouds that were streaming in from the southwest, yellow at the bottom, and then darkened to a deep reddish orange with streaks of purple. It made the top of the forest glow and reflect off the river water like a mirror.

"It's like the sun is bleeding out over the land, then igniting a fire when it touches the river."

"You have the heart of a poet," William said softly.

"And I had the empty pockets to prove it when I was a poet."

There was a long pause with no more conversation as we surveyed the land that spread out from us. If you looked closely at the tree line, you could actually see the better part of the valley that this township and the one across the river were nestled in. Now, I've been a few places in my life, and New York City itself had some vantage points where you could actually see the city's breath, but I had to admit there was something very special about this place.

Will finally broke the serenity, "So, what do you think? Did I find a good spot?"

"Damn," I answered, "The view from this height makes every trip up the rickety tram more than worth the trouble. Makes me think I don't have to look up if I want to talk to God. You could do it face to face from here."

"So," I observed, "I can see why you built here, but what made you choose here? How did you find this place?"

"I'll tell you, Charlie, I had originally planned on building in Greenport, Long Island, but one day, Ozaki and I took a cruise across the Sound aboard the *Aunt Polly* and the weather turned nasty. We looked for shelter on this river in the driving rain and anchored as soon as we were past the ferry landing to ride out the storm. The tempest passed in the night, and by the morning, the sky was bright and clear and when I stepped out onto the deck the sun was just rising on the Seven Sisters." William stopped to catch his breath. "In all my travels, across this country and abroad, I had never seen such a magnificent sight. I stared at it until the sun was high in the sky and then instructed Ozaki to head over to the town dock on the other side of the river and I began to make inquiries. A month later I owned the one hundred seventeen acres that we're standing on now."

To a city boy like me, this seemed like a lot of property, especially in the light that William had never been much of an outside person. Even his boat was like a floating home and a bit larger than the ones most of his fellow actors lived in.

"Why so much land, Will?" I asked. "Are you taking up farming or something?"

"No, my friend, but I have plans for that landscape." Then he got that faraway look in his eyes like when he was mapping out the movements in a play.

When he didn't continue, I asked, "And just what are you planning?"

He smiled, "I'm planning on indulging."

I knew nothing more was forthcoming for the moment, so I changed the subject. I stuck my chin out in the general direction of the ferry crossing the river. "Too bad Doyle wasn't here with us. I should like to hear his take on the mystery."

"I have no doubts you are right. Murder on a moving ferry, in the middle of a river in full darkness, and no one saw a thing. Even Conan Doyle would have had a tough time making that story work though I'm sure he'd come up with something eventually."

William and I had the privilege of meeting the man on one of our European tours, some years back. Doyle was impressed with William and they quickly became fast friends. From that, and the fact that Doyle had truly sickened of his Sherlock Holmes character, he not only gave him permission to use the character in his plays but told him, "Do what you will with him. Marry Him. Kill him. Whatever... I care not."

William took him for his word and totally immersed himself into the character, adding most of the refinements that are associated with Sherlock Holmes now. His briarwood pipe and deerstalker cap were both Will's ideas. Even his catch phrases, such as "Elementary, my dear Watson", or "The games afoot" came from Will's plays, not the original manuscripts. William's portrayal of the London detective had made them both more famous than ever. When William took a role, he not only acted it, he became that character. His sharp focused approach to that role was the secret of his success.

After a pause he went on, "Though I have a few thoughts of my own on the matter."

I rolled my eyes, "As you mentioned back on the *Aunt Polly*. And what, pray tell, might those be?"

"Two points, really." he answered, obviously chomping at the bit to sound out his theories. "The first being, I don't think the murder was the only crime committed that night. I believe something was stolen also." He paused, looking thoughtful for dramatization. "Something rather important, I suspect."

"Hold up now!" I said. "Where did you come up with that conjecture?"

He looked at me like I was loony, "Not conjecture, Charlie. Conclusions gleaned from observation and deduction! And solid ones, I think."

As I was still feeling no pain from whatever I had been

drinking all day, I decided to go along for the moment, but I was ready to stop him in his tracks if it went passed idle speculation.

"All right then, let's hear them."

William started dry washing his hands, a habit of his when he became excited. It took him a moment to organize his thoughts and regain his composure, and then he proceeded.

"Yesterday morning, before having no idea the crime had been committed, I awoke just after dawn and glanced out my window to observe one of the local clamming boats slowly plying the same route the ferry takes and dragging something behind it."

William continued as he rubbed his chin, "Of course, as this was not the usual spot our local bay men would try their luck. My curiosity was piqued and I quickly dressed and went to the second floor balcony. I watched it chug slowly towards the Chester side of the river until my desire for caffeine overcame my interest and I headed down to make some coffee. Ozaki, as always, was one step in front of me and had some fresh coffee brewed which I took into the conservatory to enjoy with my morning papers. I was content for a bit, but then had a sudden urge for a pipe. So, I went out to the fireplace to get my pouch and pipe and as I was passing the glass doors that will eventually lead out to the courtyard and I noticed movement on the river. I returned to my perch on the balcony, where I saw the same clam boat turning right next to the dock down below me and began to head back across the river on nearly the same route I had seen it earlier!"

"Will, Will, Will," I broke in. "It isn't unusual for a clam dragger to ply back and forth. That's what they do! Though, for the life of me, I can't see where there would be enough clams this far up river to make it worthwhile. Are you sure they weren't trawling for something else.

Shad maybe?"

William looked at me like I was speaking in tongues.

"No Charlie, because they were moving much too slow."

"Yes, but speed is deceptive at this height and distance."

He tilted his head and sighed. "I am quite aware of that. But my interest was piqued when the boat came to a stop and they winched in their lines. What they brought up was a large metal rake...you know them from your youth...the kind they use for clamming. There were objects in the rake and as they struggled to pull it up on the transom. Ozaki appeared with the pair of my new binoculars. Imagine my surprise when it wasn't the crew who emptied the basket, but two uniformed policemen, supervised by two men in business suits!"

"Is that so? It doesn't sound like they were looking for dinner, then. Who do you think it was?"

"I can't say for the moment, but I thought I saw the sun flash off of something on one man's chest. It could have been a badge." Will admitted, "But it would help our investigation if I knew what governmental branch had a stake in this affair."

This was the moment I had dreaded, but was prepared for.

"Wait a minute William! Hold up there! What are you talking about? Our investigation!" At least he had the good grace to look sheepish.

"Well, I thought as long as you were up for a few days, we could look around a bit and ask a few questions. It'll give us something to do. I'll show you the area and we can talk with some of the locals. It will be stimulating."

I shook my head emphatically, "You're not getting us into anything to do with murder or robbery! What put that cockamamie idea in your head?"

He shrugged. "I don't know, Charlie. Perhaps because all I've done for the past five years is work on my home. Now that it's nearly complete, my creative side is looking for an outlet."

"Then write a play! Go back to work! There's no sensible reason to mix us up in this mess!"

"It's not just that, Charlie." His face grew long and he turned to lean on the balcony railing, "I want to do something to help, something to integrate myself with the community." William turned to me, pleading with his eyes, "But I need your help, Charlie."

"Me? Why do you need me? You've always been the brains of this outfit. I don't have any skills in the 'observation and deduction' department." I said.

"But you have more skills with people in your little pinky than I have in my whole body. People like you and open up to you instantly. Why, I've seen you walk into a room full of strangers and twenty minutes later they're arguing who will have you over for Christmas dinner! No one around here will talk to me, unless they're on my payroll."

"What are you talking about? You're the most charming man I know! People love you! And they do argue over who's having you for Christmas dinner!"

He gave a rueful laugh. "Perhaps in our circle, Charlie, and amongst those who truly know me. But here, in the bastion of the swamp Yankees, I am shunned!"

"Oh, you're just being dramatic!" I scolded him, "You have always had more than your fair share of notoriety! These are simple people out here William. They know you're rich and famous and probably are just too reserved to approach you, much less gush over you, like your theater fans! They probably look at you like a Duke or something!"

He snorted with a bitter laugh, "Ha! I have yet to meet someone who has seen me in a play! To them, I'm just some chowder head with too much money, erecting some insane structure in their front yard! And those are the kind ones. Some say I'm mad. Some say that I am a foolish fop, playing out my fantasies. The more hurtful have declared me a warlock and accused me of practicing satanic rites by the full moon."

Ouch! I knew that would hurt him. William was brought up Christian and though he didn't jump up on a pulpit about it, I knew he truly led his life as a Christian should. But I couldn't help myself.

"Well, you know, when you consider it, Ozaki does make quite the exotic, Asian familiar. An Asian butler would seem strange to the locals."

William threw his hands in the air. "Exactly, Charlie! And that is precisely the attitude which keeps me from establishing any kind of rapport with the locals!"

He sighed, "I could bear all this if it was just I who had to endure, but I'm afraid the ones closest to me are also being affected. Ozaki has been rebuffed or treated rudely numerous times when he went to town. On one occasion he was chased by a group of drunken young men. And I'm sure both Mrs. Woods and Cattie have suffered harassment, simply because they work for me."

He paused again, looking out over the river, rapping his knuckles gently on the stone railing to emphasize his words. "I just want to belong, Charlie. Really belong somewhere for once in my life. It seems like I have been adrift since I left my parents care all those years ago. Moving from one place to the next, living a good portion aboard Aunt Polly. How ironic, now that I have finally committed to settle, that I am to be treated by the locals like some leper king!"

I knew then what he really wanted. He told me as much in his telegraph. The crime was a real obsession for him, but what he really wanted was an excuse to take me out among the local populous. He needed the one real talent I had. I was an excellent front man. I was full of manure and willing to spread it far and wide. It wasn't really what I said, nothing too profound, but it was the way I said it.

I could talk to anyone. I had a knack for reading people and relating to them on their level. Of course, it helps that I have no standards and therefore rarely judge anyone.

And William knew this. He needed me to break the ice with his neighbors and what better way than to take me to town and ask a few innocent questions along the way. I tried to stick to my guns, but the forlorn look, the slump to his usually squared shoulders, and the fact that I owed him so very much, so I changed what I was about to say.

"Will, you must understand, you will never be Tom the grocer or Hal the fishmonger to these people. You are more educated, worldly, and creative than they will ever aspire to! Not to mention rich and famous! Trouble is you've spent most of your life as a wealthy vagabond! Most of your contact with the humanity has been inside the theater world. Now, every person you've ever worked with thinks the world of you. But even those faces and places change. Continuity breeds familiarity breeds acceptance. So let's be honest, you've always been a little short on continuity."

I didn't mean to be cruel, but I could see that my words stabbed him rather than slowly sink in. So be it. William needed to hear a fact of life.

"And, let's face it, this monstrosity we're standing on won't help your cause! This is the land of clapboard saltboxes and barns and all of a sudden it looks like King Arthur moved into the neighborhood! It's going to put folks off! You may have to accept the case that you may never be able to stroll down main street, tipping your hat and 'how ya doin' to everyone you see."

He mulled that over for a moment then shook his head ruefully, "I know that. I've dealt with being an outsider for most of my life but I'm here now, Charlie, and I intend to stay. It's not that I need to establish any deep relationships with the people around here; I just would like to be some small part of their lives. The day-to-day sort. My entire social contact can't be just a visit from you and to whomever else I may extend an invitation. I just want them to talk to me. Be straight forward. I need that if I'm to live here for the remainder of my days."

In the end, it wasn't the puppy dog eyes or the resigned tone of his voice that made me agree. It was much simpler. I owed him and he wanted my help. I just looked at him after a long pause and smiled. "I suppose it wouldn't hurt to take a jaunt to town tomorrow. Maybe see what the local talk is about. As long as it has a tavern!"

William brightened right up, clapping me on the shoulder. He barked in his stage voice, "Capitol, Frohman, Capitol! I believe this has all the makings of a memorable adventure!"

Lucky for him, the clouds broke open and a steady rain began to fall, so we ducked back inside before I could process what he just said.

After Dinner Smoke

We ducked back inside just as the rain became heavy. It was pounding the stonework with big drops that exploded and formed sheets of water across the floor.

As Will never served dinner before eight o'clock, we had some extra time, so William took me beneath the castle and showed me his workroom. I was astounded by the time and ingenuity he put into the various locks and opening hardware on his doors and windows. Using wood mostly, he made each one by hand and every one was different.

It was no wonder I had seen him so rarely in the past few years. In fact, I couldn't see an end in sight and I told him so.

William replied with, "Oh, I don't think it's all that bad. She is basically built. All the doors, windows, and fixtures are installed. We've got electricity and a telephone and, I'm sure we're all grateful for modern plumbing. It's really just the finish work now and my tinkering." He gestured to the latches strewn about his workbench. "And when the courtyard goes in, the main house is really completed. Won't it be grand, Charlie? All that beautiful stone from my living room to nearly the edge of the bluff! We'll have some real parties here, my friend."

"Hell, you could hold some jousting matches," I teased him.

"With the medieval armor?" he asked sarcastically. He seemed so resolute in his disdain for my castle jokes; I decided then to lay off the subject a bit. Nonetheless, if you can't break a friend's stones, whose can you break?

"Well, then I wouldn't be putting up tapestries of St.

George or have a suit of armor in the hall."

"Not a chance," he replied, "I can assure you I have no desire to stare at those bloody battle scenes all day. Those Brits do have a strange sense of decor. I'll get some big cat wall hangings, just for you. It will be your own private cat house."

"Now you're talking," and I poked him in the chest for emphasis. "I came all the way out here because I thought the Seven Sisters was a cat house!"

Still laughing, we almost missed the faint dinner bell ringing just outside the kitchen.

I checked my watch and it was three minutes to eight o'clock. The time William had dinner every night. The bell rang louder as we made our way up the steps and back to the main level. William led us through the great room and down a short hall where Ozaki stood, alongside a bus cart with wonderful smells emanating.

Behind Ozaki was a small alcove that had a long wide dining table with benches built into the walls on either side. Damn thing was you had no room to pull back the seats and walk in!

I was about to slide onto a bench, when William stopped me and bade me to stand to one side. He took a position on the other side and Ozaki grasped the edge of the table, set into the alcove. From the smug look on his face and the way his pant leg twitched, I knew I was in for another ingenious trick.

There was a click and with a gentle tug from Ozaki, the massive table smoothly floated out away from the wall, leaving ample room to walk in and seat oneself.

I then noticed the tracks on the floor which the table rolled on. We took our seats in the rear and Ozaki pushed the table up, right under our elbows! There was another click and the table was firmly rooted again.

As I was a bigger man, it was a trifle snug for me,

though I was still comfortable and it would be more than enough elbow room for the average sized person. It was rather cozy even though you felt a little trapped. I found out later that William had a switch on the floor that he could press when he wanted to release the table and another that rang a bell in the pantry for service. What I wouldn't have given for this table when my brood was younger! Or Mrs. Woods to set it!

The biscuits I tried earlier were just one of the perfect accompaniments to her outrageous rack of spring lamb! Freshest I've ever had. The lamb tasted like I was biting down in mid 'Baaaaaaa'.

Though he was a teetotaler, William has an expert's knowledge of wine and served the perfect Bordeaux with it. We poured each other's wine, never allowing the glass's last sip to vanish, an Asian cultural lesson that Osaki taught us many years ago. Osaki explained this simple gesture would make our friendship stronger and the wine would always taste better.

After eating like a farmhand after the harvest was in, I was relieved when William released the table. I swear my expanded waist was enough to push the massive table off its tracks!

Ozaki handed me a snifter of Cognac as I walked behind William who led the way to a sitting area in front of the great fireplace. There was a couch and a few easy chairs arranged in a horseshoe around a coffee table. Owing to the chilly and rainy night, there was a roaring fire that kept the dampness and darkness at bay.

William pulled an old sock, stuffed with his pipe and tobacco, from a nook in the fieldstone hearth and packed himself a bowl. I lit a smoke of my own and watched the fire through the amber liquid swirling in my glass. I had not felt so relaxed or so content for a very long time.

Though the setting was intimate, I couldn't help but feel

I was on a stage. You could see little past the dim lights on either side of the couch, but you knew you were in a cavernous place. I told my host as much.

"I know, I know," he said, "It's just that the sound echoes in here. It will be different when it's fully furnished and the décor complete, I assure you.

I'm having some raffia mats woven in Java as we speak. They will give the room a homier feel."

"I'm sure you'll hardly be able to notice the stone walls and the twenty foot ceilings," I teased him.

As if on cue, one of the ever present felines trotted over and jumped onto Will's lap, he didn't even seem to notice as he ignored my jibe and changed the subject.

"But enough of the acoustics, tell me of this new duo you discovered. This Billie Burke and...er...who is the other girl?"

I lit up immediately. "Her name is Margaret Anglin and you know damn well who they are. They are money in the bank, my boy, money in the bank!"

"I read they were very good in 'This time its Love'. Are they the rising stars that everyone says they are or did you just give them a good piece to work with?"

"I'll leave the artsy-fartsy critiques to you intellectuals," I responded with a smirk, "They kept the hall packed for nearly two months. Every show! That Billie's a dancing fool, I tell you! I'm going to send my youngest to Harvard on those two."

William just stared at me with that 'just answer the question' look in his eyes

"Alright! Yes! They have 'it'. They are good looking, have great stage presence, and have enough wits to learn their lines on time and adapt them when necessary. They each have a good work ethic and, at least at this stage, can take direction and criticism. As a bonus, their egos haven't been inflated with money and fame yet, so they are easy to work with." I shrugged, "They'll be my focus for a while, that is, unless you change your mind and leave this inverted quarry in 'Bumpkinville' and return to the bright lights and your adoring fans."

He shook his head with a sad smile, "No, old friend, here I am and here I will stay. 'Bumpkinville' is my home now. I'm not saying that I'll never ply my trade again, but the Seven Sisters will be my main focus in life until it's completed.

I will admit, when I started this project, I was in no way certain that I was going to stay here forever. Mostly because, as you so aptly put it, I have never experienced continuity. I've learned one thing in these last five years. I am very ready to put down roots in this town."

I gestured vaguely all around me, "This is a little more than roots, my friend." Then added with a smile, "It is rather a 'Here I make my stand' kind of place!"

He shrugged, "What should I have built? Another wood and brick monstrosity with so many rooms that I would never ever use? A domicile in constant need for paint and repair? Besides, what else will I leave when I finally break these earthly bonds? I will never remarry. I will never have children. Even fame is fleeting, my friend. My name will fade in time. There will always be another John Barrymore or a Billie Burke to come and take my mantle. But, long after my plays are forgotten and characters I played have faded from memory, this place will stand. It's not immortality, but perhaps my name will be remembered for a tad longer than most childless old bachelors are allotted."

I could see his point of view. Everyone wanted to leave their mark. Most did it with family but men like my friend were driven to do more. Me? I'm not sure I made my mark yet, though I've left a lot of scuff marks in my wake.

"I'm sure it will at that, Bub." I looked up at him over

the rim of my snifter, "I suppose you mean to stay away for a while longer then?"

Will's chin came up, "That's a selfish way to put it, Charlie!" Then he grinned to take any sting out of the remark, "I am not staying away. I am simply staying put! I have my home now and enough revenue to live as I like til the end of my days. I am retiring, Charlie."

I had heard his retirement spiel before, but always in the past some new project would catch his interest and he'd be right back at it in a few months, a year at the most. Yet, this time I could see that he was earnest.

I could see from the look in his eyes that making the announcement was a big moment for him. His whole being radiated relief, as if speaking the retirement words made it the truth. He peered at me intently, as to judge my reaction.

When I didn't respond for a minute, only because I was looking for the right words of support, he asked quietly, "So does my retirement upset any of your plans, Charlie?"

The perfect opening. I smiled at him, "Not as far as you being my dearest friend."

I raised my glass to him, "Use your free time wisely, but if you ever want my company, just stock your liquor cabinet, then call."

Missed Breakfast

I slept like a newborn in my snug little room with the fire that Catty laid out keeping me warm through the night. I made my toilet run and dressed. I was surprised when I checked my watch and saw that I had slept past nine-thirty. I was usually an early riser, but I knew that William rarely got up before nine or ten. Breakfast was always served promptly at eleven, so I knew I had plenty of time to rustle up a cup of coffee.

I barely stepped off the last stairs when Ozaki greeted me, "Good morning, Mr. Frohman," he said with a toothy smile. "Mr. Girrette asks that you join him in the conservatory for coffee, if it preases you."

"Wherever there's coffee it pleases me, Ozaki. Lead on."

We passed Mrs. Woods coming across the room with an empty serving tray in her hands.

"Good morning," I offered cheerfully.

"It's a bit past that, I believe," she replied, teasing in her eyes. "There's fresh coffee with Mr. Gillette and you'll drink it hot if you hurry."

I followed Ozaki across the great room to a set of ornate french doors. Gone was the scaffolding and drop cloths from the night before, where I now could see wet grout between the stones over the door. They must have finished the work and cleaned up before I awoke. Knowing Will, he probably paid extra to have them complete it on a Saturday morning, just so it would not detract from my first impression of the conservatory.

Ozaki pushed both the doors open and bowed. I just shook my head as I walked by, "You're as bad as he is." The door closed firmly behind me and I felt as if I had stepped into the tropics.

Will explained last night that the inspiration came from memories where he was born and grew up in Nook Farm, just west of Hartford, an intellectual center that was home of Harriett Beecher Stowe and Mark Twain. Mark Twain's home has a conservatory with plants and a small pond. William took this concept and made it grander.

It took a moment to adjust to the steamy atmosphere inside. Moist heat swirled about the room to keep the exotic plants flourishing. Compared to the starkness that was evident throughout the rest of the house, it was an oasis, an Eden at the end of a long winter. Knowing my friend, he most likely had his bedroom and bath completed first, then this conservatory. He was the kind of man who always had a haven handy.

I saw William seated at a small table for two buried behind the morning copy of the New York Times. I was about to greet him as the mist thinned under the morning light, but my tongue went still. The table was situated next to a small pool at the base of a rock waterfall that cascaded from what must have been a water pipe cleverly hidden in the ceiling. The water that flowed down from slab to slab of stacked flat rock wasn't a torrent, but rather a soothing steady trickle that pattered. This corner was lit by two floor to ceiling windows on either wall. The view of the river so stunning I wondered why my friend would sit with his back to it.

Thick green vines hung down from the rafters with their broad leaves glistening in the humid air. Flowers and huge plants, domestic and imported were spread out across the room. Here and there a few benches set amongst the tropical plants. The air was thick with moisture and the

69

warmth was soothing, yet I knew I'd be sweating in short order. I stripped off my coat and vest and took the chair between the table and the pool. Fixing my coffee and taking a sip, I decided that it was a great way to start my morning.

"How did you sleep, Charlie?" William asked from behind the paper, not bothering to lower it.

"Like a baby. I liked the room, very comfy."

"Excellent. It's yours whenever you're here," he pronounced.

"As long as you give me a good rate," I replied.

Suddenly, I jumped as something green sprang out of the pond onto the ledge next to me. My heart started again when I realized it was only a frog. But I was amazed when a second frog jumped out to land next to his friend. Both just looked at me with all four protruding eyes and began to croak simultaneously.

Will, who was laughing outright now with the paper folded in his lap chirped "Charlie," between chuckles, "Meet Mike and Lena."

"Who? The Frogs? You have pet frogs?"

"Oh, my friend. Do not disparage my watch frogs, they are as faithful as any breed of canine." With that, he reached into a bowl next to the sugar and picked out some black flecks he tossed them to Mike and Lena. In short order, their long tongue shot out and quickly lapped up the morsels. "Dried flies," William said.

I made a mental note to myself to be very careful in the mornings as to which bowl I dip my coffee spoon in. They croaked a few minutes more, then William waved his hand at them and said, "No more for now." They turned and dove back into the pool together.

"Jesus!" I exclaimed, "Is that how you plan to spend your retirement? Training frogs?"

"Don't be a ninny, Charlie, I don't think it's possible to

train frogs. And please do not blaspheme."

I ignored the second part of that statement, wishing I hadn't made it. It has always been an abrasive in our relationship. William was much more respectful of "religious mores" than I. Taking the Lord's name in vain would usually elicit some form of rebuke.

Quickly returning to the subject, I challenged, "Then what do you call that performance?"

He laughed, "It's simple really. They always come out of the pool in the same place, usually when they hear sounds or see people, because they are looking for food. I just had Ozaki set the table up here and place your chair there. I figured when you sat down and started speaking, they'd show up."

"You set me up!"

He winked, "You should have seen the look on your face."

We bantered about over a second cup of coffee, and then settled in, William with the New York Times and me with a local rag, while waiting for breakfast. I was not interested in the events the yokels thought newsworthy, until I reached page four.

"Here we go, William", I commented. "Here's a story about that crime on the ferry you were talking about yesterday!"

"Really?" He asked, dropping his paper into his lap, "What does it have to say?"

"Um, let me see," I replied, giving it a quick once over, "Blah blah blah…puzzling death on river ferry … baffled... horses and carriage after dark - perplexed." I looked at him and grinned, "It says they're not sure."

"Oh, switch with me!," He ordered, thrusting his rumpled paper at me. I was more than happy to oblige.

I was just about to enjoy a scathing review of a rival's play to my delight, when an ear piercing SCREAM caused

71

me to knock the coffee carafe over. Will would have been scalded, except he wasn't in his seat any more.

With lightning reaction, he lept from his chair and began to call for Ozaki. He dashed through the glass doors to the great room with me hot on his heels. The scene we ran into made an opening night on Broadway look like a monk's meditation.

Linen was strewn along the railing, some draping down to a pile in the middle of the living area, obviously fallen from a dropped basket above.

A wailing Catty stood in the middle of the upper walkway, with Ozaki gripping her by both the shoulders and shaking her like he was sifting flour. Each time her head snapped back, she would cry out "Minicky!"

Mrs. Wood was bustling up the staircase like a rhinoceros, hollering at Ozaki to unhand the girl. By the time we reached the bottom of the stairs, Mrs. Wood had cleaved herself between Ozaki and the hysterical girl. Clutching her in a death hug, she shot Ozaki a look that would have melted the stone around us.

Ozaki didn't seem to notice as he looked at us to make sure we were watching and then pointed to a spot over our shoulders.

The room was clear behind us, but something caught Will's eye and he beelined for the french doors that led to the courtyard. His footsteps slowed as he approached the windows, having seen something that shocked him to the core.

When we reached the glass doors that led outside, he put his hands on the glass and stared straight out. "Oh, Dear Lord," he whispered.

It took my eyes a moment to focus in the bright sunlight, but then I echoed his sentiment. There was, what appeared to be, an unmoving man, in an unnatural position, lying in the middle of the unfinished courtyard.

The Authorities

Without thinking, my first reaction was to go for the door handles. "No! Wait Charlie!" William grabbed my wrist, never taking his eyes off the lump in the sand.

"Wait for what?" I asked in confusion. "He may need help!"

He slowly shook his head, deeply troubled. "He's way past that point."

I looked out at the shape again, but all I could tell was that he wasn't moving. Yet, I also knew William had far better eyesight than most, "What am I missing here?"

Without turning his head, he replied, "There is sand on his left eye."

I waited for more but he was focused, I hated when he did that, "And?"

"He hasn't blinked," he replied, as if it was the most obvious thing in the world. "He has lain there for hours."

"We need to go out and see who it is." I suggested.

He turned to face me, "I already know. I'm afraid it's young Nickolas. The first mate on the *Aunt Polly*."

"What the hell is he doing lying out there in the middle of your courtyard?"

"What indeed."

Before I could voice a question, he swung around to face Ozaki, who had come up from behind to join us.

"Be sure that Mrs. Wood keeps Catty in the house, then please call the...no, wait, have Mrs. Wood...,". He broke off as he saw Catty sobbing uncontrollably into her shoulder on the couch where we had just sat the night

73

before.

I put up a hand to stop him, "I'll call the police, Will. I'll tell them to bring an ambulance."

"Thank you. I do not wish to lose this train of thought. When you return, we shall see if we can move closer, along the wall. There is something I want to look at closer."

I just sighed. "Got it. Telephone is in the kitchen?"

"Yes, and thank you Frohman."

William moved to unlock one of the french doors with Ozaki right behind him muttering in his native language. Knowing him, he was furious that the lad had the bad grace to get himself killed in sight of the house. I put it aside as I went to find the phone.

It took a few minutes to navigate the rural telephone system. An operator named Pauline finally put me through to the police station in Haddam. A few questions on their end and a few I-don't-knows on mine and I was assured that they would send someone post-haste.

I hung up the phone and went out to join William, passing the two women who were seated on the couch. Catty still mewling uncontrollably as Mrs. Wood tried to comfort her.

My friend was not in sight, but the door was wide open so I quickly left the drama in my wake and stepped outside onto a narrow path that had been laid along the wall. When my eyes adjusted to the morning sun, I found William, standing alone in his shirtsleeves on the wall that surrounded the unfinished courtyard. He was perpendicular to the corpse with binoculars dangling from his shoulder. The wall had a wide, flat top and he was facing a twenty foot drop off the other side if he lost his footing. He was standing rock still, staring intently at the corpse that lay far enough towards the middle of the courtyard that I could not see any details.

"What the hell are you doing, Will?" I called out. "You're going to break your neck!"

"Nonsense," he replied in a loud voice, not taking his eyes off the heap of mud splattered clothes and waxy flesh directly across from him. "Join me. You may find this interesting!"

Morbid curiosity pulled me up onto that ledge and I made my way carefully out to my friend. I didn't want to break his concentration as I sidled up to him, so I just stood still and shaded my eyes to squint for a better look. What I saw made my stomach flip-flop in a way that made me grateful we hadn't gotten around to breakfast.

The corpse lay in a twisted position. His torso was flat on his back but the hips and legs were twisted up and back in a way that was most unnatural. I could hardly tell it was a person and it was covered with sand and soil which hid most else from me. I could only assume it was a man by the flat chest and the clothes the first mate wore.

"How the hell did you know it was your first mate, Nickolas?" I asked a after a moment. I wasn't really sure if I wanted to get him going, but curiosity got the better of me.

He looked at me, "Catty of course. She was screaming 'My Nicky' over and over." He gave me a curious look, "Are you getting hard of hearing, Frohman?"

There was the 'Frohman' again. "No. I just don't speak hysteric, so I didn't understand," I replied. "How the hell could she tell who it was from so far away and with the sun in her eyes?"

"A lover always knows," he replied simply. "I've had my suspicions about those two for some time."

"Ooooooh, I see."

"I suspect she was just through collecting the bed sheets and laundry when she looked out the upstairs windows and saw him." Will was about to expand when something caught his eye and he shouted around the back of my head.

"You men there! Stop! Please stay back until the police arrive!"

I looked to where he was shouting and I saw Ollie and his crew, jumping off two wagons filled with poles and planks. They pulled a ladder off the side of the first wagon and started towards the wall at a frantic pace.

They immediately stopped dead in their tracks, to stare up at their employer. It took Ollie, talking fast and firmly, to quickly herd the workmen back to the wagons.

"Thank goodness!" Will said looking at me. "Their mucking about could have complicated an already herculean enigma."

"What the hell are you talking about, Will?" I could not believe the insensitivity! Very unlike the William I knew. "One of your best men is laying out there, man! It's tragic - not fascinating!"

Will looked at me like I was insane. "You really don't see it do you?"

"See what?"

He shook his head and sighed. Pointing to the body he asked, "Tell me what you see?"

I really wasn't in the mood for guessing games, but I owed him enough respect to listen to him when he's in this mode. I took a good hard look at the scene before me. Nickolas obviously hit the ground hard. The body was crumpled and embedded in the center of courtyard. I could just make out the twisted limbs, splayed in an unnatural position. The one mar on an otherwise perfectly smooth courtyard table of sand.

Something overall was nagging at me, but I couldn't put my finger on it so I reverted to sarcasm. "A dead Russian sailor," I replied, looking up at the castle's upper balconies, "who either lost his footing or decided life wasn't worth living."

He ignored my tone, "And how far would you say it lies from the nearest point of the house?"

I shrugged, "I dun no. Thirty maybe thirty-five feet."

"And how far from the nearest point of the retaining wall?"

"Twenty, maybe twenty-five feet on the outside."

"A rather far leap for anyone. Even with a running start." Will gestured to his upper balcony. "Which is highly unlikely given the balcony is only a few feet wide."

"He could have gotten on the roof where we were last night."

Will shook his head. "No. Even for a young man as fit as Nickolas it's not likely. The balustrades are five feet high. He would have had to launch himself over that obstacle first and his momentum could not have carried him this far out! I doubt he could have cleared the lower balcony from there."

"Well, he certainly looks like he took a fall! I think your speculations might be a tad off this time."

"Not speculation, Frohman! Physics! However he made his way to that spot, he did not begin from my rooftop!" Then he added in an afterthought, "Nor, I fear, did he act alone."

"You think someone put him there!"

Will made a sweeping gesture at the courtyard. "A possibility though not plausible with the evidence before us."

"Evidence?"

He sighed, "What do you see on the ground around the body?"

I looked around as hard as I could but I came up with nothing of interest. Except where the body lay, it was flat and unblemished. Smoothed by the crew yesterday in anticipation of the stone laying. Then it struck me. The ground all around the corpse was empty of marks. No footprints. No drag marks. Nothing. I looked at my friend incredulously, "How in God's name did he get there?"

Will looked down his nose at me, eyes glittering with anticipation, "That is what we must discover and what makes this case most unusual. Let's go down and take a walk along the wall until the police arrive and look for some evidence of an explanation, shall we?"

So we made our way back to the main house, walking in to see Catty's face still buried in Mrs. Woods' bosom. The older woman gestured for us to slip past and we made our way to the side door. This led us outside again just a few paces from the courtyard's curved retaining wall. It was only a few feet high where it met the house to nearly twenty feet in height due to the sloping ground.

Will put his arm up to keep me from walking past him, and put the binoculars to his face again, slowly scanning the ground before him. I stood there staring at him for a long minute. It had all happened so fast it was still a blur in my mind. Yet I know Will was focused.

Calling me by my surname and referring to this whole incident as a 'case' was a sure sign that he was going into character. I wasn't sure how I felt about that. Parlor tricks and little bouts of deduction was one thing, but this was a serious matter. A man had died.

Still, it was his home and it would definitely put him off from pursuing the river robbery with another mysterious murder. I decided to play along; confident the police would arrive shortly.

I followed along behind him as he walked bent over, to examine the rock wall and the ground around it. Will finally straightened when we reached the apex. There was little more than twenty feet of ground left between the steep wooded slope that led to the river.

"Find anything?" I asked.

"Nothing of relevance." He turned and abruptly walked over to the small knot of workmen who were awaiting instructions.

"Any of you men see anything or know anything about this?" Will asked. I was wondering how they knew the body was there at all. You could not see the center of the courtyard from this angle below.

They all shook their heads and mumbled their responses at the same time. Ollie stepped forward.

"No Sir, we did not." He answered for the crew. "We had just crested the rise in the driveway back there when..." he jerked a thumb at a young man standing next to him, still holding up his end of the ladder, "Dylan sees someone lying in the sand."

"The sand we spent three days leveling out!" Dylan spat out, almost indignant that his work was marred.

Ollie glared at the kid so hard I thought his ears would catch fire.

"We could all see that he wasn't moving so we pick up the pace and then we heard a girl screaming from inside the house, so we double timed it over. Of course, we weren't going to barge through the house, so I told the boys to grab the ladder as soon as we stopped and we'd get to him that way. I hope I didn't overstep my duties, Sir, I just thought that you and Mr. Frohman might need a hand when we saw you standing on the wall."

He paused and asked, "One of the lads says he's sure it's Nicky. Is it?"

William clasped him on the shoulder. "I'm afraid it is, Ollie, and you did nothing wrong. I only wish to preserve the scene for the authorities to examine."

He turned and looked over to the men, "Any of you lads have any idea what might have happened here?"

Again, there was a spat of head shaking and mumbled denials, though there was one under the breath mutter,

"Ain't natural, I say!"

Ollie's eyeballs popped out of his skull as he wheeled on his crew.

"Who said that?" Without waiting for a reply he plowed on, "If I hear anyone flapping their gums like that, they'll be flapping their arms next, when I throw them off my crew.... right over the bluff! I...."

The rest of his tirade was drowned out by the sound of motorcars and sirens which approached the front of the house.

The Chief

The coppers made a great show of their arrival with sirens blaring and both vehicles screeching to a sliding halt, kicking up great clouds of dust from the dirt road.

Their dramatic entrance was marred by the fact they had to sit in their cars until the dust settled out of the air or they'd be filthy the moment they stepped out. Will smirked and rolled his eyes at me.

As we waited for the local yokels to emerge and I turned to my friend. "What was that all about? Why did he say 'ain't natural?'" I asked.

William rolled his eyes. "One of them must have seen the same thing we did; that there was no evidence of the corpse reaching that point in the sand. Which, of course will be more than enough for these swamp yankees to prove there is black magic at work?"

He gave me a stern look and admonished, "Now, please, there have been more than rumors about me since I began building here years ago. I am feared and despised by some of the more simple folk in these parts, with views more suited for the sixteenth century. I am sure some locals have decided because of the design of my home, my desire for privacy or that I was not born here, that I am either a demon, warlock, or one of those blood drinking creatures that Stoker wrote about."

"I hate to say, but a mysterious death is only going to result in more warlock gossip for certain." I pointed out.

He sighed, "People can be so ignorant."

"You know Will, now that I think about it," I teased, "you are a rich recluse. You do live in the only castle on the east coast, and you have a uniquely exotic Asian master servant." After a pause, I shrugged, "Who knew?!"

He gave me a withering look but the authorities reached us before he could reply.

One was a large man with a cigarette dangling out of his mouth. Taller than William by a few inches and packing more pounds, but looking pretty dapper for a public servant.

The second was of a slighter frame, still athletic, wearing an ill fitted suit of last year's cut. Two constables waited by the car until, I assumed, they were needed or called for.

William stepped forward to greet them, but the big man just held up a finger then pointed at our feet, a clear signal to wait and not move, and then walked right by. The second one had the grace to stop for a moment. He checked his watch, then flipped open a small note book and jotted down the time.

"Good Morning, Inspector Rowan," William greeted him, "I-"

Rowan cut him off, "Morning. I'll be with you in just a moment, Sir," he said hastily as he rushed to join his obvious superior.

Will and I looked at each other again.

"That was rude." I observed.

The big oaf made a beeline for Ollie, whom he obviously knew, but I was more concerned with the reaction of the rest of the crew. As he approached, they all took a collective step backwards. If I was a dog, I could have smelled the fear in them.

Ollie didn't look too thrilled to be singled out, but he held his ground. The man asked Ollie a few questions, who pointed to the wall and courtyard beyond, and then to the ladder that was lying just a few feet away.

A couple of the men set the ladder against the wall, halfway down the wall, a good eight feet high at that point, and the big fellow climbed up it nimbly. After a few minutes, he climbed down and Rowan took his place. He walked over to William, took his glasses off and wiped them carefully before replacing them back on his nose. He took a deep breath, "I understand the deceased, Nickolas Ivanovich, is in your employ."

When he didn't continue, William spoke, "Yes, he was. He was the first mate on my ship, the *Aunt Polly*. She's berthed down below us."

"Have you noticed anything strange about his behavior lately?"

"His behavior?" Will returned. "Oh, I see. You are thinking this must have been a suicide." He shook his head, "I would not make that assumption if I were you. I'm certain that Nickolas did not leap to his death from my roof."

The big man's face pinched until his eyeballs met and he looked like he was about to take a big bite out of my friend's ass. The younger man was off the ladder by then and sensing that there was going to be an explosion, hustled over.

The big man managed to get control of himself and clasped his hands behind his back. When he spoke, his voice was not unkindly, as he must have misunderstood William's reaction.

"I'm sorry. I know these things are hard to fathom sometimes. It's hard to believe someone you know would do such a thing. If you look the area over carefully, you will see that there is nowhere else he could have come from. And he couldn't have slipped off by accident or been pushed and landed where he did. It took determination and speed to make a leap like that."

"You are wrong, Sir," William stated. "A leap like that is impossible for anyone."

The cop snorted and his face turned beet red. "Come

again? What do you mean- wrong? I hope you can explain just why I'm wrong!"

Will didn't back down an inch. "Plain physics, Sir. The highest point of the structure that faces the courtyard is seventy-two feet. It is set back twenty-two feet four inches from the lowest balcony. The body is around twenty-five feet farther out than that. As all objects fall at thirty-two feet per second, even allowing for thrust and momentum, gravity would have pulled him to earth a great deal shorter than that."

The flatfoot stared at him in amazement and with little amusement. "That's quite a mouthful. Are you some kind of college professor, or something?"

This pompous ass was starting to grate on me. I made a big show of writing numbers in the air and mumbling until I had their attention. "And carry the one." I stabbed the air with my finger and looked directly at the rude bugger. "He's right, Chief. Do the math."

"Watch yourself pal," he jabbed a finger in my direction. "I've got a special program for smart asses!"

He turned back to Will. "And you must be Mr. William Gillette, the famous actor. When you're not teaching physics."

"I am."

"And you built Buckingham Palace here behind us."

"It is hardly of that scale, but you are correct. This is my home."

"You were pretty sure of your measurements. I am Michael Luboff, Chief Inspector for the Haddam district." He gestured to the other man, "And I think you already met Inspector Rowan."

Rowan stuck out his hand and he and William shook again. Will was about to introduce me, but Luboff spoke right over him. Carelessly tossing his spent cigarette in my direction, he asked, "How and when did you discover the body?"

I wasn't used to being snubbed, as it never happened in my purview, and I didn't much like it. Fuming, I only half listened to William as he gave a dissertation about our morning, but I'm sure it was precise and accurate, as was his nature. Luboff listened while Rowan took notes on a small brown writing pad. Luboff was silent for the most part, almost bored it seemed, until William mentioned Catty and her reaction.

He put up his hands in a silencing motion and asked slowly, "Oh Really? Are you telling me they were an item?"

That got Will's dander up, "It appears that way, though I could not say with any certainty."

"Don't pay much attention to the help, Eh?"

"As long as a person in my hire performs their duties, I have no say, nor interest in their personal lives."

Luboff slowly looked him up and down, then up again with contempt. "I see. I would think even a famous actor would keep a closer eye on a young girl in his employ."

"Just what are you implying?" William's face never betrayed a wisp of his emotions, but I could see the steam coming out of his ears.

"Oh, I never imply Mr. Gillette."

William drew himself up to the fullest of his impressive height, his usual prelude to a scathing remark, but Luboff cut him off.

"Is the staff inside?"

With a supreme effort, William reined in his tongue and replied stiffly, "I believe so, yes."

"Then take me to them."

"Do you not wish to examine the scene or the body? The poor man is just lying out there!" William said.

Luboff dropped any pretense of civility and snarled, "That may be just the way you write it in your silly plays,

Gillette, but this is the real world! Here we follow procedure and method! The medical examiner has been sent for and I'll take his findings into account. Though, frankly, despite your theatrics and the math lesson, it's fairly obvious what happened here. Until then, he can just lie there."

Will began to argue with him some more but Luboff was having none of it.

"Enough! Take us in to your staff or I'll haul the whole lot of you to the station and we can spend the day sorting it out there!"

Will looked as if he might start up again, but bit his tongue and made a half mocking bow and gesture towards the side door.

Before we could start out, Ollie called out to Will from the wagons, "Mr. Gillette? What about the Italians? They're due here by midmorning."

William drew in a deep breath to answer him, but Luboff cut him off.

"What Italians?" he asked out of the side of his mouth that didn't have a cigarette sticking out.

"Masons. The courtyard was to be paved today."

Luboff took the butt from his mouth and turned to Ollie, "Tell them to beat it! There will be no work today or until I say so. Tell your men to keep this area clear until either myself or Rowan here tells you otherwise."

William's eyes shot daggers at the copper but he said nothing and turned on his heels to walk towards the side door.

Luboff took Ollie by the arm, "You know this place?"

"Been working here since we dug the hole for the foundation," he answered with pride.

"Then follow my instructions and come inside."

Ollie nodded and went over to his crew.

Luboff caught me staring at him from the corner of my

86

eye and growled, "What?"

I shrugged, "You just cost my friend a lot of money."

Luboff made a grand show of sweeping the castle with his eyes, then he grinned, "And?"

I just followed my friend towards the door.

Love Revealed

I came in on Will's heels and I caught Mrs. Woods
hustling a still sobbing Catty into the kitchen as we
entered. The furtive look Mrs. Woods gave us as we
entered made me certain she was trying to keep Catty out
of sight. I was puzzled by her reaction, and then it
occurred to me that her romance with Nickolas would
most likely not be viewed acceptable to these clannish
people.

Ollie came in shortly after us and when William gave
him a questioning look, the old man just shrugged and
jabbed a thumb over his shoulder. The chief Inspector
came barging in behind him with inspector Rowan and a
constable in tow.

"Gillette," he said without preamble, "I'm going to have
Ollie here show my men the upper levels and the roof. I
hope you don't have a problem with that."

William was too shocked to answer. I knew he was
horrified at the prospect of complete strangers poking
about his home.

So the words just poured out of my mouth before I could
form them in my head. "Who do you think you're dealing
with, bub? You think you can just bully your way into a
man's home and conduct a search. Do you have a
warrant?"

He just turned his head and looked at me like I was a
pesky fly. He put his finger in the air and made a twirling
motion. "This entire property is the scene of an active
death investigation. I don't need a warrant! BUB! Now

that's the second time you've spoken out of turn." He looked at me over the rims of his glasses, "I better not hear a third."

With that, he dismissed me and turned back to William. "Is this going to be a problem?"

William straightened up, oozing dignity and replied softly, "No. Do what you must." He turned his head slowly and addressed Rowan. "I'll trust in your discretion to protect my privacy, Inspector."

Ollie waited for a nod from his boss before he led the way to the staircase. Rowan held back a moment as Luboff whispered something to him and Rowan replied in kind. As the young inspector bustled across the room to catch up, Luboff turned his attention to Ozaki, who was standing nearby. He looked Ozaki up and down, as if he didn't know what to make of him. Then suddenly took him by the arm and propelled him along into the center of the room.

Ozaki looked to William, his face showing none of the rage I knew he must be feeling. He loathed to be touched by anyone. I knew William was about to explode himself, for he was as protective of Ozaki as the little man was loyal to him.

But I put a firm restraining hand on William's arm. I knew what these small town dictators were like. My Uncle Jack was the sheriff of the Hampton's when I was growing up and he ruled his fief with an iron fist. It was better just to let them blow smoke. Otherwise we could just have bigger problems.

William looked down at Luboff's hand then at me and I shook my head. He trusted me enough to give Ozaki a nod, letting him know to co-operate. Luboff removed his hand from Ozaki, and then stepped in front of him. He gave Ozaki the once over again then raised his head. Looking over the top of Ozaki's head and snapped, "Does he speak anything but Chinaman?"

Remarkably, William kept his composure as he stepped over to the Chief inspector. "I believe the term is Chinese, Chief Inspector." he said in his best stage voice. "And I doubt very much if any of us in this room speaks Chinese, despite the irrelevance!" Will stared Luboff right in the eye and added between clenched teeth, "Ozaki is Japanese, and besides, he speaks very good English!"

"Good! Then he'll understand what'll happen to him if I think he's lying to me! Now, step back, Gillette." the Chief instructed with barely concealed impatience, "Have a seat until I get around to you."

Now, I knew it was going to get ugly, unless I defused the situation, so I stepped over and took William by the arm to lead him across the room and sat him on the couch.

I know just what straws would break Will's back and Luboff had a bundle of them. But I also knew his type of bully, the big fish in a little pond, and whether or not he came to regret it, - as he most assuredly would-, he would toss William in a cell for as long as he could and rough him up a bit for good measure.

So I made sure we just sat quietly as Luboff questioned Ozaki for a quarter of an hour or so. The questions popped out of him so fast I could hardly keep up with the answers.

What did he see? What did he hear? When did he go to bed? When did he awaken? What was he doing before the body was found? Why did Catty see it before him?

His questions went on and on, each one seeming more to lead Ozaki into a position where he had failed in his responsibilities in some way.

William cringed at the bent the interrogation was taking, but I kept him in his seat. Ozaki was doing fine without our help.

His story was the same as you have already heard. He kept his answers short and truthful, giving Luboff no opening to attack him until Luboff's last question.

"One more, then you are free to go about your business." he said in a calmer, almost congenial voice, "Did you get along with him?"

Ozaki looked confused, "Sorry. Get arong? I don't understand."

"Get along! You know, ever pal around?"

"Par around? I'm so sorry, but I do not understand."

"I mean, were you friends with this Nickolas fellow?"

Ozaki's facial features rippled and he tensed from head to toe. "Not friends"

"Good!" the Chief barked a laugh, "I don't much like foreigners myself!"

He spun away from Ozaki and gestured to his underling, who was just coming down the stairs, Ollie and the uniform in tow. "Let's go! We're burning daylight."

As he approached us on the couch from one direction and Rowan from the other, we rose.

"We didn't find anything out of the ordinary." he reported. Just stone mostly. No scuffs or scrapes or any sign anyone had been up there recently. Of course it did rain earlier last night."

Luboff nodded thoughtfully.

"Call the women out here, Gillette." he demanded in his next breath.

"Chief Inspector," William replied in a steady voice, "I'm sure I could answer any questions you may have. Nickolas's death has upset them greatly."

Luboff just took a deep breath in through his nose and rubbed his forehead.

"Just call them out here," he ordered, through clenched teeth. Then added in a menacing tone, "And let me put this in some lingo you might understand. Now!"

Rowan, at least, had the good grace to look embarrassed

at his superior's bad manners. "I'll fetch them, Sir." He offered and quickly half trotted towards the kitchen before Luboff could object.

In a moment, Mrs. Woods and Catty came out together with their arms interlocked. William and I stood to allow the women a seat.

Rowan herded them over to the couch and Mrs. Woods gently lowered Catherine and sat so close to her their thighs were touching. He and William took up positions on either end of the couch and I elected to move off a few feet to lean against the fireplace. Close enough to hear but far enough to observe everyone.

Luboff sauntered over to loom over the two of them. He looked down at Catty and heaved a theatrical sigh, causing her to cry again.

Mrs. Woods whispered in her ear and gave her a comforting nudge, then rubbed her on the back until Catty lifted her head to look up at the Chief Inspector.

She had regained at least some measure of composure. Perhaps a little too much as she began to look a little catatonic to me. If Luboff noticed the same thing it didn't alter his mode of questioning.

"Well, Catty! You're not having much of a day, are you?"

"Chief Inspector!" Mrs. Woods gasped, showing the shock we all felt at Luboff's insensitivity. He just stuck his forefinger at her with a look that was clearly meant to shut her up.

Catty recoiled like she'd been slapped. Tears welled in her eyes again and she squeaked, "No sir."

Luboff just stared at her and made a gesture for her to continue.

"I'm a busy man, Catty. Don't make me drag it out of you!"

I thought she'd break right then and there but the girl had

some grit yet and there was a spark in her eye as she regained control of herself and looked the stern behemoth looming over her dead in the eye.

"I was collecting the linens from the upstairs when I glanced out the window where the new courtyard was going in. I was thinking how nice it would look, facing the river and all. And Nicky was lying there on the ground, not moving. I knew he was gone." Abruptly, she went quiet again.

"You have any ideas about how he ended up out there?" He pointed in the general direction of the courtyard.

"No! He shouldn't have been here!"

"And just where was he supposed to be?"

Catty was taken back by the question and just lowered her eyes and said nothing. Luboff pounced.

"So what made you scream like a stuck pig when you saw the body? I've never known you for a squeamish girl before."

Mrs. Woods shot off the couch, her body ridgid with indignation, "Chief Inspector! That's enough! Can't you see this poor child's been--"

"QUIET!" Luboff roared, "Not another word! If you can't shut your trap you can wait in the kitchen until I need you!"

She gave Catty a look as if to say, -be strong -, and rose from the couch with a quiet dignity to walk into the kitchen. She hadn't crossed the threshold when Luboff began to badger Catty again.

"So what's with all the weeping and wailing, Catty? There wouldn't be anything between you two, would there? No! I can't see that! I know you were raised right and good girls don't spend time with godless foreign sailors." He leaned in close and almost whispered, "Because we know what those kind of men want. The only thing they want, don't we?"

I have to admit, his methods were reprehensible, but he did get results.

"It wasn't like that!" she snarled. "He wasn't like that. He was my fiancée!" She started to sob again, "We loved each other. We were going away to get married!"

Ozaki's Last Word

Jaws dropped, eyes crossed, and everyone stared at her in disbelief. The Chief, the uniforms, and William were struck speechless. You would have thought she just announced she was going to have Ozaki's baby!

Ozaki was the only one, besides me, in the room who seemed to have any compassion for the young lady as he looked at her with sad eyes.

Luboff starred at her for a moment then lunged again.

"Really now? With flowers and a priest? In a nice church? Where's the ring? Or do you only wear it when nobody can see it? Like your family perhaps?" He sighed and gave her a look somewhere between disgust and pity. "Or maybe that boy was just stringing you along? There is a reason they call them 'sweet nothings' when they're whispered in your ear."

"There is too a ring!" she screeched. "I've seen it! And I could have worn it if I wanted! If people weren't so stupid and mean!" She looked as if she was about to burst again, but she pulled herself together and went on more slowly, "I...I just didn't want to wear it until I could in the open. Nicky was keeping it for me until we left."

"Left? Left for where Catty girl?"

"New York City. We were going to be married there."

"Oh, I'm sure." Luboff barked out a laugh. "A pretty girl like you, from a good home, was going to elope with a dumb, penniless, boat mate?"

"He wasn't Dumb! He graduated from college! With a degree! From a good university! After we were married we were going to travel Europe until he found a position!"

95

"And how were the two of you going to manage that! Does Gillette here pay you that much?" He jerked a thumb in William's direction.

"I'm good with my money and Nicky has been saving almost everything he makes. And he was getting more sent over from his family soon. He comes from a well-to-do family in St. Petersburg!"

For a moment it looked as if she was about to attack Luboff physically, a lioness defending her mate, but she broke under Luboff's glare and burst into tears. Keening and crying as if she wished for death herself, Luboff was forced to let up for a few minutes until the onslaught subsided and he could address her again.

"Best you tell us everything, Catty." Luboff said, not unkindly, "So we can begin to put this behind us."

Catty regained her composure and droned on in a monotone for quite a while. Apparently, she had been secretly seeing Nicky for quite some time. Their love grew faster than her parent's disapproval. Nicky assured her that he was expecting a good sum of money and they could finally make their move. They were going to go to New York City and marry there. Afterwards they would be taking the next passenger ship to Europe.

He instructed her to pack what she needed and tell her folks she would be staying with Mrs. Woods at the castle for a few days. Apparently, this was common enough for big cleaning projects or when William was to have guests. They planned on sending her family a telegram after they had boarded a ship for Europe.

I rather thought it all idyllic. They were young, in love, and had money which was a better start than ninety percent of us. I also noted that I was in the minority as Luboff looked disgusted, Rowan disapproving, and William kept his head down out of sincere sorrow and loyalty.

She went on to say that she had seen Nicky yesterday in the early afternoon because William had given him the day off. She noted that he seemed a little nervous but in high spirits, describing all the wonderful sights they would visit promising her good things were going to happen soon, though he wouldn't say more.

"I don't understand! Why did this happen? How? We were going to meet last night at eight o'clock, but he never showed. I thought that nasty Captain Roy had put him to work. He was always doing that and trying to keep Nicky and me apart!"

I could see that William was itching to ask something, but hesitant because of Luboff's manner, but Rowan stepped up to the plate.

"Where were you supposed to meet him?" he asked Catty.

"At the Chester ferry landing." she replied. "Then we were going to catch a train to the city."

"Do you have any idea why Nickolas would be anywhere near the castle last night?"

"No! He almost never came up to the house, especially if Mr. Gillette was home and certainly wouldn't have while he had company!" A puzzled look came over her.

"What happened to him?" she demanded suddenly. "Why is he dead?" She nearly whispered, but then burst out, "Ask that nasty Captain Roy! He spent more time with my Nicky than anyone!"

The Chief Inspector just looked down on her, a stern look on his face. "It doesn't matter Catherine. Not to you anymore. Let me give you a bit of advice. Put this all behind you as soon as you can and be thankful this foolishness ended before it could have ruined your life, not to mention your family's name."

Luboff turned away from her, not bothering to see the devastation he caused the young girl and bellowed, "Mrs.

Woods! Come here please!"

The woman poked her head around the jamb of the kitchen door and then walked out, head held high, eyes ablaze, with a look designed to strike Luboff dead. "Yes, Chief inspector?" she said coldly.

"I know you were listening, so let's skip the dance. Do you have anything to add?"

She hesitated a moment then replied, "No. Not really. I last saw Nicky yesterday afternoon, from afar, as I was getting ready to go. I'm not sure he saw me, or if he did, he didn't wave or anything. He was coming out of the boat house and heading towards the *Aunt Polly*."

"What was he wearing?" William asked.

"Wearing?"

"Yes, how was he dressed?"

"In his usual work clothes, dungarees and a blue shirt."

"If you both are quite through." Luboff cut in, "I'm asking the questions."

Mrs. Woods glared at him, "And you could have asked me first! I could have told you everything without your brutal manner."

"How could you let this go on?" he shot back, "You know her family."

"Catty is my friend." she replied calmly. "I helped her as best a friend can."

Luboff shook his head. "Women!"

He looked Mrs. Wood dead in the eye and then pointed at Catty, and then the door.

"Get her and yourself in the car. I will drop you on my way back from the station." He leveled a challenging stare at William.

"The Ladies are taking the rest of the day off." He glanced back towards the door where the two constables had placed themselves. "Gibson." One of the bobbies stepped over to escort the two women to the car, and after a few exchanged looks with William and a reassuring nod from him, the girls gathered themselves and took their things that Ozaki had already fetched for them.

Luboff turned to Rowan, "That's it for now. I'll go with Gibson back to the station. You and the rest of the men can wait for the doctor and the meat wagon. Tell him to call me with the results. After he takes the body, get a statement from the captain. Meet me at the station when it's tidied up." With that walked toward the door.

William shot after him in a snit and they both stopped five feet short of the door where Ozaki stood to assist.

"Chief Inspector, am I to understand that this is to be the length of your investigation? And the browbeating of my servants is the span of your attention to this matter? Are you not curious about the condition and the position of the victim? So disinterested that you are not even going to look over the scene?"

Luboff turned toward William and with a great sigh, he said, "Nothing I have seen or heard so far goes against my original thought. It was either a suicide or just plain old clumsiness on the part of a 'Ruskie' in love."

William was aghast, "Even when your own men reported that there was no evidence that Nickolas was in the house, which I assure you he was not!"

"Well, if you don't mind," he replied sarcastically, "I'll let the doctor's report speak for itself."

Luboff's face broke into a crocodile grin, "I have no intention of wasting time just because some foreign boat mate decided to die on your door step! So, yes it is, Mr. Gillette. It may be a little over the heads of laymen, such as yourself, but professional investigators gather all the information before they come to any conclusions."

Will was on his stump and had no intention of stepping off it.

"And how are we to know whether it was a natural death

or otherwise without an examination of the scene? Or is that simply too inconvenient for you?"

William took a breath to rail on, but Luboff rode right over him.

"If I were you, Gillette, I would pray it was a natural death. Or you're going to see just how 'inconvenient' I can be! This isn't one of your plays where the answer is revealed in three acts! This is real life, not Broadway. Say! Perhaps when it's all said and done, you can adapt it. You can call it, *The Case of the Flying Corpse!*" With that he broke into a chuckle at his own wit as he turned and walked towards the door.

"Sir, I find your methods erroneous!" William called to his retreating back.

Ozaki was there to open the door and bowed slightly, clearly giving Luboff a chance to walk out. Instead, the Chief Inspector froze and turned slowly to face William. He pushed his glasses higher up his nose, hitched up his pants, and asked "Err...what-us?"

"It means, without effort or merit" Ozaki explained with a toothy smile.

Luboff went beet red. I thought he was going to blow a gasket, but he simply glared at Ozaki and stomped out the door. Ozaki pulled the door firmly shut.

The Meat Wagon

There was an awkward silence. No one spoke until we heard the motorcars start up and roar away. Rowan turned to William with a sheepish look on his face, "I am sorry, Mr. Gillette, Well, no, damn it! Actually sir, I'm not!"

"I beg your pardon?" William asked.

"I am not going to apologize for the man! He's a lout and a blowhard and some days working for him is what I always envisioned hell to be!"

"You certainly have my sympathies son," I said.

Rowan looked at me and hesitated. William realized that we had never been introduced. "It is I who should apologize, Inspector, for not introducing you to my dearest friend, Charles Frohman."

We shook hands and said formal greetings. Ozaki slid over to William's side with our coats draped over his arm to inform him of something. William nodded and threw his arm in his coat.

"It seems that the doctor is about to arrive, Inspector. Just let us get our coats and hats and we can proceed."

"Us? I think not, Sir!" Rowan said in a voice trying to be authoritative. "The doctor and I will examine the scene. It would be best if you stay in the house until we finish."

"Nonsense Inspector," William said firmly, "This occurred on my property and Nickolas was my employee. This event, be it foul play, misdeed, or accidental, has some mysterious points and I want some answers!"

Rowan looked at him like he had three heads, "Sir, the Chief was right about one point, this is not the theater. The

101

blood will be real and there are no scripts to guide us. It could be extremely gruesome."

"Still," I pointed out, trying to stave off a confrontation. "A couple of extra sets of eyes couldn't hurt. Besides, I really do believe you need a warrant to keep a man off his own patio!"

You could see the wheels turning in the young Inspector's head as he mulled over what I said. He opened his mouth to retort, but no sound came out and he turned back to William.

"What you do on stage is wonderful, yet nothing like real police work, Sir. Most of what we do is mundanely unpleasant. I see no need for you to involve yourself further unless you're needed. Not to be rude, Sir, but what could you possibly contribute?"

William took his cue like a true master of his craft.

"Inspector, besides the obvious facts that you are happily married to a blonde, have a daughter, two cats, one of which is an outdoor pet, police work was not your first choice of careers. Although your father was one, God rest his soul, and the fact that you're going to have another child which you hope will be a son, there is just one point I'm not clear on. Are you a mason or was it your father?"

Now, I had seen this act before and I was still impressed, but the young Inspector was floored. "We both are or rather were. I mean, he was and I am." He was speechless for a moment, but rebounded quickly. "I'll grant you that every word you spoke was true, but I am a public figure and this is a small town. You have obviously listened to wagging tongues."

"I do not engage in gossip, Inspector. Every fact was gleaned with observation and deduction. Though you wear no ring, the blonde hair stuck to your cuff link tells us she's blonde and the smudge of lipstick on the back of your right ear tells of happiness. A second blond hair between your coat collar and shirt tells me you received a fierce hug this morning from a young child. The bright blonde shade and the curl and length could only come from the head of a pretty young girl. Likewise, there are two distinct cat hairs on your pants and a muddy paw print on your boot, hence the outdoor cat."

Rowan said with a nod, "I see."

"When you opened your notebook, aside from your notes, I could not help but see you had filled a page with boy's names, all with your surname. A sure indication you were planning on being a father again and you wish for a son."

Rowan looked at him, eyebrows raised, "You can read shorthand? Upside down?"

William merely shrugged and plowed on, "The shorthand is what told me that you had attended a university and had studied business. Not the courses a man plans on for a career in Police work. That and the fraternity pin hanging on your watch chain. I observed when you checked the time earlier, that the watch itself was your father's, given to him at the time of his retirement, as told by the date engraved on the lid. A watch I'm sure he would have worn himself until his death." Will waited a moment before continuing.

"The frat pin is much newer than the fob, therefore yours, but I could not tell, for the flapping of your jacket, whether the mason pin was original to the fob or that you added it."

At that point, Rowan didn't know whether to squat or wind his watch. Before he could say anything, a constable stuck his head in the door and announced that the doctor had arrived. Rowan gathered his thoughts and said, "Come along then. But remember! This is my investigation. Stay in the background and follow my instructions." Then he pointed his pencil at both of us and added, "And the Chief must never know about this!"

We nodded and gave him heartfelt assurances of our discretion, and then we headed for the door. Ozaki was there to open the door and to hand each of us our hats as the doctor and his meat wagon approached.

The Scene

We went out the front door and out the portico just as the meat wagon rolled to a stop. For its grim name, it was really just a simple Ford Model T with a box on the back. The three occupants piled out of the front seats.

Two were your regular constables, the older man wore the stripes of a sergeant and the younger, in a crisp, creased uniform, looked as if he just came on duty for the first time this morning. They introduced themselves and shook hands with William but I hadn't really heard their names. The object of my attention was the man between them, wearing a country cut suit of neutral brown and carrying an old battered valise.

Doctor Thomas Blum was a slight man, certainly of the Jewish faith by his features and cut of beard. He carried himself with that air of self-confidence that made you confident of his abilities. I myself always sought out a Jew when I needed medical treatment. They were the best in my opinion.

William brought us all back inside to the doors that led to the courtyard. We all stopped for a moment, standing shoulder to shoulder, noses practically pressed to the panes in the doors to look at the corpse before we went out. It lay there in the morning sun, only it and the sand that still bore the pockmarks of last night's rain which marred the smooth surface.

"Hard to believe," Rowan said, breaking the silence, "Nicky and I have had pints a few times over at the Widow's Tavern. We weren't the closest of friends, by any means, but he was a very smart and likable fellow."

There was a melancholy timber to his voice that

endeared me to the lad. It gave him a more human side, in stark contrast to his despot boss.

"What makes it harder to understand," he went on, "is that he did it on the night he was supposed to elope! Why would he do such a thing? Leave a sweet girl like Catty in trade for oblivion?"

"Coldest feet I ever heard of" I joked. It went over like a belly laugh in a confessional.

Will peered down at me from the corner of his eye and sighed as he turned his head to Rowan. "You seem certain it was a suicide, Inspector?"

Rowan looked surprised, "What else could it have been, Mr. Gillette? There are no foot prints, or any other marks for that matter, in the sand! Even if there was someone else and they smoothed out their tracks, it would be impossible to duplicate the pattern the rain drops made hitting the surface of the sand. He had to have dropped from somewhere above us."

With a tilt of his head, a new thought came to him.

"I suppose it could have been accidental."

"How so?" William asked.

"I wouldn't want to speculate, this early in the investigation, but what if Nicky was delayed and missed his meeting with Catty? He would have known she was here because this is where she told her parents she would be. Perhaps he was trying to climb up to her room and slipped on the wet stone."

"Don't waste your time perusing impossible scenarios, Inspector. There is no way Nickolas jumped or fell from my home to where he landed. Whatever happened to young Nickolas was not initiated in the courtyard but somewhere farther from the house or the immediate area."

Rowan didn't appreciate being brought up short. "Are you saying he was killed and the killer tossed him out that far? I doubt if even two strong men could toss him that far!"

"We agree on that point, Inspector," William said. "The impact Nickolas made would have been somewhat muffled by the sand, but I have to believe there would be some commotion leading up to his death that would have been accompanied by some noise, perhaps a scream or a shout. There certainly wasn't a gunshot. Yet, no one heard a thing last night."

"Will," I pointed out, "It was rainy and windy, so the windows and doors were shut tight, and those walls are three feet of solid stone. I doubt if we would be able to hear anything."

"In regards to us? Perhaps you're right Frohman, but no one heard anything."

I thought that over for a quick moment and got his point. "Ozaki."

"Exactly," I grunted in agreement and explained when I saw the look on Rowan's face, "Ozaki doesn't miss much of what's going on around William here. He's damn near clairvoyant that way. If someone had been acting up out here, or inside, Ozaki would have been on it in a flash. He is very protective of his master."

"I am not his master."

"You ain't his sister either."

"If he didn't jump or fall, then where did he drop from?" Rowan pressed.

"I could not answer that, Inspector, not without facts! As of yet, no explanations fit the circumstances." Will replied. "We can only be certain that he came from somewhere!"

That sparked a possibility in my head, but I decided to keep my thoughts to myself and think it through a little more, else William, in his frame of mind, would be sure to shoot it full of holes and make me look foolish.

Rowan mulled it over for a minute then squeezed eyes shut and shook his head.

"All I need. Another enigma!" Rowan muttered under his breath. "Two dead men in a few days!"

"Two?", Will asked, all innocent like.

"Well, Doctor?" Rowan asked, turning to Blum and ignoring William. "Any first impressions for your part?"

Blum looked around for a quick moment and replied, "No, Inspector, I do not. And to be frank, it goes against my nature to stand here in idle speculation, while a patient lies within eyesight. Even deceased, he needs attention."

"You're right, Doc. Let's go see what we can do for poor Nickolas."

The three of us stepped into the courtyard. The sand was still moist and firm. Still, it was not much different than any New England beach. Except for the uniform tiny craters from the rain and the corpse, the courtyard was as clean as a fresh brushed billiards table.

Despite the obvious, the Inspector bade us to spread out, walk slowly, and look for anything unusual on the surface. "If you see something, bring it to my attention immediately! And, please, do not touch anything, unless I say its o.k."

The doctor just glanced in Rowan's direction and made a bee line for the body, albeit at a moderate pace. Rowan looked annoyed but said nothing as he took up a flank position to the left of him, about ten feet away.

Wiliam went farther left, between the Inspector and the wall and began to study the ground before him. I moved to the Doctor's right that took me more towards the center of the courtyard. I saw nothing that marred the plane of the surface.

As we made our way out, my perspective changed the closer we got to the body. By the time we reached the body, I came to the conclusion that it could only have gotten here one way. I would have shared my reasoning with the others right then had I not been struck dumb by the gruesome sight before me.

Never had I seen a body so battered and broken. The lad laid on his right side, at least his torso did, except for his left arm that was oddly out of place, jutting out of his side at a right angle like he was dancing on the ground. More so with his legs splayed out in almost the opposite natural direction. One of his thigh bones tore a swath out of his pants where it had exploded out of his leg. Its jagged white edges glintered in the sunlight, contrasted by the bits of bloody gore that still clung to it. I just stared at it, bile rising in my throat, until I saw Rowan casting a doubtful eye in my direction. I swallowed several times and forced my feet to move again.

Sand and soil covered his suit, clinging to the dampness of the cloth. His shirt and torn coat had ridden up slightly, exposing a strip of white flesh. His shoes, where they showed through the grit, were gleaming in the morning sun. All this I noticed but my legs froze again when I looked at his face.

The mouth hung open, slack jawed but whole, as was his nose. His eyes were another matter.

Both open and staring straight into the sun. The left was peppered with sand and dirt, but the right was fairly clean, but sunken unnaturally into his head. The forehead above it actually bulged out a few inches where it had broken away from his skull.

While I stared in morbid fascination, the doctor went to his knee and began his examination. Rowan made a circuit around the body, and then took up position next to the doctor as he took out his notebook.

William made two circuits around the body and came to a stop next to me. He too went to his knee and put a glove on his right hand. Then I'll be damned if he didn't take out a magnifying glass!

The doctor looked the corpse up and down and put two

fingers to the throat. After a minute he looked at his watch and spoke,

"I declare this man dead, at 10:09 am, Saturday, March third. The patient has multiple contusions." Both he and the inspector were making notes in their own little books.

I didn't really hear all the gory details of Nickolas's injuries because I was too busy watching my friend do something incredibly strange.

Kneeling next to the body, William began to examine the left hand under his magnifying glass!

Rowan beat me to the question. Pencil paused, he raised his head, "What are you doing, Mr. Gillette?" he asked, annoyed at the disruption of Blum's report.

"Oh, I am just examining the fingernails, Inspector."

Rowan blinked. "Whatever for?"

I could see his point. It was hard to look at this battered and bloody husk of a human being lying between us and think of looking at something as minor as a manicure!

Will hesitated, the glass reflecting one large eye as he peered intently through it, then replied, "Scraping under the nail," he murmured, then raised his line of sight over the glass, "For signs of poison."

"Poison?" Rowan straightened up, "Why would you be looking for poison? And why look for it there, of all places?"

"Oh, he's quite right, Inspector," Doctor Blum cut in as he gave William a respectful nod, "many poisons will discolor the nails."

"As to why?" William said, as he continued his examination, "Eliminating possibilities will only aide us in the discovery of the actual cause of death."

That answer made Rowan hesitate, but he regained his stern look and admonished, "Please just stay back until the doctor is finished."

"Of course, Inspector," Will put away the glass and

straightened, "My apologies."

The doctor began to drone on again, while the inspector scribbled away, but I just stared at William in disbelief.

Before he got up, I saw him put his thumb, which the other two could not see, on a ring Nickolas wore and pressed it into his palm, deftly lifting it off and pocketing it as he made his apology. Before I could ask, he shook his head slightly and mouthed the word, "Later". The other two hadn't noticed.

The doctor finished his narration for the death certificate and started duck walking around to the head and gently placed his fingers into the sand below the back of the head. "It's quite pulpy, Inspector. Feels like a summer melon."

"Nice analogy, Doc," I blurted out, "I'll never eat cantaloupe again!"

He smiled and straightened up. Blum walked slowly around the body, checking the extremities, especially noting the femur bone that jutted from his pants and the surrounding area. Moving to the torso, he poked and prodded, listing the additional injuries, such as broken ribs. Finally he stood and took a towel from his bag to wipe off his hands.

"I would also note there is a strong smell of alcohol, so it seems he was in his cups when it happened."

This got Rowan's attention and bent over to take a whiff.

"You're right, Doc. He reeks of something. I'm not much of a drinker, though, so I can't say what."

William looked at me and raised an eyebrow. I sighed and bent lower to smell it. "Scotch! Bar stock." I gave my expert opinion,

"He must have been a sloppy drinker." I remember thinking to myself that it must have been a damn near lethal amount for it to still carry its acrid smell after a night of rain and the morning dew. "He got as much on him as in him."

Rowan made a note in his book.

"This could explain a lot." he mused.

"Well, inspector, that's about all I can do here. When you're finished, have your boys bring him to my office and I'll do a full autopsy."

"How about a time of death then?"

Blum mulled it over for a moment then shook his head, "Hard to say out here in the open. I'd rather look him over first, in a more sterile environment. There are a few points I want to examine closer."

"So do I write it up as an accidental or an intentional?" Rowan asked, pencil posed over the paper.

"Sorry again, Inspector. I won't attest to either. I will need to undress him and clean him up before I can do a thorough examination and make a final ruling."

Rowan looked at him quizzically, "You think that's necessary? Wherever he came from, it seems pretty obvious to me that he didn't survive the impact."

"That is because you are making false assumptions on misinformation," William groused.

"What do you mean by that, Sir?" He demanded in a surly voice. No matter how impressed by William's knowledge, he wasn't about to be called down by him. He was in for a bit of a surprise.

"Nickolas did not survive, because he was dead long before the impact."

Futile Search

Rowan looked to Blum, who raised his left eyebrow and nodded, clearly further impressed with William's insight.

"I'd say he was dead at least a few hours before he ended up here," the doctor said, looking around.

"How did you know this?" Rowan asked Will.

"The femur and the lack of blood in the surrounding area, actually. I noticed it as soon as we walked up."

Rowan looked to the doctor again.

"That's right." the Doctor confirmed. He pointed to the bone and continued. "If his heart had been pumping when that bone broke free, there be enough blood pooled to fill your hat Inspector and it would have sprayed everywhere. Nor is there much, if any, leakage from the other wounds. That, and just a general feeling I get from the damage he suffered, but I'm sure my examination will bear me out on this."

"That was very astute of you, Mr. Gillette," Rowan said, in a much less churlish tone. "Have you had any medical training?"

"Just the regular anatomy and so forth one picks up at university." he replied modestly.

Rowan nodded his head thoughtfully, and then shook it ruefully. "If he was dead before he landed, well, that changes everything."

I decided it was time to let my cat out of the bag, "Gentlemen, I think I know how he got here." Everyone turned my way and looked expectant. I formulated my reasoning and plowed on, "Airplane or balloon. If he couldn't have jumped or been tossed from the ground, he must have been dropped from the sky!"

William patted me on the back sympathetically, as if I just lost the school spelling bee. "I applaud your attempts at reasoning, but both are of a low possibility. Those possibilities have already crossed my mind and were dismissed."

"I know I'm going to regret this," I sighed. " But – why?"

"Really Frohman, there isn't an aero plane in this county, nor have I ever heard of or seen a balloon big enough to carry two men. Aside from that, it would be most improbable that anyone would kill Nickolas, put his corpse on board, just to drop him on my property! I highly doubt an aero plane could fly so close to the house, in the dead of the night, and dump Nickolas without some notice. They are rather noisy, after all."

I went to open my mouth to defend my balloon theory, but William went right over my words.

"And the balloon theory just won't fly, old boy." he said, with a twinkle in his eye at his pun, "aside from the monumental task of building and flying a balloon big enough to carry several men."

"Hard to miss something like that," Rowan put in with a smirk, "Especially in this town that is full of nosy parkers!"

"Add to that, the wind was blowing hard and with the gusts and rainfall, there would be no way to control it or land it in the dark. A person would have to be insane to even try it. Third, why would Nickolas be in a balloon on the night of his engagement?"

"I don't know," I sputtered. "Maybe he's a romantic! Maybe he just rigged something big enough to get him up to the skirts room and he messed up and crashed!"

Will laughed, "I am beginning to wonder about your

sanity Frohman. Your theory would be a neat wrapping for this package, but you are failing to see the whole picture! That is why you must never try to make facts fit the theory. Rather you must let the facts form the theory."

"If you two are finished," Rowan cut in, "I would like to turn out his pockets and see what that might tell us."

The doctor, who had patiently remained silent during our discourses, picked up his bag, "However he arrived, it's time for me to depart. I'll leave you gentlemen to your investigation. I'll go round up the men and the stretcher. Let me know when you're ready for me to take him away."

I envied him as he started walking back to solid ground. My wet feet were frozen and a slight breeze had brought a chill in the air.

Rowan looked to William. "Why did you ask Mrs. Wood what he was wearing earlier?"

"I haven't seen him wear it before and I wanted to know if he was wearing this suit earlier. Since he wasn't, I assume he put it on to meet Catty, as she said they had planned."

"Did he usually gussy up for his courting?"

"Not that I could attest to, although I would have no idea what they did on their off times."

"Not much to do around here that you need a suit for," Rowan noted. "But I guess if you are going to elope, you would put on a new suit to do it in."

"It's not new, Inspector." I said. "It's a European cut, tailored and he's had it a while. If you look at the cuffs and collar, you can see the fraying. Also, the button holes are stretched from use." Then I stuck his nose near to the breast pocket of the jacket. "Mothballs, he had it stored. I would bet it was the suit he came to this country wearing."

"You sure about that?" Rowan asked.

"Fairly," I shrugged

"My friend is a bit of a clothes hound," William said, "and he travels quite a bit. He would know."

Rowan made a few more notes in his book and looked at us with sly smile, "You boys are turning out to be a big help. Let's see how we do with the next step."

"Now," he took a small cloth bag from his pocket, shook it out, and handed it to me. "If you would be so kind as to hold this open, I can catalog the items as they are removed from the corpse." He continued, looking right at William, "If you wouldn't mind retrieving the effects."

If he was testing William to see how squeamish he was, he was barking up the wrong tree. My friend immediately dropped to one knee and started going through Nickolas's pockets.

"One pocket watch, Russian made, with fob and one charm - a small silver cat."

"Did you give that to him?" I teased.

He just gave me a level look and added, "Cat, Frohman. Catty?"

"Makes sense," Rowan said.

William continued to root around, "A pocketknife, spring loaded, five-inch blade; forty-two cents in loose change; pocket handkerchief--blue. No markings. That seems to be all from his outer pockets." William seemed disappointed.

He patted the jacket once more and cried out, "Aha!"

Pulling the shirt tails that had come partially out of his pants, he revealed a pouch around the chest area. "A money belt. It must have ridden up when he hit." William looked to Rowan, "May I remove it Inspector?"

"Of course. This may explain a lot."

I wasn't envying my friend at that moment. Reaching under the body to find the buckles and fumbling around with the hooks was a gruesome chore when your face was just inches away from the battered corpse.

"C'mon William!" I chided him after a moment

watching him struggle. "Pretend you're back in the east wing with one of your father's maids!"

Rowan chuckled but William ignored me and suddenly he grunted and pulled his arms away, holding the belt.

Will looked down his nose at me, "That comment was completely inappropriate, Frohman."

"But oh so droll, my friend." I retorted.

Rowan gave us a look like we were a bad vaudeville act. "Can we please get on with this?"

"Of course Inspector," William replied and he carefully opened the main compartment.

This money belt was similar to one I used to own and sometimes used when I carried large sums of money from the theatre to the bank. It saved me a lot of trouble as gold and silver are heavy and a wad of cash will make a bulge in your pocket that any hard case could see from a block away.

About seven inches wide by fourteen inches long, it strapped around your midsection by way of twin belts sown onto it. Usually, it was separated into sections, the main being for bulkier items like cash and the smaller for important papers.

Will's eyebrows shot up and he reached in to remove a stack of bills first.

He handed it to me, "Count it please," and dove back into the pouch.

I flipped through it quickly, "Three hundred-eighty-seven dollars," I announced.

"And another eighteen in gold," William added, dropping the coins into Rowan's bag.

"Four hundred and five dollars. Not bad for a boat hand," I said.

"Did he make all that working for you?" Rowan asked William.

William thought about it for a moment. "I suppose if he

were frugal, but he would have had to save carefully. His room and board were part of his pay so his salary would have been his to do what he wished. I certainly never paid him a bulk sum such as that."

I made a low whistle, "He must have been a smooth talker to woo a looker like Catherine and hold onto most of his money!"

"Maybe he did have a rich family. Would that be enough cabbage to get married and book passage to Europe?" Rowan wondered, tapping his pencil on his chin.

"I don't think they could go first class." William noted, as he resumed riffling through the pouch. "Yet, they could certainly get a good berth on a cross Atlantic line. He was a sailor, perhaps Nickolas knew someone on a ship."

He pulled out a sheet of folded paper and a small booklet and leafed through them.

"His Passport, Visa, Seamen papers, and what looks to be two photos of his family, perhaps back in Russia."

"Well, now," Rowan said, "That suggests to me he was planning on pulling up stakes. Did he give you any indication he was leaving, Mr. Gillette?"

"No. None whatsoever. The last I saw of him was early last evening when we brought Frohman here from New London. I gave him and the captain the weekend off and fully expected them to resume their duties on Monday morning. Of course, Catherine gave me no notice." he added in a soft voice. I knew he was hurt by the realization. He tended to treat his help like family.

"She's young, William, and obviously in love with the boy. We both know how little women consider when their emotions take over. All she was thinking about was her new life with Nickolas."

"If they could outrun her brothers," Rowan mused. "And start a new life somewhere on just over four hundred bucks!"

"They're young and in love," I pointed out, "Nothing else would have mattered."

Rowan seemed to concede my point, but William hadn't heard a word I said. He was running his fingers over every inch of the money belt and peering into each pocket. Satisfied it was truly empty, he handed it to Rowan and stared off into the sky.

He broke out of his deep thought and suddenly swung a leg over the corpse until he straddled it. Rowan's eyebrows shot up and we looked at each other with a 'what-the-hell-is-he-doing' look.

William just bent over and began to run his fingers over every inch of exposed clothing and rummaged through the pockets, seemingly oblivious of the mangled human that filled it out. After a solid three minutes of fruitless searching, he straightened, puzzled and empty handed.

"Mind telling me what you might be looking for Mr. Gillette?" Rowan asked.

"A symbol of all that we have just been discussing Inspector – a ring."

Compromise

We waited a moment for him to elaborate, but he just pursed his lips and stared down at the body.

"I'm not sure I follow that." Rowan said, breaking the silence.

After another moment, William turned towards him, eyebrows raised, and looking down his nose, "Really? I would think it obvious."

Before Rowan could reply, William changed his stance and flashed the Inspector his best smile, "So, what is your next step Inspector?"

It took a second for him to change gears, but the Inspector replied after some thought. "I'm going to have a talk with your Captain Roy. I'll see what light he can shed on this matter, and then I suppose I'll head back to the station to wait for Doctor Blum's report. Once we know how he died, I can see what direction..."

"If that's what you think best, Inspector." William cut him off. "Though I fear our killer's trail may grow colder, the longer we wait."

Rowan was taken back. He raised both hands and said sternly.

"Killer? Who said there was a killer? Until we get the doctor's report, we don't know if it was murder!"

"Now you sound like that blowhard, Luboff!" I cut in. "Only he didn't bother to take a few minutes to examine Nickolas's body for himself!"

"I'll ask you to watch your tone, Sir. Chief Inspector Luboff is the head of our police force and the office demands some respect even if you don't care for the man. And he is right about the proper procedures of an investigation. Once we have determined if it was an accident, suicide, or a murder...we can proceed."

He turned and signaled his men waiting at the wall. They got to their feet and, picking up a stretcher, began to make their way out to the courtyard.

I wasn't through yet, "Son, I make 'make believe' for a living and even I know that something's screwy here!"

William cut me off, "What my friend is trying to say is...no matter what the manner of death was, the fact that Nickolas was dead before he ended up here gives us the undeniable fact that there were others involved. And as no one has come forward after ample time and opportunity, we must conclude there was foul play."

Rowan sighed, "Be that as it may, Mr. Gillette, we have our procedures. Unless your captain can tell us what happened here, I'll wait for the autopsy report and I'll move forward from there."

The men arrived at our location, cutting off any more conversation while we watched in silence as they loaded Nickolas's body onto the stretcher. It was a particularly gruesome sight.

Aside from being embedded in the sand and damp to boot, none of Nickolas's body parts seemed to be connected. When they tried to lift him by the arms, his head rolled back so far he looked like he was trying to kiss his own back. When they tried to lift him by his torso, the bone in his thigh jutted out farther and fresh ichors oozed from the wound as his other leg stuck fast in the ground.

I was thanking God by then that I'd only had a chance to drink half a cup of coffee as I watched these hardened constables trying to keep their breakfast off their coats.

Finally, they each took a corner and the four of them managed to pull the poor bastard out of his temporary grave in one piece. I'll never forget the sucking sound the wet sand made when the body came free, nor the taste of the bile that was bubbling at the bottom of my throat.

With small steps, they walked the body over and set it on the stretcher. With a fair amount of grumbling, they each took an end and began to walk toward the meat wagon.

Ozaki stood by the french doors, the stern look on his face guaranteed the bearers would pass swiftly through the house, as it was the only exit, unless they simply heaved him over the wall and picked him up below.

We turned our attention to the cavity the body left in the sand, in case we had missed something under the body. But the sand showed us nothing but a rough outline of the corpse and some small blood stains dotting the surface.

Rowan repeated himself. "I simply cannot fathom how he ended up here."

William flicked his wrist into air. "It is an enigma, yes Inspector. But still merely a curiosity, and not the question you should be asking at this point. And one I fear you will find no answers to in the autopsy report. There is leg work to be done."

Rowan mulled that over for a moment.

"Perhaps, Mr. Gillette. But maybe if we knew how he died, the rest would fall into place!"

"If you truly believe that, Inspector, then you are on a path that will lead you nowhere!"

Now it was Rowan's turn to see red. "You seem pretty damn sure of what I might be doing wrong Sir, but I haven't heard a theory from you yet!"

"Because I have not yet gotten all the facts I can!" Will chided, "Once one collects all the facts- then it will coalesce into a theory. The opposite is just turning ignorance into incompetence!"

Rowan rose up again, but Will just rode right over him. "But I digress! Data is what we need, so after we question the good captain, I suggest we have a look about Nickolas's cabin. We may find something of interest there." Will suggested.

He turned to walk away and Rowan exploded in his boots.

"We will do no such thing Sir!" he stated, putting both hands on his hips. "You have no authority in this matter and I'll not have you muddling up this investigation with your own amateur investigation! Best you go back inside to your breakfast and leave this matter to the police."

"Inspector, are we really going to have this discussion again?" William asked in his most condescending voice. He then sighed and looked down his nose, "Very well then. Let us get it over with."

"Christ Almighty! If Luboff heard you were conducting your own private investigat..." Rowan was stopped.

"Kindly leave our lord out of this discussion. I do not care what your superior may or may not feel about this matter. His boorish manner earlier has shown that he is unwilling or simply too narrow-minded to conduct a competent investigation. Furthermore, I am a tax paying landowner and a free citizen, who has every right to tend to affairs that happen upon this property and to my employees!"

"Mr. Gillette, please be reasonable. The last thing I want to do is place you in custody for obstruction!"

"Ah" William retorted, "But obstruction of what? You have yet to declare this a murder investigation! Are you not planning on waiting for the autopsy report?"

I let them bicker back and forth like school boys while I mulled over the options. On the one hand, my gut was telling me that this would be one ugly mess in the end and there was no way we should get deeper involved. The safe play was to let the coppers handle it while we went back inside and finished our breakfast. But my sense of misadventure got the better of me and I stepped into the fray - and I'm sure the Sherry Ozaki put in my flask helped.

"Gentlemen, Please!" I cried out. "We are wasting valuable time!"

They both stopped talking and turned to me a bit stunned. This is why William summoned me here. To reason with the unreasonable.

"Yes Inspector. You could take William into custody and keep him away for a while. But the moment you lay hands on him, I'll go in the house and make a few phone calls and I promise you, you'll spend the rest of the day under a pile of lawyers and politicians! I promise you that William will be released by lunch time and we will just go about our business then. You, on the other hand, will have several very long days."

That got his Irish up. "I don't like being threatened, Mr. Frohman!"

I drew myself up. "I don't threaten Rowan. I deliver."

Before it could escalate, William stepped in.

"Gentlemen, there is no need for this. Inspector, I would very much like to observe as you question the Captain. It would certainly help smooth the way for you and I may have a few insights that would be helpful. Please allow me to accompany you. I feel as if I could be of some small assistance and I feel I owe Nickolas that much."

Whether it was William's carefully modulated tone or his easy demeanor, the tension seemed to flow out of Rowan and he carefully considered William's words and my threat.

Again, I could tell by the look on the young Inspector's face, our tough guy, sweet guy routine got us our way.

"Alright then. You may accompany me, but the rules stay the same! I'll ask the questions and you two keep your eyes and ears open."

A Short Hike

Thank God, when we finally stepped off of the frigid wet sand with our bare feet, onto the walkway outside the doors. Ozaki was right there, hats, coats, and even my cane draped over a butler cart.

He stopped us at the end of the retaining wall, next to the house, and placed small towels on the wall and motioned us to sit. He produced a flat stick and with smooth strokes scrapped most of the sand off our legs and feet. Then he grabbed a bucket of warm, soapy water that contained a sponge and he proceeded to wash away the rest of the grime. He finished William and handed him a towel then went to work on me. The warm water was a godsend as I was starting to lose feelings in my toes. I grinned at my friend who was putting on a fresh pair of socks and his boots.

"Ahhhh. A French bath by a Japanese man in an English castle! By Jove, America really is a melting pot!"

Ozaki gave me a withering look, "Even the French have more sense than to wark around in wet mud on a cord morning!" He slapped the towel into my chest and William laughed.

As soon as he collected our wet outerwear, he whirled back towards the house carrying Will's socks and the bucket, all the while muttering about sickness and wet feet.

"We had better get going," I teased William, "before Old-zaki makes you go inside and take a full bath!"

He gave me a sly look.

"If he hears you call him 'Old-zaki', you'll suffer for it

my friend. Remember, we probably won't have a maid for the rest of your stay."

I was about to make a smart mouth remark to that, when I felt an object in the coat pocket that Ozaki brought me. I pulled out my flask, which I am sure I left empty on my dresser, and now it was full. I opened it, sniffed it, then took a long swallow of sherry and beamed. "It's Prince Ozaki from here on out!"

We set out for the *Aunt Polly* to speak to Captain Roy. To my dismay, we were to take the tram back down to the pier. Ollie and another one of his crew was looking down and hollering instructions to someone below. As we neared, the worker noticed us and jerked his head in Ollie's direction. Ollie turned and whisked over to us.

"Excuse me, gents, but the tram isn't safe to use just now."

"What's the problem with the lift?" William asked.

"Well…er...the braking mechanism is... well…we think it might be stripped. I've got the lads working on it now, but I'd rather we knew it was safe before you use it Sir."

"Well, imagine that" I whispered at William out of the side of my mouth.

William ignored me and asked, "Stripped? How did that happen?"

Ollie looked at the ground sheepishly.

"Well, I had two of the lads up top here with the truck, unloading the sacks of mortar that came yesterday. The lunkheads forgot to pull the last load off when the boys below sent it up. It was past quitting time, the rain was coming and I honestly don't think they knew there was one more load coming up. In any case, the load was left on the platform and, under all that weight, it must have given way in the night. Thankfully, the deck was just banged up and the mortar stayed in the bags, but we had to tighten the lines and grease the braking mechanism before we could get the platform to move."

William took a few steps to the edge of the precipice and looked down. He returned to Ollie and commented, "Yet the platform is still intact?"

"Oh, yes Sir. Just knocked a few of the floorboards loose. One needs to be replaced but we can have that taken care of in a jiffy. I'm real sorry about this Sir, and I'll understand if you want their jobs. They are good lads for the most part, Sir. They are just young lads thinking about girls and ale as they got to the end of last night's shift."

We all looked at William for his reaction, but he just smiled and shook his head, "No, no, Ollie. There's no need to take away their livelihoods. Accidents happen, just make sure they pay more attention in the future. Thankfully no one got hurt and that's the most important thing. Last thing we need now is another death."

He turned to us.

"Well, gentlemen, shall we take a stroll?"

Fortified with the spirits Ozaki supplied, I was game for a walk. The sky was clearing and it was warming up with the air fresh and clean from last night's rain. At least it was downhill.

As we got a ways down the road, we all smiled as we heard Ollie lambasting the lad that left the mortar on the tram. "You idiots are lucky Mr. Gillette is a good man and you still have your jobs! And you're damned lucky no one was hurt or I'd be kicking your skinny hairless butts across the river myself! How you could be so stupid..."

Feet warmed by dry socks, the walk down the road to the docks took us no more than fifteen minutes. As William and Rowan made small talk about the town and county, I took the opportunity to take a closer look at the scenery I hadn't noticed on our arrival yesterday. The view was stunning. Massive oaks, maples, and a smattering of white birch made an impressive backdrop for the wide river that divided the central Connecticut forests in half. One could just see the town's steepled church across the river and a few homesteads that dotted its banks.

As we reached the bottom of the slope, we could see the *Aunt Polly*, secure at her dock, sitting on water so flat it cast perfect reflections. There was another launch, motoring across the river in our general direction and I was amazed to see how far back you could trace its wake on the still water.

Curtains drawn all over the ship and still and silent as a tomb, there were no signs of life on the *Aunt Polly*. But that wasn't surprising as we knew where at least half the occupants were.

To the right, a rather large structure, windowless and covered with natural wood shakes. It was nestled against the river bank surrounded by trees just starting to show spring buds.

The same building I thought was a garage when we arrived yesterday came into view. It looked as if it had been there for years; only the bright white wash and just slightly weathered shakes gave its age away. What I mistook for a garage yesterday was the boat shed, open on the river side, and the two doors on the side were facing us and looked large enough to drive a horse and buggy through.

By then, I had rejoined the conversation, where Rowan and I ended up throwing out various possibilities, including variations of my balloon theory, as to how Nickolas ended up in the courtyard.

William was silent, refusing to speculate. He was deep into the role now, so I stopped badgering him. There was nothing to do but go along when he got this focused. We had just come abreast with the boat house, when Rowan brought us to a quick halt.

"Before we see Captain Roy, gentlemen," he said, looking us both in the eye, "You will remember that this is a police matter and you must respect my procedures. I will ask the questions. You are here only as observers. I respect your insight and would be happy to hear your opinions and or remarks," he paused and looked at us sternly, "Afterwards! Do I make myself clear?"

I mumbled my acceptance; William just gave him an amused smile and nodded.

"Lead on, MacDuff!"

Rowan gave him the eye but held his tongue. We made a brief detour to a police launch tied up next to the *Aunt Polly*. Apparently they had heard of a fatality and put in to see if they could be of any assistance.

Looking for gossip was more likely, in my opinion. Rowan was of the same mind, so he gave them very little information and instructions to wait for him.

While we waited for the Inspector, I looked the *Aunt Polly* over. The old girl looked fine in the morning light. Her windows reflecting the still water and her brass softly glowing. Her woodwork shined and her hull was clean. I wondered if she'd stay so pristine without Nickolas around any longer.

Then we walked down the dock and boarded William's yacht. I noticed some mud clumps on the gangway and remember thinking to myself that the kid had been dead for less than a day and already things were going to hell.

When we were all aboard, Rowan looked around and asked, "Where might Captain Roy be this time of day?"

William began to walk along the starboard railing, calling out the captain's name and when he got no response, returned to us.

"I suppose he may still be in bed. I did give the Captain and Nickolas the weekend off. Perhaps you and Frohman could wait in the salon and I'll see if I can rouse him."

"When you do find him, please tell him nothing. Just bring him to me."

"Of course," William smiled and gave a slight bow. "I shall be the soul of discretion."

It was his mockery at its best, so I took Rowan by the arm and led him through the glass doors before he realized he was being insulted. William could be somewhat abrasive when he was in role.

It was still chilly as the cold air settled in the river valley, but the saloon was warm and toasty, so we shed our jackets and I bade Rowan to have a seat while I made a beeline to the cabinet. Deciding it was too early to be swilling gin, I poured myself two fingers of William's brandy, then some for Rowan. I carried them over to the sofa where he was seated.

"Oh, I appreciate it, Mr. Frohman, but I'm on duty."

I continued to hold out the offering, "and it's cold, damp, and you have sand in your shoes."

He shrugged, "That's all true." Then he took the glass and tossed it back. I was beginning to warm up to him then. William came bustling back into the room, looking disgusted.

"I just woke the captain up and he reeks like a distillery."

"The sot." I commented and took a slow sip of my drink.

William ignored my comment as he took his coat off and took a seat next to me.

"The captain will need a few minutes," he announced. "He was quite indisposed when I woke him. I told him to pull himself together and we would meet with him in the galley shortly."

"What reason did you give for waking him?" Rowan asked.

William gave him a level look. I don't think he liked the probing question and its implication.

"Why, none, of course," he replied coolly. "He is my

employee. I simply told him I required him immediately and somewhat coherent.

"What's he like, your Captain Roy?" Rowan asked, as he flipped out his handy notebook, "For that matter, how did he and Nickolas come to be in your employ?"

William thought that over for a minute and answered, "In the fall of last year, facing another winter, I began to realize that, in the pursuit of building my home, I had virtually ignored the old girl's maintenance. I have not had time to sail as I wanted to do and I have done little or no entertaining in these final stages of my construction."

"You're still short in the entertainment department," I teased him, but I had to laugh at his wounded look. I winked just to let him know I was kidding.

He smiled and patted my arm and continued. "So to remedy the situation, I decided to advertise for a crew. As fate would have it, Captain Roy showed up on my doorstep the very day the ad was placed in the newspaper. He had Nickolas in tow, who was presented as an excellent mechanic, and Roy had the papers and references to prove his years of experience and education. They seemed to be the perfect team for what I needed.

Despite his 'salty dog' persona, which I could appreciate as a man of the theatre, I sensed a deep intelligence. So I made him an offer of a modest salary with room and board on the *Aunt Polly*, which he accepted without negotiation. Our contract was for one year."

"Why for just a year?" Rowan asked. "Don't you need a crew to sail a ship this big?"

"Oh no Inspector, though I have in the past employed crews many times, depending on the length of the jaunt." he replied. "Ozaki and I can handle her quite well on our own. I simply did not have the time to maintain her as she should be."

"I see," Rowan said. "What are they like?"

"I am more than satisfied with the way the Captain and Nickolas have kept her! She is clean and polished, and ready to sail at a moment's notice, should I want or need to. They have done a remarkable refit on her engines, though I think Nickolas is mostly responsible for that aspect, and the captain had designed and implemented an ingenious rope and pulley system for mooring her, along with a modestly innovative safety system.

In addition, Roy supervised the building of the boathouse we passed on the way in and they are currently working on another project for me, a nice motor launch.

Despite a tendency to go over budget on a regular basis, they have been excellent employees and I thought I was fortunate to acquire them."

"Yes, well that's all well and good Mr. Gillette, but I was wondering what they were like."

William looked confused by the question, so I explained, "He wants to know what kind of persons they are. Are they decent men? Boozers? Religious? Are they rakes?"

"I cannot answer those questions." William admitted, "I have never interacted with them on a social level. As I have stated repeatedly, I am a busy man, as of late. I'd say that Roy was a bit of a spendthrift with my money, though I never suspected him of keeping any for himself. Nickolas was a bright, a likable fellow, obviously a great mechanic, and he was always proper and respectful around me.

They lived and worked down here at the docks and, until we fetched Frohman yesterday, I have not sailed on the *Aunt Polly* for any journey of length since last summer. For the most part, it has been just short trips to procure building material for my home. Aside from checking on their progress and the occasional scolding over his expenditures, I have to say I have had little social contact with the two of them. There have been no incidents, either on my property or in town as far as I know. Though I will say this, Inspector. Despite his almost buffoonish bravado, Captain John Roy is a sharp man. I would bear that in mind during your investigation."

"I'm still not sure it is an investigation yet, Mr. Gillette. At present, I would categorize it more of an inquiry. And I still say, until Doctor Blum gives us his report, we're not sure there was a crime."

"And I reiterate," William replied, "The fact that young Nickolas was dead before he was placed in the courtyard means there were at least three felony crimes committed and any number of statutes and regulations broken."

"Not to mention the few ethical ramifications," I pointed out.

"Please Frohman! Let us stick to the facts." he said with a sigh.

"Assuming, just assuming, this was a crime, how did you arrive at the figure that there were three felonies, Mr. Gillette?" Rowan asked.

William's eyebrows shot up at the question and the smug little smirk appeared again, "Really Inspector, you should know the laws you are appointed to uphold."

Rowan looked like he had bitten a lemon, but before he could retort I suggested quickly, "Maybe we should take a look at Nickolas's room, while we wait for the Captain to make an appearance."

"Oh course, Frohman, excellent suggestion!" William replied and he shot out of his seat, leaving Rowan and me to catch up. Rowan's face was a thundercloud as he got up to chase after him.

"Don't mind him," I clasped the young Inspector on the shoulder. "He's just got an inordinate amount of focus when he's onto something. He means well."

"If you say so." he replied warily. "Just as long as he minds his step."

133

I just smirked as I we followed William. Trying to play peace keeper with these two was going to get old. Fast.

Crew's Quarters

We cut through the pilot house then down a set of stairs towards the bow where the crew cabins were. I usually stayed in one of the guest cabins when I sailed on the *Aunt Polly*. Not as roomy as William's stateroom but comfortable enough for a single person.

Will stopped at the door of the smallest cabin and tried the handle. It moved just slightly, the door was locked. I knew it wouldn't matter, and William proved it as he hauled a set of keys out of his pocket. He had a master key for everything he owned with a lock. He quickly found the right one and unlocked the door.

The cabin was compact and efficient in a nautical way. A bunk was recessed into the right wall, with built-in drawers below. On the opposite side of the cabin, a floor to ceiling cabinet and shelves were half sunk into the wall. Between them there was a closed wall desk, complete with work pants draped over one corner, and chair. The ensemble sat below a small porthole. If you stood in the center of the cabin and spread your arms, you could barely make a circle without touching something.

In a typical young man's fashion, small neat piles of clothing dotted the floor and fixtures making it all the more cramped.

The cabin was too small for the three of us, so I stayed outside the doorway as William led the Inspector inside. Rowan had barely made it over the sill, when William asked Rowan to turn around and pointed at the wall. I stuck my head inside to peek and saw a key ring hanging on a peg near the door.

Rowan had his pad out and began scribbling God knows what as he slowly circled the cabin, but it was William who had my full attention. He stood in the center of the cabin. Ramrod straight, only his eyes moving as he swept the room, he slowly rotated his head. I thought he was doing an owl imitation. The very intensity of his concentration seemed to thicken the air.

Rowan opened a small closet door which contained an empty valise. Rowan jotted down some notes and Will began the search of the cabin. He turned to face me through the door, but he didn't even seem to see me as he ran his fingers across the top of the door frame then dropped to his knees and looked under the bed, reaching back with his long arms to retrieve a few dust bunnies and something else he could not identify.

William lifted a small throw rug, and then regained his feet to begin searching the bed from pillows to foot. Not finding what he sought, he started on the piles lying about. He took out each piece of clothing and ran his fingers along the seams before he placed it in a heap on the floor by his feet. So industrious in his efforts that Rowan had to practically squeeze backwards into the tiny closet to keep from being knocked over.

"Now, just a minute!" he protested. "Just what are you doing?"

William stopped and gave the young man a withering look, "Searching, Inspector. As you also should be doing."

Rowan's face reddened and I knew that he had no clue as to what he was looking for.

"Perhaps you should not be disturbing what may be a crime scene," he shot back.

"As you have so vehemently stated Inspector, there is no established fact of a crime," William retorted sarcastically. "This is simply an inquiry at this point. Aside from

Nickolas' personal effects, this is my property," he gestured to the room around them, "and I have every right through a contractual agreement with Nickolas, to inspect this room at my discretion! Now please, inspector. Could we not continue this incessant quibbling and stick to the matter at hand."

With that said, he stepped over to a small wall desk and chair in the corner between the bunk and the hull. He rifled through the pants that were draped over the chair and finding nothing, tossed them on the seat. After turning the chair over, he checked the underside. Upon pulling the desk top down, he found it empty, but for a half full inkwell and a couple of old pens. William quickly abandoned it and went to the set of cabinets built into the wall on either side and began rummaging with his hands on the backs and undersides of the shelves.

"And just what is the matter at hand? May I ask just what it is you are looking for?" Rowan asked, more than a bit miffed at his brashness.

William didn't look up, "For the same thing I searched the body for, Inspector."

"Which was?" Rowan asked in an irritated tone.

William paused and arched his eyebrows, a sure sign he was going to say something between condescending and snide, but before I could intercede, someone politely cleared their throat behind me.

I jumped like a little girl, whirling to face a grinning Asian. "Ozaki!" I snarled, when I could breathe again, "I've told you not to do that!" The man was quieter than one of Will's cats and twice as sneaky.

"Prease, if you would excuse me, perhaps I can be of some help."

It didn't surprise me to see Ozaki standing there even though we left him at the castle, muttering to himself. He was always popping up unexpectedly and I realized he must have been standing behind me for some time if he thought he could assist William. I just wanted to wipe the smug look off his face as he squeezed into the room.

Even with his small stature, three was too many for Nickolas' cabin so Rowan, looking a little flustered, stepped out to the hallway with me. William spoke to his Ozaki in a low voice, then tapped the third finger on his left hand. Ozaki nodded and glided over to the wall desk. He took a pair of work pants draped over the chair and carefully folded them before laying them gently on the floor. Kind of like a flag ceremony at a military funeral.

He opened the desk and set the chain to keep the top at a right angle. He gestured and spoke in a low voice to Will, who nodded and reached for the center drawer in the desktop. He removed it completely from its slot then stuck his long fingers in the opening. There was an audible click and a side panel to the left of the drawers popped open.

Grinning with success, he pulled a small drawstring bag from its hiding place.

"How did he know it was there?" Rowan asked under his breath, then looked at me. "And what is it?"

"Because he's a damned snoop," I whispered.

"And because this was Ozaki's cabin when they lived on the *Aunt Polly* all those years," William reminded me. I had forgotten the keen hearing that he had along with his eyesight. "Ozaki bought the small desk in Delaware and installed it himself. I had no idea of the hidden compartment."

"Somehow I don't see Ozaki letting Nickolas in on his little secret." I pointed out, skeptically. "How would Nickolas know about it?" I stared pointedly at Ozaki. Ozaki shook his head then shrugged. William spoke.

"As I have told you, Frohman, Nickolas was quite intelligent and good with his hands. I have no doubt he was able to discover it all on his own."

William opened the bag, which he identified as sable skin, by way of a small drawstring. Fishing around with his long fingers he pulled a small piece of jewelry from inside. Any man who was ever in love could tell you what kind of ring it was. The small diamond glowed in the soft lights as William held it up, like a trophy.

"Ozaki, you are a treasure" he complimented.

William looked at it in triumph for the briefest moment then stepped over and handed it to Rowan. "Here you are, Inspector. I expect you will want to hold that as evidence."

I could not fathom why he had such an obsession with that ring, and Rowan was as lost also.

"I'll put it with his other things, to be sure, but I fail to see the big significance, Mr. Gillette. We already knew it existed. Catty told us earlier."

"My dear, inspector," Will started, in his patronizing tone, "to progress any investigation, one must follow the chain of events. Link by link. The existence of the ring was never in doubt. Where we found the ring is quite meaningful, as it establishes a timeline."

"Timeline? What timeline?" I asked. Rowan looked as confused as me.

"For Nickolas' last movements, of course," he replied as if it were the most obvious fact ever.

"Shall we go see if Captain Roy is available now?"

Without waiting for an answer, he pivoted and walked out the door to squeeze past me and headed down the hall with Ozaki hot on his heels. Rowan stood there, holding the ring and looking poleaxed. I just couldn't let the look on his face pass.

"Still feel like you're in charge, Inspector?" He shook his head and put the ring in a vest pocket. "Not really."

I clapped him on the shoulder, "Get used to it, my boy, get used to it."

Poking the Bear

Ozaki informed us that the captain was in the galley
making tea. William thanked Ozaki and then sent him back
to the house. Will said it was because the girls had gone
home early and no one was left up at the house but the
work crew, but I suspect it was more because there was
bad blood between Captain Roy and the faithful servant. I
had noticed it when I was introduced to the pair and made
my faux pas with Ozaki.

I'm sure that Roy thought he was captain of the *Aunt
Polly* and therefore due proper respect while Ozaki, in the
position of majordomo, would look down on him as he did
all the other servants. I had witnessed the animosity
between Ozaki and Nickolas and it was bound to be twice
as bad with the captain.

William ducked through a doorway on the right side of
the hallway and Rowan and I followed him into the galley.
Despite the circumstances, I felt a nostalgic twinge since I
had so many happy mornings spent on the *Aunt Polly*.

It was bigger and more comfortable than the name galley
implies. The countertop, cabinets, and sinks were as large
if not more so than most apartments in the city and the
stove was larger, as was the icebox. William had spent a
good portion of his years on the *Aunt Polly* and he had it
refitted for his comfort and daily use.

I was surprised how little the décor had changed. If not
for a coat and gloves hanging above the heater and two
empty bottles of hooch on the sink, it looked exactly as it
did the last time I stayed aboard. All was shipshape, not at

all what I would expect two sailors to keep it.

Captain Roy was standing at the stove, waiting for his tea kettle to steam. Though he could not miss the three of us in his peripheral vision, he made no acknowledgment of our presence. He just stared at the kettle.

When we got inside, I could read the two empty bottles by the sink. One I recognized as a mid-priced scotch whiskey and the other was an empty glass jug. Thus, I surmised this was the cause of Roy's ugly mood. After a long minute, he snatched up the kettle and with quick precise movements, poured a cup, added sugar, milk, and took a noisy sip.

He put the mug back on the counter and turned to face us. "Well, well. Good morning, gentlemen," he said in a raspy voice. "though when your employer, a peeler, and some dandy lawyer come a' waking me from my beauty sleep, perhaps 'good' isn't the word I'm looking for."

I would have taken umbrage at being called a 'dandy lawyer', but one look at the captain made me decide to let the remark go unchallenged.

All six foot five of his two hundred plus pound frame filled the cooking area. In the bright morning light, his blood shot eyes, ruddy cheeks, and hair sticking out in all directions made him look like a hibernating grizzly bear that was awakened too soon. Menace seemed to radiate from him and I found myself wishing I had brought my cane.

"Perhaps, Captain." William took up the gauntlet, "But that is no reason..."

"Mr. Gillette!" Rowan cut him off, trying to reassert control. He flipped open his notebook and stepped forward.

"Captain Roy, I need to ask you a few questions. When did you last see your first mate, Nickolas?"

Roy ignored him and looked at his employer, "What's

141

this all about, Mr. Gillette?"

"I'll ask the questions, Roy, if you please." Rowan said firmly.

Roy slowly turned his bale fire orbs on the inspector, "And why should I be answering them?" he said deliberately.

To give Rowan credit, he wasn't intimidated by the surly response. He tucked the pencil behind his ear and tucked the notebook into his back pocket as he stepped closer to stare Roy in the eye. Then Rowan started poking the bear.

"Because this is a police investigation, because I am the law, and because you are going to answer them, sooner or later, easy or hard."

"Oh really?" The bear was aroused now, "Police investigation, is it? And is that why you brought my employer and his lawyer along? No offense Mr. Gillette," he glared at Rowan.

Gone was the drunken sailor and in its place stood the grizzly bear with his massive paws balled into mace sized fists ready to pummel Rowan.

"Either someone tells me what the hell is going on or I'm going back to bed," he growled.

"I think not," Rowan said grimly, pulling back his lapel to show his shoulder rig and the pistol grip resting in it.

"If you be thinking you and that peashooter could stop me, I'd best be fetching those bully boys you got tied off on me bow!" Roy growled as he stepped forward with his large taut frame.

"Nickolas is dead," William said quickly, in an effort to stave off trouble. Rowan glared at him but said nothing as he went on. "His body was found this morning."

"Nicky?" Roy staggered back a step and grabbed the counter for support. In a voice just above a whisper, as if he hoped he may have heard William wrong, "Are you sure?"

"Absolutely, unfortunately."

The tension melted from his posture and his eyes widened in surprise and sadness. His hands uncurled and he brought them up to clutch his head, "Oh, no, no, no," he murmured. His knees shook and it looked as if he would collapsed until William stepped up and took his arm, helping him to the table and a chair. He put his elbows on the table as he continued to hold his head. William and Rowan took seats across the table from him. I remained standing, wanting to stay out of arms reach of him in case the captain's mood went south again.

"Could you please tell us when you saw Nickolas last?" Rowan asked again, in a more gentle tone.

Roy's mouth moved but he couldn't seem to get the words out. I reached into my jacket, unscrewed the cap, and handed him my flask, knowing firsthand the benefits of a couple slugs of alcohol after a rough night.

He took a healthy pull, chased it with his tea, and handed it back to me with a nod. I wiped off the neck and took one for myself before I stowed it away.

He gathered himself and asked, "What happened? How did it happen?"

William was about to answer and Rowan shot him a look. He opened his notebook again.

"That's what we're trying to find out. Now, when was the last time you saw Nickolas?"

Roy hesitated, one eye closed as he tried to clear the fog from his head, "Twere yesterday. Bout sunset or near enough. No, no, it was after dark, as far as I can remember."

"And that was here on the boat, I assume?"

Roy shrugged, "Yes, right here in the galley."

"What was he doing?"

"Trying to match me drink for drink with that God-awful potato vodka he makes."

"And?" Rowan prodded him after a moment.

"And what?" Roy countered. "It wern't no contest. The boy doesn't have my tolerance and he's much smaller."

Rowan winced and sighed, and then William cut in.

"Please tell us exactly what happened after you let Mr. Frohman and me off at the dock yesterday."

Roy's eyes narrowed and flickered between the three of us. "Just how did he...die...anyways?"

Rowan and William exchanged a look and Rowan nodded. "That has not been established." William said in a grave tone, "He seemed to have suffered multiple grievous injuries. Until the doctor gives us his report, it is unclear if the injuries were accidental, or inflicted."

Rowan was studying Roy's reaction closely. I assume that's why he let William break the news, so he could be ready for any reaction, but even he recoiled as Roy pounded the table with both fists!

"If he was laid out, ye'd best be looking to Catty's brothers! Looks as if them lads made good on all their tough talk!"

"How's that?" Rowan asked all ears.

"Bah! I doan have to tell you what these swamp Yankees think of their sister sparking it up with some Russian sailor! They've been around a few times before, a-tellin Nicky to stay away from the girl. Most times, Nicky just run them off himself. He could lick the lot of them! Only once I had to step in and send them back to their mama. That time they had ax handles and were talking real serious." He got a little misty eyed, "Nicky, though, he just grabbed a gaff hook and was ready to lay right into em. I showed them my pistol and they put their sticks down and left double time."

"When was this?" Rowan asked.

The captain shrugged, "A month ago. Six weeks at the most."

"So you think they might have finally caught up with Nickolas?" Rowan asked. "Do you really think they were serious enough to kill him?"

Roy leaned forward, "No man knows what lies in the heart of another Inspector, but they are young and youth is hot blooded and reckless in my experience. Truth be told, I might feel the same way if I were in their shoes. I loved that boy like a son, but he was foreign. If you say Nicky was beaten, they'd be the ones I..."

"Perhaps!" William barked out, stopping all conversation. "Before we toss any more conjecture about, could we hear what happened last night? Captain, please tell us precisely yesterday's events, up to the last time you saw Nickolas."

Roy, taken back somewhat, gave Will a hard appraising eye and shrugged. Rowan flipped to a new page, and I took another swig.

"Well, as you know, we took you down the river to New London, where we picked up your friend here and returned to the estate. After we docked, you gave us the rest of the weekend off and disembarked with him and your man, Osaki. Nicky wanted to drain the oil and flush the system, so I gave him the go ahead, seeing we were docked for the next two days. I fiddled about the galley and fried up some sausages while he did that. Then when he came up, we had a late afternoon ploughman's lunch. After he cleans the galley, Nicky says he's going to clean up himself because he'd be goin ashore. Me, having no duties and, soon enough no company, I decided to have a drink. Then one turned into a few. Nicky came back to the galley, all duded up and raring to go. I knew he be going to see the girl, but he was dressed in his best and smelled like a virgin's fart, so I had to josh him a little. 'wedding or funeral?' I asked him. Nicky said 'Tis a special night" and then Captain Roy paused.

"How so?" I asked. But he wouldn't say anything more for a long minute, no matter how I pressed him. Then Roy moved forward...

"By then, I had a wee bit too much to drink and I got a little peckish with him. I regret that now." Roy hung his head and said, "I told him, like I had a hundred times that he was wasting his time and money. There'd be no chance for a Russian boatman like him and the daughter of New England prudes! Well, the boy got mad, as he always did when I tried to give him advice bout women."

"How mad? Did you fight about it?" Rowan interjected.

"No, No," Roy said quickly, "it didn't come to blows. No, this time Nicky seemed special hurt by my talk and I felt a bit bad about me remarks. So, I said me apologies and talked him into having a drink with me. Course, that led to another and another and by the time Nicky says he's late and has to go. I could just about find my way to me berth and lay down. Next thing I know, it's morning and Mr. Gillette was waking me."

"Did Nickolas tell you his plans, or where he might be going?" William asked.

Roy thought about that for a minute. "No, not that I recall. We didn't talk about the girl after he had a drink in his hands, and I've found, when two men disagree, it's best to leave lie while you're drinking. So I held me tongue. I thought he was most likely taking her out to dinner or dancing maybe, being the way he was dressed to the nines and all."

"How much do you think Nicky had to drink?" Rowan asked. "How drunk was he?"

Roy barked a little laugh, "I couldn't say, Inspector. I was well past the point of good judgment myself by the time I went to me bunk."

"I'd say 'good judgment' was in short supply," I said, causing everyone to look at me.

Roy snorted, "At least I had the 'good judgment' to wake in me own bunk!" Then, as memories of Nicky came to his mind, he looked saddened. "That crazy Russian kid! I can't believe he's gone."

"Is there anything else you can tell us, captain?" Rowan asked, "Any other details you can remember?"

Roy wiped his eyes. "No, I don't believe there is. He was walking and talking when I went to bed." Roy shook his head sadly. He turned to William and asked, in a miserable tone, "What happens now, Sir?"

"We'll worry about that later, Captain," William answered, "when we have cleared this matter up. For now, could you please ready the *Aunt Polly* to sail? I realize I gave you time off but under the circumstances, we may need to take a few runs across the river over the next few days."

Roy heaved a sigh, "Yes Sir. Aye, of course. If you could just spare me a few hours to refill the oil and start her engines up. I'm sure I could manage alone."

He wiped his eyes again and dramatically hung his head.

William nodded, "Take the morning to compose yourself, Roy, and ready the engines when you can. We will likely return this evening. Perhaps we'll have some news by then." With that Roy stood and headed to the doorway.

Rowan, a bit startled by his brisk ending of the interview, nonetheless, rose and followed him out the door. I stayed a moment, having just enough out of the flask to bolster my courage and said, "I am not a lawyer."

"Eh?" Roy lifted his head to squint at me, "What's that you be sayin?"

"Twice you referred to me as a lawyer. I am not a lawyer, I am a stage producer."

Roy sneered with his frizzy hair nearly touching the top of the hallway. "Beggin your pardon for pairing you with an honest profession, Sir."

"Come along Frohman," William called out from the hallway and his receding voice convinced me to leave a retort on my tongue instead of throwing it in the captain's face.

Just as well – we poked this bear enough for now – a rather witty bear at that!

Boat Ride

We collected our outerwear, bundled up and made our way off the boat onto the dock. Addressing the inspector, I said, "Well, I suppose you'll be off to find Catty's brothers and ask them a few questions."

"Perhaps, at some point," he replied, making yet another notation in his little book, "But I have some doubts about their involvement in this."

"Why?" I asked, "You heard the captain. They had a motive and have come after Nickolas before!"

He mulled it over and shook his head, "I know those boys and while I'm sure they would have beaten Nickolas to a pulp if they had the chance, between the four of them, they aren't cruel enough to toss his corpse where Catty might find their handiwork. They wouldn't think that way. They would have been scared and either bury or sink the body as fast as they could. They may be overly protective but not too that level of vindictiveness."

"I doubt also that they had a balloon at their disposal!" William said with a slight smirk. Even the four of them could not possibly wrestle Nickolas up the retaining wall and toss a hundred eighty pound body that far. No Frohman, further speculation will do us no good. We must wait for Doctor Blum to complete his autopsy."

"Can I offer you a ride, Gentlemen?" Rowan asked graciously, "Since your yacht is incapacitated for now?"

"Thank you, Inspector," William answered, "That is very kind of you."

"A ride where?" I asked.

Rowan looked surprised, "Across the river to Doctor

Blum's, of course."

He looked at William. "I'm sure you're headed there, in any course, no matter what I had to say. I assume you want to hear his report first hand."

William had the good grace not to gloat and he simply nodded once and looked my way.

I shrugged, "In for a penny, they say."

"Excellent, Frohman," he said, "Your company is practically essential!"

"I'm sure," I replied sarcastically.

We climbed aboard and made our way to the small cabin of the police launch. It was cramped and smelly, but it got us out of the damp cold wind.

"I'm sorry about the accommodations, Mr. Gillette," Rowan said, half teasing, "I'm sure your yacht would have been more comfortable, however this launch will get us there quickly."

"Perhaps," William had to concede. "That is why I did not call Captain Roy on his lie. We must wonder why he did not want to run us over when he could have easily done so."

"Are you saying that he was lying about the boat not running?" Rowan asked.

William pulled his coat collar up and asked, "Do you notice how chilly it is on the water, Inspector?"

"Well, sure. It always feels colder when you're out on the river. Especially if you come outside from a warm place."

I smacked myself in the forehead. "Jesus! How could I miss that? It was warm on old Polly."

"There's no need to show how unobservant you are." William teased me. "Certainly no need to hurt yourself!"

"Did I miss something?" Rowan asked.

I ignored William and answered him, "It was warm, Inspector. The heaters on the *Aunt Polly* don't work if the steam isn't up and the engines aren't running. Therefore, he must have been lying about Nickolas changing the oil. The boat would have been an icebox if they had been shut down all night!"

"Well, I'll be damned," Rowan said. "Why did he lie about it?"

"Because the lazy bum just wanted to go back to bed and nurse his hangover!

Why did you let him get away with it?" I ranted at Will, "For Pete's sake, the man works for you. Why didn't you call him on it?"

"Because I'd rather leave the *Aunt Polly* at berth until I hear the Doctor's report and I was sure the Inspector would offer us a lift." he answered but from the faraway look in his eyes, he wasn't going to elaborate further.

Though cold, damp, and extremely bumpy due to the wind, the trip across the river went quickly. With William in la-la land and Rowan going over his notes, I was left to my thoughts and flask for the ride. The image of Nickolas' broken body kept flashing in my mind and I found a swig comforting. The flask was almost empty before we arrived.

Thankfully, we were tied up and on solid ground before I could finish the contents. I was grateful for the chance to walk some of the effects off as we made our way over to the doctor's office.

"So, just what town are we in now," I asked out of curiosity. "Is this still East Haddam?"

"Well, yes and no," Rowan answered. "This entire area is in the Township of Haddam. It's just broken up into sections. Actually, right now we're in Chester."

I nodded, "Just like where I grew up. The town of East Hampton is the entire South Fork of Long Island, but everyone has a name for their patch."

"I suppose," he replied, "Everyone wants their own

identity."

"Names mean little," William observed, "It's who collects the taxes that matters."

"So true!" Rowan barked with a laugh. "And since those taxes pay my salary, they can name themselves as they please. He looked to me, "So you grew up on Long island. It must have been quite different than our sleepy little burg."

"Not really," I answered, "Money in the summer and fishing all year round."

It wasn't really all that different. From my observation, every town on the coast was pretty much the same, from Maine to New York. Near the water, towns weren't built, but rather they evolved. A few houses, built close together for protection or to be near a certain area, became stores after a few generations and more people settled the region. Eventually those come to intentionally build a store or business in a modern fashion and these are sized to fill the empty spaces between the original homes. Before you know it there's another Main Street, USA.

Chester was no different, although most of the buildings were still the two storied clapboard saltboxes that they've been building in New England for the past hundred years. Each with a shingle or sign out front describing their practice, be it grocer or barber, or haberdasher. Their windowed fronts lining a wide street that went from the water to the main road inland and out of town.

Change the shapes and the names on the signs that swayed in the breeze and I could have been home in South Fork, on the bay side anyways, just like I was walking down Main Street in Sag Harbor, past the Bennett house.

Shortly we came to a simple, white clapboard saltbox, with just a small brass plaque next to the door, naming it 'Dr. Blum's Practice'. Though only two windows on either side of the door graced the front, it looked spacious for a single doctor, so I assumed it also served as a local hospital in these parts.

Rowan opened the door and entered with Will and me in his wake. A set of stairs was directly to our left and Rowan hooked a right that brought us into a spacious room with a few chairs and a large oak desk. The room was vacant.

"Hello?" Rowan called out, "Doctor?"

A door that led to the back of the house burst open and a rather large woman, dressed in a generously sized white dress, complete with blood stained apron, burst through and shut the door behind her quickly.

In three steps she was standing in front of us, looking at us like we were seagulls trying to land on her fishing boat. "Is this a medical emergency?", she boomed.

Rowan answered, "No, nothing like that Susan. We're here..."

"Then I'll have to ask you to leave. The office is closed at the moment. The Doctor is performing a delicate procedure. He cannot be disturbed!" All this she proclaimed like it was the eleventh commandment.

"Now Susan," Rowan said trying to sound reasonable, "I'd hardly say examining a cadaver was 'delicate'. I'm here in an official capacity to hear what the Doctor found out."

She had that woman's look that said she was ready to fight about it some more, but she just huffed and went back through the door, slamming it behind her.

She was back in a flash. "The Doctor says he needs another hour or so and that you're to come back later." She looked as if she was ready to beat us all into submission. "Those are his instructions. Good day!"

She gestured towards the door and with subtle hand motions, herded us out the front door. As I was last in line, she was breathing down my back the whole way. I had long past reached the point in my life where I let people give me an annoying bum's rush. Before she could push me out and slam the door, I turned so abruptly, her belly almost knocked me backwards into the street.

She was too shocked to move and I asked her, "Be honest with me now. Do you think the Doctor will be able to pull Nickolas through with that 'delicate' procedure?"

She grabbed the door and swung it shut so hard that if William had not pulled me backwards onto the front step, it would have certainly broken my nose.

With William giving me a withering look, I decided to go on the offensive and said to my friends, "You two aren't even trying to have fun!"

Inn's Lunch

Rowan shook his head, but I could see he was trying not to laugh, "Whatever made you say a thing like that?"

William piped up before I could open my mouth, "I am sure because he needs to get something in his stomach. Care to join us for lunch, Inspector?"

"And just what are you implying, my good man?" I asked.

He snorted, "You've been pulling at that flask all morning and that is on top of whatever you got out of my stock on the *Aunt Polly*! If you don't get something to eat soon, we'll have to carry you home. We have seen this play before, old friend."

"Yea, well, you think any of this would be more fun sober?"

Rowan clasped me on the shoulder in a friendly manner, "I can assure you, Charles, it's not."

Rowan turned to William, "I'd be delighted to join you, while we wait on the Doctor. So, let's go see what Jimmy's cooking up today at the Inn."

The Inn turned out to be a quaint, rustic, and a quite popular establishment. A short stride through the foyer and it opened up to a common room, what my uncles called a tap room. Its paneled walls were covered with memorabilia, a few mounted fish skeletons, and the inevitable ten point buck's head with dusty antlers.

A huge mahogany bar started just a few feet from the door and stretched to the back of the large room. Its wide top gleamed, though time and countless elbows had worn the finish down to the wood grain along the edges. The beveled mirrors that covered the upper wall behind the bar made it seem larger, though I would have guessed that twenty men could drink at the bar at the same time if they were friendly enough to swill shoulder to shoulder. The back left corner had an unmanned reception desk with a key rack behind it that was attached to a staircase that led to the overnight rooms. The rest of the room was a common area, the furniture arrayed in a semicircular pattern, radiating out from a huge stone hearth.

The tables were solid oak, the larger with benches and the smaller squares with chairs. Rowan led us to one and we sat. It was obvious the Inspector was a regular here. He waved to the woman behind the bar and held up three fingers. She came bustling over with three glasses on a tray. She put a tall glass of ale in front of Rowan and me and a darker liquid before William.

"There you are, Mr. Gillette. It's iced tea with a little honey and lemon and thank you for coming to see us again." She beamed and turned to the Inspector, "And hello to you, Inspector. We haven't seen much of you lately. How's the missus doing? She's getting close if I remember right?"

Rowan smiled, "Just a month or so is what the Doctor thinks, Kitty. She's a bit run down trying to keep up with my hellion. Auntie Beth is practically living with us and she's been a big help while I've been busy.

So I haven't been home for dinner for the last few days." He winked at William and me, "Beth could burn water for tea, so I am dying for a good meal. What's Jimmy making today?"

"You know, I thought he was all set to dish up his pot roast today, but then old Bill Wickers stopped in earlier with a pile of fresh stripe bass he took last night. So bass it is!" she said.

"Sounds great! Bring it when it's ready."

Kitty gave him a wink and started to turn away, when I spoke up,

"Actually, my dear, if it's all the same, I'd like to have the pot roast instead." Something heavy was just what I needed to soak up all the liquor that was starting to sour in my stomach.

"I'm sure you would, hun," she replied with a sympathetic smile, "but Jimmy made bass." With that she turned away and hustled off to the kitchen.

Rowan smiled at the confused look on my face, and then explained, "This probably isn't what you are used to in the city, Mr. Frohman. There's no menu here at the Inn." He laughed, "Heck! It doesn't have a real name. Everyone just calls it the Inn. And here at the Inn, Jimmy only makes one dish a day. Take it or leave it."

"That's nuts!"

"I wouldn't say that." William chimed in. "From a business point of view, it keeps things simple and it's better to do one thing great than many things mediocre." Will then swept his hand around to encompass the room that was more than half full of diners, "It seems to work for the Inn."

"Please don't tell me Jimmy is just the busboy and it's his turn to cook. At least tell me he is a chef." I said with a worried look. They both laughed at that one.

"Do not fret so, Frohman. I've only had good, or I should say exceptional meals here." William assured me, "Jimmy knows what he's doing and I am sure you will be more than pleased. It will be better than that pricey New York City food you are so used too."

And, by God, Will was right. The three plates came steaming hot. A thick filet of fresh striped bass accompanied by buttery root vegetables and creamy mashed potatoes. The bass was cooked perfectly, with just the right amount of butter and seasoning. I had eaten a boatload of fish in my life, and bass wasn't my favorite, but this was the best I ever had.

By some unspoken rule, none of us mentioned the murder while we ate. We were ravenous and the food disappeared quickly. Mary came to clear the empty porcelain promptly and told us that Jimmy was making us some dessert. We accepted her offer of coffee which she brought right away, and another great surprise – the coffee was a rich dark roast in an oversized mug that was just perfect.

Soon after, the old gal Kitty came back with three bowls of warm bread pudding. A specialty of the Inn. Jimmy acquired the recipe from a farmer in Mystic, now in his eighties – it's Charlie Rippel's buttery bread pudding. The bread pudding produced a taste and texture I'd never had before, and it was smothered in a bourbon sauce that came alive in your mouth and sent a warm tangy scent up your sinuses. Combined with raisins and cinnamon, it was a perfect dessert. Not a word passed between us until our spoons scraped the bottom of our bowls.

We all sat back and I fished out a cigarette. As I sat smoking, I looked around the room. To my surprise, almost everyone else in the room was peeking at our table, out of the corner of their eyes, and whispering quietly to each other.

I had experienced this before, when I was out and about with famous actors or others of notoriety, and I was mildly surprised to see this same behavior out here in the boonies. Not that they weren't as star struck as most folk. They were just too clannish in their do-for-yourself-ways to act like it. I commented on it to William.

"Oh, it's not me there talking about, Frohman" and he gave the Inspector a knowing look.

Rowan heaved a sigh. "I suppose not. Not exclusively

anyways." Then he muttered under his breath, "Incredible how much trouble can fit into a briefcase!" Then he raised his voice an octave. "But I think a man should be able to enjoy his lunch in peace."

Will patted Rowan's arm, "Believe me, Inspector, that won't work. It will just hone their curiosity. You might as well get used to it. Like it or not, you are going to get a taste of celebrity life now."

Rowan leaned in and lowered his voice with some strained conviction, "Celebrity? More like the laughing stock. We're no closer to a solution now as we were when we started! I can tell you this, men from half the law enforcement agencies are out scouring the eastern half of this country, and will soon enough descend on our quiet little town! The murder on the ferry has reached the boiling point." Rowan snorted and shook his head, "And the Chief wants it solved so he can hand them the affair in a neat package when they get here!"

"And now you have another bucket of clams to shuck, with Nickolas's death." I pointed out.

He smiled ruefully and shrugged. "But if this is what celebrity fame is like, I'd gladly leave it to you, Mr. Gillette."

"Thank you, but no, Inspector. I'm trying to put all that notoriety behind me now. I just want a quiet retirement," Will replied.

"Which is hard to do with a corpse on your doorstep," I wisecracked.

Rowan looked around furtively and said in a hushed tone. "We may have a bit of extra time in that regard, Mr. Gillette."

"You don't say."

The inspector looked left, then right, and leaned closer, "I know for a fact that the media has been barred from the area until further notice. Even our little weekly has been told to lay low on the ferry murder."

I knew the information was beneficial to Will, but somehow, it didn't sit too well with me.

"That seems a bit un-American, don't you think? Freedom of the press is guaranteed by the Constitution!"

"I'm sure there is good reason, Mr. Frohman. Treasury Secretary, George Cortelyou himself called Luboff demanded we keep a tight lid on the situation. If you knew the dire consequences, or the enormity of the ferry crime, I think you would agree that keeping a few gossipers in the dark was the lesser of two evils."

He shrugged. "I'm just following my instructions." Then Rowan smiled to take the sting out of his words and joked, "My wife eats like a horse! I need my salary!"

"I meant it just seemed odd to have Washington officials and the federal police involved for such a small town crime. Even for murder and robbery. Just who got killed and what the hell did they steal?"

Rowan seemed surprised by my bluntness and from the way his eyes quickly scanned the room. He was more than a little worried.

"I must be very clear about this, gentlemen," he said in a low voice. "I, or rather we, shall not discuss yesterday's events. That case is sealed from the public from the highest positions."

He leaned forward, putting both hands on the table and said quietly, "Our orders are coming right from Washington and by tomorrow, half the federal force will blanket this area. Believe me when I tell you, you're better off not knowing. And if Chief Luboff ever knew I was talking out of turn, we would all be in a cell within the hour!"

I thought that was a bit melodramatic, as William told me, everyone in town knew at least something about the ferry crime, but I thought it better to heed the Inspector's advice on this one. I've often thought 'involvement' was the root of the word 'inconvenience'.

William, who I thought hadn't heard a word we said, suddenly came out of his trance and focused on the Inspector with a pointed comment in a very hushed voice.

"The new currency plates. The set destined for Philadelphia."

I Settle the Bill

I didn't know where my friend came up with that statement, but the near violent reaction to it from Rowan was the only confirmation I needed. You would have thought Will backhanded him instead making a simple observation.

Rowan gripped the arms of his chair and started to rise, sputtering like he had an ice bucket dumped in his shorts.

In one fluid motion, Will uncrossed his legs, leaned towards the young Inspector, and put a firm hand on his arm. Smiling ear to ear, he spoke in a low tone, "Please calm yourself, Inspector! Unless you want everyone in this room to know our little secret and the rest of the town within the hour!"

To his credit, Rowan saw the wisdom in William's advice and returned a strained smile as he settled back into his chair.

"You can't possibly know about the plates!" he whispered fiercely, looking more like a gaffed fish now.

"That's what was stolen from the ferry?" I asked.

Lord knows, I had a genuine reason to be concerned. If someone was to start printing their own money, with the actual plates, the economy could be compromised. For a guy in a mostly cash business, I saw a lot of headaches in my future.

"Of course, 'off the ferry', Frohman. Have you not been listening to our conversation?" William said.

I just rolled my eyes at him and snorted. This persona could be mildly irritating, but it was worth it to watch him pull the truth out of thin air like he just did. Rowan, on the other hand, was not entertained at all.

"I'm afraid I'm going to have to take you gentlemen down to the station."

I was about to laugh in his face, but William made a subtle gesture for me to stay still.

"Whatever for?" Will asked, the slightest hint of a smirk lurking about his mouth.

Rowan's face was stone, his voice iron. "I won't insult you by trying to deny what you said was true. You got me there. There is no legitimate reason for you to have that information! The goddamn President doesn't even know they are missing yet! You have a lot of explaining to do, and you can start by telling me just who gave you that information." and his face grew even harder if that was possible, "And God help you if you can't!"

A wave of dread washed over me as I noticed Rowan's hand creeping towards the butt of his pistol under his jacket. William really stepped in it this time. First a death at his home and now his revelation about the robbery, it didn't look too good for my friend.

"Please, Inspector," William said sharply, with a touch of disdain, "Gather yourself! Of course, no one relayed this fact to me, and I am not involved in the crime! And in no way is our Lord involved, so kindly refrain from using his name in vain! I can overlook the fact that you would even consider me for a murderer and a thief, as we have just gotten acquainted and your profession is suspicion by nature, but I assure you, I only came to my conclusions as you and Frohman were talking just now. Had I known it was a briefcase that was taken, I would have come to the same conclusion earlier. You cannot fault me for drawing conclusions from words you yourself spoke."

Rowan winced, and sat back in his chair to let his mind review our table conversation. He wore an utter look of bewilderment, but had the good grace to mumble an apology for his language.

I didn't see the connection either, but I had seen this act before, so I sat back with my coffee and waited, feeling a bit smug. After a moment, Rowan shook his head and threw his hands up in exasperation.

"How?" Was all he could manage to ask in a hushed voice.

"Simple deduction really."

William may have looked patient and crafty on the outside, but I knew he was well in his element and having the time of his life.

"I had already considered the fact that the object, or objects, that I assumed were stolen could fit into a briefcase. The only reason why your murderer would slit someone's throat, then delay his escape long enough to sever the victim's hand, is obvious. To get at something locked about the wrist. I briefly entertained the thought that it might be papers of some kind."

"Oh, right!" I cut in, "like that diplomat from Norway we sailed with that time. He had that case full of treaties or something hanging from his cuffed wrist the entire trip."

"Exactly, Frohman," he turned back to Rowan, "I was following that course until you mentioned Washington." He broke off when he saw the look of dismay spread across the Inspector's face. I think Rowan was just realizing how much smarter William was than he. Yes indeed, Will's intellectual mind is truly amazing. Poor Rowan was wishing we had skipped lunch.

William, letting his persona overrun his sensitivity, plowed on.

"You claimed the crime would have 'dire consequences' for the economy and that your orders came from Cortelyou, our current Secretary of the Treasury. That brought forth in my mind an article I read in the journal on

February second."

"Hey," I chimed in, "I remember reading something about those plates too!

Weren't there three sets made? One for Boston, one being for New York, and the other for Philadelphia."

"Bravo Frohman! Quite so. Assuming they kept one for themselves, the Boston mint would have to ship the other two."

Will paused to take a slow dramatic sip of his tea, then concluded, "So, we are looking for objects small enough for a valise and light enough to be handcuffed to a wrist, yet important enough for the fifth most powerful man in America to be personally involved and the rest of us kept in the dark, less we suffer some financial disaster. Elementary my dear Rowan. It was the money printing plates."

"Damn," I turned my attention to Rowan, "If you don't catch this guy soon, we might as well stack our cash in the outhouse, at least it will get some use in there." I turned back to William with a smirk but he ignored my comment.

"That case must have been heavy. How do you think they got it off the boat?" Will asked.

Rowan leaned in again and hissed, "Gentlemen, please just stop talking! If someone hears us, we will end up in serious Dutch." He wagged an accusing finger at us, "You are too smart for your own good! What am I to do with you two?"

He just sat there, dejected and shaking his head. I believe he was seriously still thinking about running us in just so his ass was covered.

William was in no way concerned as he tapped my cigarette case and raised an eyebrow. I was mildly surprised by the request, because he never smoked in public, but we were halfway through our smokes before Rowan looked up at us again.

"What am I going to do?" he repeated.

William took a long drag on his smoke and slowly let it out towards the ceiling. He turned to Rowan with a benign face and said, "Perhaps you should take advantage of an opportunity."

"Come again?"

I saw where this was leading so I leaned forward and gestured for them to do the same, "We already know what's what and we still have a little time before we head back to the Doctor's, so…"

"Are you serious? I'm in enough trouble as it is! If anyone else on the force knew that you knew, I'd be without an income and you gentlemen would be seriously inconvenienced."

"Then we will just have to keep this among ourselves, Inspector. I assure you that you can rely on our discretion. I have no desire to be persecuted for a simple deduction." William assured him calmly.

Rowan looked to me and I said, "Mum's the word, Inspector! A stay in your jail is definitely not on my vacation itinerary!"

I could see in Rowan's eyes he was still uncertain, but wanting to pick William's brain some more. I pressed him a bit, "Seems to me, Inspector, you could use a fresh perspective." I shrugged and put my palms in the air. Nodding in Will's direction and added, "Look at what he figured out already. Imagine what William might come up with if he had all the details?"

I planted the seeds and was willing to let them stew in his head for a while but he surprised me with a quick decision.

"What the hell," he said with resignation, "Chances are the perpetrators are halfway across the country by now. It's been days and we're no closer to a solution."

He looked right then left. "But, I think we should have

this discussion somewhere else. I certainly cannot take a chance that these gossipers hear our discussions."

Will shifted his gaze to the room and it seemed everyone tried to look like they were doing anything but gawking. "Perhaps you are right, Inspector. I'm sure we can find somewhere to sit on the way to the Doctor's." He raised his hand and got Mary's attention.

She dropped what she was doing and hustled right over to see what we needed. I hastily reached into my billfold and handed her a large denomination, enough to pay for our lunch ten times over.

"The rest is for you and the staff, dear lady!" I said as we rose and shrugged into our coats.

Her jaw dropped and she stared at the bill then us, "That's far too much, Sir. Are you certain?"

I waved her off, "It was the best meal I've had in a long, long time. And be sure to take care of Jimmy, that striped bass would have been proud how he was served!" I tapped the bill and waggled a finger at her, "And make sure you do something fun with your portion." I figured I better pass my bills around now, just in case someone starts printing money.

When we stepped outside, the sun was shining brightly, bringing the temperature up to a comfortable level. My head was much clearer and I had that certain glow you got from doing something incredibly nice and unexpected for a stranger. I looked up to see William eyeing me speculatively.

"What?" I asked him.

"Nothing, Frohman," he said with a smile, "I was just wondering what sins you may have committed to bring about that extravagant penance."

"Ha-Ha," I retorted, "The whole day's been nothing but blood, gore, and mysteries!" I shrugged. "Someone should have a good day. I hope she spends that money on old wine and young men."

Rowan looked at me, open admiration on his face, "You're a good man, Charles Frohman."

"Bah! Get between me and a box office receipt and see what happens!"

Rowan's View

"I'm still not sure about this," Rowan started off. "Perhaps-"

"We have been through all that!" William huffed. "We have just enough time to hear you out before we adjourn to the doctor's if you stop your dilly-dallying. So, please. Relate the facts only, in sequence, and leave nothing out."

Then he simply leaned back, eyes lidded, and waited for Rowan to begin.

We were seated in a town gazebo, situated on the town common, near the docks. The day had turned warm under the afternoon sun. Warm enough for a group of youngsters to launch a couple of old canoes off the wharf. I envied their resilience to the cold water, but I was more than content to sit under the roof of the gazebo, where the slatted walls blocked the slight breeze coming off the river. There wasn't another soul within a hundred yards of us, so we could talk freely.

I'm sure Rowan wasn't too taken with William's imperial tone, but he said nothing before he flipped open yet another of his ever-present notebooks. The Inspector scanned his notes for a moment then spoke.

"First, I'll give you my side of the story; it'll help put things into perspective. Afterwards, I will fill you in on what we have learned so far in the investigation."

"However you deem it to be the most expedient, Inspector," William said like he was some limey lord.

Rowan drew in a deep breath and let it out his nose before he began.

"The night before last, Thursday, I was about to check out and head home when Luboff got a call. When he came out of his office, he gave me orders to have our police launch manned and ready to sail if necessary. Then he instructed me to take another constable and to go down to the docks and wait for the ferry to come in. My orders were to simply observe the unloading of a single carriage, and when it was on its way out of town, I was to return to the station and report to the chief. I wasn't too happy about the assignment, I can tell you. The very pregnant wife was expecting me for dinner, and well, you know how they are about a change in plans."

"And did he tell you why you had to pull this extra duty?" William asked, without opening his eyes.

Rowan chuckled, "All he said was, "To do what you're paid to do and keep an eye out for trouble." When I asked him why the launch, he replied, "insurance." He wasn't any more forthcoming than that and he doesn't like to be questioned too closely, so grudgingly, I came down to the docks here. At first, I just sat right here in the gazebo, but I got restless and took a walk down by the banks. I was talking to the men manning the launch when the red lights came on."

"Red lights?" I asked.

"Three red lights, lit over the wheel house, is the signal for trouble." William explained, and then he motioned for Rowan to continue.

"Wait," I asked, "Doesn't the boat have a horn? That's the usual signal for distress."

William sighed and shook his head, "You are absolutely correct, Frohman. Only...the vessel was not in trouble, just its occupants. The horn is used only when the vessel itself is in danger. The lights are used when there is a problem with the passengers like drunken disruptive riders or a serious dispute breaks out on board."

"Right," Rowan said, "Which is why the captain didn't think to blow the horn three times for an S.O.S. If only he had, I might have had the lads out quicker.

As it were, the ferry was still about two or three hundred feet from the dock, so I told the boys to fire up the engine on our boat and make ready to cast off if needed. The constable and I hightailed it over to the ferry landing. We could make out the shape of the ferry but it was still too far out from the dock lights when we heard someone shout,

"Stand where you are or I'll shoot!"

Well, Sirs, I can honestly say I didn't hesitate for a moment! I told the lad to call Luboff from the Inn and get as much back up as he could muster to the dock right away. The lad took off like his pants were on fire and I drew my gun to wait for the boat to get close enough to the ferry landing lights for me to see a target."

I thought we had discovered another side to this soft spoken, intelligent man. "You sound like quite the gunslinger," I said.

He laughed, "No, no, just scared and confused mostly." Then he added in all seriousness, "But I'll do whatever it takes to fulfill my duties."

"Commendable! Commendable!" William grumbled. "Continue."

Yet another sigh, "I didn't have to wait long. In just a few minutes the ferry came out of the gloom. Though, what I saw when everything came into focus, left me still in the dark! The first thing I saw was the horses and a carriage behind them, just like Luboff said there would be. I noticed the door to the cab was open and gently swinging back and forth with the motions of the waves. The horses were fidgeting, but calm enough.

The person that wasn't calm was a man wearing a bandanna wrapped about his head. His hair was sticking up like an Indian headdress and he was holding two pistols sticking out from his body in two directions. He was aiming at the two crew members, Gordon and Perkins. Perkins was just a few feet away from him and Gordon was standing outside the wheelhouse doors. Both had their arms raised. I waited until the ferry had come close enough for a reasonable shot and I shouted, "Police! Drop your weapons or I'll shoot!" Of course, I didn't know the situation. All I saw was two citizens I was sworn to protect being menaced by a bleeding, shouting madman."

Rowan shivered slightly and continued. "You don't know how close I was to dropping him on the spot! My finger was tightening on the trigger when he screams,

"My name is Rashleigh! I am an agent with the U.S. Treasury department! Send for the Police! When we dock..."

"We can't dock until you let them man the ropes!" Burke screamed from the wheelhouse. Seeing me, he shouted across the water, "There's been murder done, Kevin! You have to make him..."

The two crewmen started to lower their arms , now I was the focus, but Rashleigh pulled the hammers back on both pistols and shouted right over the captain's words-

"Move a muscle and I'll kill you where you stand!"

Rowan took a deep breath and let it out in one whoosh, his cheeks puffed out like a horn player. "I still almost shot him when he said that, but also realized that he may well have been telling the truth, or why would Luboff have sent me here in the first place? Though I doubt he had anything like this in mind. So I identified myself and ordered him to hold his fire. I could see the situation was getting nowhere fast, so when the ferry was close enough, I jumped onto the deck."

"You're lucky you didn't break your neck, lad," I observed. I knew how tricky it was to board a moving boat.

"Luckily, I landed on my feet and caught my balance as I bounced into the front gates. Holding my gun pointed up and my other palm open, I approached the man who claimed he was a Treasury agent. Still holding his guns level, his eyes never leaving the crew, he opened his jacket and I could see the federal badge pinned inside. I showed him mine and got quite the shock when he turned towards me.

The entire left side of his face was bloody. One eye was nearly swelled shut and the other was fluttering. He started to sway on his feet and so I reached out to steady him. He collapsed in my arms and I lowered him to the deck into a sitting position. The pistols dropped to the deck and he clutched my sleeve. "Gone.... stolen," he croaked, "Arrest crew...search boat. ....search river...you must find..." Then Rashleigh fell unconscious."

"Damnation!" I said, "What did you do then!"

He shrugged, "First, I let the crew dock the ferry. They stayed well clear of me and the bleeding man, which was understandable, as he had just threatened to shoot them all. By the time they had us tied off, the lads on the launch had come alongside. Burke and the boys were just standing around me, looking like the last thing they wanted was more trouble, so I ordered my men to search the river."

"That was quite intuitive, Inspector," William said. "But, whatever did you tell them to search for? You were not aware, at that point, that the plates had been stolen."

Rowan gave him a hard look. "I'll tell you the same thing I told them, Sir.
"You see anything but a fish, you bring it to me right away!"

In any event, as Rashleigh was still breathing, I was debating whether to send one of Burke's men to fetch the doctor, in spite of Rashleigh's instructions about taking them into custody, when to my surprise and I admit, my

173

relief, Luboff arrived."

"Before you continue," William commanded behind closed eyes with his hand raised, "Describe what you saw at the scene before Luboff arrived."

Rowan sat back and took his hat off. He ran his hands through his hair a few times and then stared off into space, like he was reading his notes in his mind.

"I'll try, but it's all kind of like rolling downhill after I saw the three lights, like trying to map out chaos. After Rashleigh had passed out, I stayed with him as the two crewmen went for the mooring ropes and Burke returned to the wheelhouse to maneuver the ferry for docking.

Between trying to stop the blood flowing from his head and trying to decipher his last words, the scene is burned into my memory. I took a deep breath and then looked the scene over, mostly concentrating on keeping the crew in sight. Your familiar with it, Mr. Gillette, but I'll describe the layout for Mr. Frohman.

The ferry is basically a rectangular barge with sides. Facing the boat, on the right is the wheelhouse that sits eight feet or so above deck, fifteen feet from the front, glass on all four sides, with an access door from the deck. The back right corner is an open area with just a three foot sidewall that wraps around to the engines that run the ferry, which are located in the center stern."

"What type of engines?" I asked, getting an arched eyebrow from William for the interruption.

"Steam, I believe," Rowan replied. "Why?"

I shrugged, "Just wanted to know if they were manned. A steam engine requires constant monitoring and stoking of the boiler with coal."

"Excellent point, Frohman!" Will said exuberantly, "An astute observation. You astound me! Continue, Inspector."

Rowan gave us both a suspicious eye, then put his fingers to his temples and closed his eyes, "The left rear corner is a mirror image of the right. The wall leads to a passenger area, which is directly across from the wheelhouse. The front has two simple wooden gates, as I already described."

William suddenly swung his legs off the bench and sat up. "So, now that Frohman is up to speed, what was your position and what did you observe?"

"I was on the left side, about ten feet or so from the passenger area. Well, the main thing, from my perspective, was the carriage and horses. The horse team was calmed down, perhaps because the ferry stopped moving and I saw that the door to the cab must have shut and latched because it wasn't swaying anymore." Rowan hesitated for a second, "But, as far as I could tell in the dark, the only thing out of place was a pair of wooden buckets rolling back and forth in a big puddle of water. Those I'll get to in a moment."

"Very well," William said, "So you were assisting the man called Rashleigh when your superior arrived. What happened next?"

"Like I said before, I was relieved to see Luboff show up. I didn't have the foggiest notion what the hell I was going to do beyond that point. I wanted to stand but I had Rashleigh's head cradled in my arm, trying to keep it off the cold deck. The Chief stopped in front of us, holding a lantern, and bent over. He straightened right back up and waved one arm, never taking his eyes off of Rashleigh."

"Is he going to live?" he asked me.

"I don't know, Sir. He's breathing steady but it looks like he lost a lot of blood! He definitely needs a doctor!"

"Think so?" he asked in his most sarcastic tone. Just then two constables rushed up with a stretcher and took the wounded man from me.

"Get him over to Doc Blum's and then one of you come back here. The other one stays until he wakes up or he

dies. Either way, report back to me immediately. Got that!"
They'd have saluted like army recruits if they weren't
carrying Rashleigh away.

I could see that over towards the wheelhouse, the captain
and crew had finished shutting down the ferry for the night
and were whispering as they stood under the faint glow of
the running lights from above. You could tell they were
scared and I wondered again why Rashleigh had them in
his custody. I'll admit I wasn't tracking too well at that
point. So much was happening so fast, I knew I was
missing something important.

Suddenly, the thought occurred to me! Luboff's timely
arrival was far too precipitous! At that time of night,
Luboff should have been home. There was no way he
could organize a squad and get to the scene as fast as he
did.

That was why he assigned me this duty and had the
launch readied. He knew something was going to happen
and he sent me in blind! Angry, or perhaps just scared and
confused by the circumstances, I was about to lay into the
Chief and demand that he tell me what the hell was going
on!

But before I could open my mouth, I saw his eyes widen
behind his thick glasses. He snapped his gaze at me.

"Why is that key in the door?"

I turned to follow his line of sight and the Chief blew
right by me. Then Burke's words came to the front of my
mind!

"There's been murder done."

So I stepped right on Luboff's heels and that's when I
saw the key sticking out of the door to the carriage. Luboff
reached it in a few steps and, kicking one of the rolling
buckets aside, flung the door open. He said something
softly, in Yiddish. It..."

"Before you continue," William said, cutting him off,

"That is the second time you mentioned those buckets. What is their part in the robbery?"

Rowan was about to answer, then changed his mind. "I'll get to them in a bit. They are important, but not for this part of the story.

Anyways, Luboff said something in another language.

"Most likely 'Got bashitsn aundz!'" William observed, "It translates to 'God protect us!"

Even I was knocked off my seat by that one. My friend never ceased to amaze me.

"You learned Jew talk at that Catholic college you went to?"

William just gave me his most dignified look and replied. "No, at your wedding. Your mother-in-law kept saying it over and over."

He turned back to Rowan, "Go on, Inspector."

Rowan's smile at our exchange quickly disappeared and he took a deep breath and exhaled slowly as relived the events in his mind.

"It was as bad of a scene as I had ever had the misfortune to witness. Not until this morning, when we saw Nickolas in your courtyard, had I ever seen such damage to a human being. The victim's throat was slit and he had been stabbed through the eye."

"Jesus wept!" I blurted out. "You'd think one or the other would have sufficed!"

"Our Lord had nothing to do with it," William chided me.

"A sliced throat for silence and a thrust to the brain for an instant death. Our killer wanted no struggle it seems."

"I thought that too," Rowan replied, "But he wasn't done yet! The stump of his left arm was resting on the seat next to him and the severed hand was lying on the floor of the coach!"

"And so the plates were taken," William mumbled under

his breath.

"Ha!" he cried out, startling the both of us with his sudden animation. "Our killer shows a remarkable talent for speed and efficiency!"

"For Pete's sake, Will!" I said, "Maybe you could show a little compassion! We're talking about a man's life here!"

He just looked at me like I had two heads. "Frohman. Please don't be so tied to your emotions. Of course I in no way wish to diminish his sacrifice in the line of duty, but emotions will not rectify the situation. Only total objectiveness will give us the deductive reasoning needed to resolve it. As in any crime. I am sure the Inspector would agree."

William then turned to Rowan and asked, "What was Chief Inspector Luboff's reaction?"

"As you can imagine, we were all in shock. Except for the Chief. He seemed to size up the situation in a heartbeat. Of course, he knew a bit more background than the rest of us. But, I'll give him credit. He didn't miss a beat! He sent one man back to the station to grab more men. He put one man to watch Burke and the boys. Then he organized an inch by inch search of the ferry.

'Find a case,' Luboff bellowed at the few free men. He spaced his hands out in front of him to indicate the size, "Probably metal but that's just a guess."

Rowan chuckled and shook his head. "One of the younger men, just a few months on the force, asked, 'How will we know if it's the right case?'

Luboff went as red as a beet and stuck his face right in the boy's and said softly, 'It'll have a bloody handcuff attached to it!'

As they scattered, he turned to me with instructions.

'Take the crew down to the station, shackle them, and keep them separated and quiet on the ride. I need...'

"Shackles, Sir?" I cut in. "I've known these men all my

life and..."

'Do it!' Luboff cut me off in return. He pointed to himself then poked me in the chest, 'Let me tell you something. This is bigger than our town or our state! So listen and listen well. You will handcuff them and keep them quiet with no talking amongst themselves! And when you get to the station, you will strip search them and then get their stories. I want to know everything that happened from the time they laid eyes on that carriage until this very moment! Everything! You understand?! Question them separately, then together. You want to press them hard, son. When the big boys arrive, they're gonna want answers!'

Then he poked me in the chest again and said, 'I'm trusting that you'll have them ready.'

"So, I was sent off to the station with the ferry crew. Truth be told, as disappointed as I was to be taken off the scene, I was more than happy to be away from that bloodbath."

The Skinny

Rowan paused with a haunted look in his eyes. I reached over to pat him on the shoulder and it was easy to see, in that moment, that he was a gentle, sensitive soul at heart. He had young children and a loving - expecting wife at home and just this week had to step out his door into a cruel hard world that he probably never thought he would see, even as a detective in this sleepy New England burg. It was sad to watch the world drop on a man's shoulders.

William, on the other hand, was oblivious to the young inspector's tortured memories. He was a hound on a scent.

"So am I to infer from our previous discussions that the illustrious Chief Inspector Luboff found no trace of the missing plates? Nor any clues to their whereabouts?"

Rowan gathered himself, shook off his doldrums and came back to the moment. I knew then that Rowan was truly a professional. "Not a trace, Mr. Gillette. No evidence of a stowaway. No trace of an intruder and no way for a boat to pull alongside and board her anyways."

I was skeptical. "How can you claim that? A man or even a few men could row a skiff alongside and board that ferry! I grew up pulling the oars on a Bennett dory, Sir, and I can tell you without doubt it is possible!"

"AH!" Rowan held up a finger, "But to escape without notice?

I tell you I had the launch sweeping the river just minutes after I saw the three lights. Even a small boat can't hide on top of the river."

"Maybe they made it to shore before your launch spotted

them."

Rowan shook his head. "Not possible. The ferry was almost directly in the middle of the river when the crime occurred. There was no way it could get far enough away from detection! Even in a sculling skiff. Impossible!"

"That is a bold statement, Inspector," William said with a smirk, "in lieu of the events."

I suddenly realized that my balloon theory could fit this scenario. "Then that leaves but one way to board that ship."

"Before you recycle your aerial assault theories, Frohman, perhaps we should hear the story from the crew's perspective. And that of agent Rashleigh. Perhaps then we shall have enough data to make an intelligent deduction. Proceed Inspector, if you would be so kind." He pulled his watch from a vest pocket and checked the time, "Though perhaps you can keep it concise. We are to be at the Doctor's in less than half an hour."

Even though I knew it wasn't really my friend talking, his tone just made me want to slap him. Rowan was amused enough to let his pushiness roll off his back.

Rowan leaned forward. "Steven Burke, the owner and operator of the Haddam-Lyme Ferry Company, was contacted a few weeks ago, on March third, for a special charter by a representative of the U.S. Treasury Department. He was asked to make a separate run, minimum crew, for a single carriage, on March twenty-third. As part of the charter, he was instructed to take no other passengers or freight. He was instructed to be at the east ferry landing no later than seven p.m. and wait for a single carriage.

Burke was offered half again his usual charter fee, so he was quick to take the job. The crew loves these extra trips because it's all dolly money for them.

Will's eyes snapped open and he tilted his head slightly

towards us. It reminded me of a reptile who just saw prey. "Irrelevant!"

Rowan sighed and went on. "After the passengers disembarked from the six p.m. run to Chester, they made a quick re-crossing and waited for about twenty minutes or so before the carriage and six lathered horses thundered up. The driver introduced himself as John Rashleigh and handed over a voucher to pay for the trip. It took a few more minutes to back the carriage onto the ferry and secure it."

I cut him off. "Why back them on?"

"From what little I know, it's easier to back horses onto the ferry than make them walk forward. If they can see the water, they're reluctant to walk out onto it. Unnatural for them, I suppose."

"Hmm," I commented. "I didn't know that. I won..."

"Gentlemen! Please," William growled, eyes snapping open once again. "Could we save the equestrian discussion for another time and get on with it?"

Rowan continued. "So, as the ferry set out, the captain and Gordon Steele were in the wheelhouse and Glenn Perkins was in the stern, stoking the boiler. The horses and carriage took most of the length of the ferry, straight down the middle.

After a check of the horses and a walk about the ferry, the driver knocked on the door of the cab, then used a key to open the door. The occupant handed him out some food and they spoke for a moment before locking the door. He climbed up onto the driver's seat to eat it. Perkins and Steele checked the perimeter of the boat and lit the running lights. Both men returned to their stations. For the first half of the trip everything seemed normal."

"Was Perkins the only crew member on deck in clear view of the carriage?" William asked.

"Actually, no. There is a wall that separates the cargo

deck from the engines."

"Bulkhead," I corrected him.

"Excuse me?" Rowan said.

"Bulkhead," I explained, "A wall on a boat is called a bulkhead."

"Thank you for that illumination, Frohman," William said snidely. He looked to Rowan, "If Steele was in the wheelhouse with the captain, who was on deck watch? There has always been a crewman assigned to that position whenever I have taken the ferry."

"Technically, it was Gordon, Mr. Gillette, but as there was only the one carriage which they were told to stay clear of, the captain kept him in the wheelhouse with him. Later he admitted he did so because he was afraid Gordon would try to strike up a conversation with the man if he got half a chance. I have had a pint with the man and he could talk a seagull off a fishing boat! Burke wanted no trouble with the Agents or Luboff."

At another raised eyebrow from William. Rowan went on quickly before William could chide him again.

"As you know, the wheelhouse is elevated, so when Rashleigh got back in the driver's seat, he was almost level with the captain and Gordon. They had a clear view of the man and the rig."

"Yet their view of the right side of the vessel must have been impaired," William observed, then looked at me and snapped "starboard," then went back to Rowan. "So we have one agent upon the carriage, one inside, the captain and Gordon in the wheelhouse and Perkins attending the boiler in the stern, for the start of the trip, anyways."

"Right," Rowan, "It wasn't until they were halfway across the river when things went to hell in a hand basket! Burke and Gordon testified that the horses began to fuss. Rocking back and forth in their traces. Rashleigh shouted at them and pulled at the reins in an effort to calm them down, but they continued to fidget, so he threw his sandwich down in disgust and climbed down to tend the team."

"But the crew could not see Rashleigh once he dropped off the seat?" William said, his tone making it a question.

"No. Gordon thought he may have seen the top of Rashleigh's head as he tended the horses, but it was dark by then and their night vision was ruined by the light in the wheelhouse."

"Did Perkins see him get down?" I asked.

Rowan shook his head. "He was busy keeping the steam up as the ferry went against the tide. It wasn't until about five minutes later that he heard a commotion and stuck his head out of the engine area. That's when all hell broke loose. Perkins said he heard what sounded like all the horses snorting and stomping around. Having grown up on a farm, he thought that some water might calm the beasts down. He was worried that they might dislodge the blocks they placed against the wheels to keep them from moving, so he filled a couple of his buckets from the water barrel and stepped out onto the deck to see if he could help and offer the water to Rashleigh."

"And did the captain and first mate have the same concerns?" William asked.

"No," Rowan replied. "They saw the horses fidget but assumed that Rashleigh would handle his team. Neither one of those boys knows one end of a horse from the other. When Perkins rounded the bulkhead, he realized that something was terribly wrong.

Rashleigh wasn't calming the horses; he was underneath them, unmoving! Glenn saw his legs sticking out from under the team, so he immediately threw down the buckets and rang the aft warning bell to alert the captain. Then he rushed over to pull Rashleigh to safety before the horses finished stomping him into the deck. There were hoof prints all over his torso and arms and he was bleeding from a deep gash in the back of his head.

Thinking quickly, he took a bandana from his pocket and had it tightly wrapped around the wound by the time Burke and Gordon burst out of the wheelhouse to join him."

"Good man!" I put in.

"And what were their reactions?" William asked without opening his eyes.

As soon as Glenn rang the warning bell, Burke put the engines in neutral, letting the ferry go into a drift. His first thought was that there was a problem with the engines, until he heard Perkins hollering from the other side of the carriage. They rushed out the door and ran around the back of the carriage to find Glenn cradling Rashleigh as he began to regain consciousness.

Gordon fetched the medical kit from the wheelhouse and they wrapped some linen around the wound and splashed some cold water on the man.

As soon as his eyes focused again, he asked them, "Where's Jim?"

They didn't understand at first but he pointed at the cab.

"Still in there," Burke told him, "Haven't heard a peep out of him."

When he heard that, Rashleigh clawed his way to his feet and staggered over to the door, the boys right behind him. Rashleigh pounded on the door and called out to the rider as he fumbled the key out of his vest, but there was no reply at all. Rashleigh unlocked the door and flung it open.

Nothing moved inside when the door was swung out, and when Gordon raised the lantern high enough to light the interior, the sight caused Perkins to turn and run for the gunnels, where he vomited all over the passenger area."

Rowan paused, giving time for the image to grow in our

imagination.

"And what were your impressions, Inspector?" William asked. "And what was the agent's version?"

"I'll answer the latter first. Rashleigh stated that he had perched himself on the driver's seat because it gave him a clear field of fire if needed and he was watching the last of the sunset as he had his supper. He had almost finished eating and was admiring the view when the..." Rowan checked his notes carefully and added, "...right hand horse in the middle team, suddenly jumped forward, bumping into the horse in front of it and pulling the horse behind it. He quickly climbed down and went to calm the animals. He said that he had just gotten the animal settled and was walking forward to check the lead horses, when something struck him in the back of his head and he went down. He awoke, surrounded by the crew and, well, you've already heard the rest. Though perhaps you may have missed one of the more salient points," he added, a sly grin on his face, obviously baiting the hook. To my utter surprises, Will didn't bite.

"And this Agent Rashleigh, he saw or heard nothing of his assailant? I would have thought a trained agent of the Secret Service would have kept his guard up to a greater degree than that."

William's condescending tone finally tweaked me.

"Give over, Will! He was only one of two passengers on a barge, crossing a half mile of water in the middle of nowhere! If it had been me, I would have been catnapping the whole trip!"

"More likely tipping your flask and drunk!" Will responded dryly. "No matter the reasoning Frohman, the outcome was grim."

"Oh, you can bet on that! His career is in ruins and if those plates aren't recovered quickly, I'm sure his livelihood is sure to follow." Rowan said still not elaborating on the 'salient point'!

"Yes, that is most unfortunate," William said, "What of the murder scene itself?"

Rowan sighed, "It was as gruesome as I have ever seen, and I can tell you that! When that carriage door was opened, I nearly followed Glenn's lead and vomited myself. The corpse was slumped, sitting up, in the corner of the cab. There was a gaping hole where his right eye socket had been and what was left of his eye ran down that side of his face. A deep slit ran right through the middle of his neck, clean edges and deep enough to cut his trachea nearly in half. His chest was coated in blood and more pooled in his lap.

Then there was his arm, the right one, lying on the seat. He was handless, with a huge amount of blood on the seat that had run down the front and pooled on the floor."

"And yet," I pointed out, "you said earlier that there were no signs of a struggle? I can't imagine a trained agent just sitting calmly while all that was done to him!"

"That was the same thought we all had, Charles, but I think he was dead before he knew what was happening. His feet were flat on the floor of the cab and he had his arm lying next to his side, hand open and unmarked. His gun was still in its holster and by the way the blood ran down the front of his coat, there was no indication that he tried to open it and pull his weapon.

Aside from a few drops on the backrest of the seat and the sidewall, there was no blood splattered anywhere. Which there surely would have been if there was any kind of a struggle. Even after we removed the body, we found nothing and I personally went over that cab with a magnifying glass. And a few more agents after me did the same!"

"I assume you sent the corpse to the doctor's for an examination? What did his report say?"

After the required page flipping, Rowan answered, "Not much more here than what I have already told you. Though the Doc was fairly certain the first wound was to the throat, the knife thrust through the eye is what killed him. Doc said it was 'vicious'. The blade went clean through to the back of his skull and then it was twisted around to cause as much damage as possible. Judging by the amount of blood, the hand came off quickly. No other bruises or contusions, nothing to indicate a struggle." Rowan shrugged, "Neither hand had anything under the fingernails. He could have been in his night clothes, asleep in his own bed when it happened, for all we could see!"

"Except for the missing eye, the slit across his neck, and a missing hand," added. "So, you're saying that..."

"Hold that thought Frohman!" William roused himself to cut me off. He looked at Rowan, "What did the Doctor Blum have to say about Rashleigh's injuries?"

"Oh! Well! That was a bit of a debate!" Rowan replied, "Doc says that he thought the blow to the back of his head most likely came from the horse's hoof! Claimed it had the same shape and depth he's seen on other men kicked in the head!"

"You seem skeptical, Inspector." William observed.

Rowan harrumphed. "Well, are you thinking that the horse coincidentally conked Rashleigh over the head just when someone was about to commit mayhem and steal the engraving plates? Or are you thinking that the horse was trained to do it?"

He chuckled at his own wit and continued,

"Bear in mind that Blum is a simple country doctor. He is an excellent physician but he has had little experience with forensics."

"For-whatsics?" I asked, having never heard the term before.

188

"You wouldn't understand it, Frohman. It is a relatively new science and you cannot make much money off it."

Rowan laughed, "It's the science of modern detecting. It can help bring physical evidence to light in many new ways."

"Well put Inspector! In any case, the good doctor seems a sensible and competent man." As William stood and pulled on his gloves, he said,

"I have one last question for now. What became of Captain Burke and his crew?"

"We released them the following afternoon. We had no evidence against them and they held to their stories under a long, and sometimes hard questioning. Besides that, the town was screaming for the ferry. It would have been a week before we could get a replacement crew. So the chief let them out and they're back to work. But we're keeping a close eye on them."

"Tell your men to be vigilant." William didn't bother to explain his statement. "I believe the doctor should be ready by now to receive us." William was halfway to the road before we caught up to him. That old hound just picked up a new scent.

To Relieving Duress

"Oh! Hold on sir. Don't hang up! He's here now, Sir, he just walked in the door."

We had barely cleared the doorway, when our crabby nurse, Susan, made this pronouncement and thrust the telephone's mouthpiece at the inspector.

"Your boss," she mouthed in a hushed tone and gave Rowan a smile that was just a hair off of a sneer. Rowan looked like he didn't want to take it, but he was trapped and he knew it. He stepped up to the wall where it hung.

"Rowan here."

Though we couldn't make out specific profanity, the caller was certainly livid. Rowan wince a few times then replied, "But sir, I haven't got the doctor's report yet."

The voice on the other end went up a few more octaves and continued in a stream of abuse for quite some time.

"Yes, I heard you clearly, sir. I'll be right there."

Another stream of curses came out of the earpiece and then we heard an audible 'click' as the line went dead. Rowan snarled and slammed the mouthpiece back in the cradle, then whirled on the nurse.

"And thank you, Susan, for holding the line." He glared at the girl for a moment and turned to us with a embarrassed look on his face. "Thank you for the lunch, gentlemen, but I guess this is where we part ways. That was Luboff on the phone. He has ordered me back to the station immediately." He heaved a sigh. "Seems one of his little birdies told him we had lunch and it stuck in his craw. I'm in Dutch for sure!"

"Why?" I asked, feeling a little sympathetic for him after an obvious dressing down by Luboff. "You get to eat, don't you?"

"I believe it was the company, not Jimmy's bass that the Chief Inspector objected to," William observed.

Rowan nodded, "He ordered me to send you home. He used the terms 'unauthorized personal', and 'trying to interfere with a police investigation'." Rowan looked a little embarrassed and added, "He made me give you this message, "It's a bad time for meddling amateurs.""

William actually smiled at that. "As there is never a good time for bungling authority figures! How on earth can he possibly hope to resolve this if he pulls you away while we are still in the midst of your inquiries? What about the doctor's finding?" William pressed, "Surely he needs it to proceed."

Rowan's eyes were already heading for the door, "Says he's already got Nickolas's autopsy report. Doc gave it to him on the phone and he claims to have already made an arrest!" He looked as bewildered as I must have.

Will rolled his eyes and sighed, "Most likely one of Catherine's brothers. He seemed far more focused on Catty and Nickolas' romance than the cause of death. A foolish waste of time!"

"So," I said, making sure I had things straight. "One must infer, from the fact that an arrest has been made, that it was indeed murder?"

"I guess he thinks so, Charlie," Rowan replied, "But you guys know as much as I do. Even if the Doc did prove it was murder, I can't imagine who he pinned it on and where he got enough evidence so quickly to make an arrest!"

Rowan stepped closer to us and said in a low voice so Susan would not hear. "My advice to you, though I'm sure you two won't take it, is to do what the chief ordered and return home and wait any developments. I can't stress this enough, Michael Luboff is a nasty man! Petty and as vindictive as they come."

I thought William might have taken umbrage at that, as I noticed a tightening in his shoulders. His character would never take orders, or let a threat go unchallenged, but to my surprise, William just nodded.

"Of course, Inspector," he replied pleasantly. "We shall take the next ferry. It should return within a half hour or so, if it is on schedule. You may inform your superior of our intentions. I promise we will not make a liar out of you," Will said solemnly. Then he put a slight smirk on his face.

"In the meantime, Frohman is suffering from a dash of striped bass indigestion. We'll just get a little something for it from the doctor, as long as we are here."

Rowan opened his mouth to say something, but then just shut it and smiled. "Of course, you have every right to seek medical attention. Just follow the chief's instructions as soon as possible. Please. If I still have my job, or a butt to sit at my desk, I will be at the station for the rest of the afternoon. I will let you know if there are any developments as soon as I can."

"And we shall do the same, Inspector," William assured him. "We should be back at my home in a few hours. Please feel free to telephone or call on us as soon as possible."

"I certainly will."

As he stepped out the door and walked away briskly, I turned to William, "Who in the hell could the Chief have arrested already?" I asked.

"Nobody guilty, I'm sure, and the doctor's report may shed some light on that."

"A-HEM," We both looked to nurse Susan we had

forgotten was still standing there during the discussion, "I'll have to ask you gentlemen to leave. The doctor's office is closed for the rest of the day." If she knew who William was, and I'm sure she did, she wasn't star struck for sure. In her defense, I had the feeling she looked down her nose at everyone the same. She struck me as a maniacal Florence Nightingale.

"First we shall have a word with the doctor," William said in a voice that brooked no argument. "My friend here is in need of a consultation."

But the cantankerous hag just had to try anyway, "The doctor isn't seeing any patients today and..."

"Nonsense!" Will barked, "He is a physician and he is in his office! Please be so good as to tell the doctor we want a word with him. Now!"

To give her due, she stood her ground, "Inspector Luboff gave him clear orders not to talk..."

"That's enough!" This time the directive came from behind the cracked door to the doctor's examination room. "Send them in Susan." Doctor Blum ordered.

We both brushed past her and went into the office, with the nurse hot on our heels and jabbering away, "But doctor, you know very well what the inspector told us-"

The doctor stood up behind his desk and slapped the surface, "Stop talking, Susan!"

That brought her up short, and he continued, "You may go home now, Susan. Please pull in the shingle and lock the door on your way out."

She huffed and puffed but she finally turned to leave, hesitating at the door when the doctor spoke again, "And remember, Susan, Luboff may think he rules this little kingdom of his, but I'm still the only doctor within thirty miles. Nurses on the other hand, I can find, if mine doesn't know how to keep her mouth shut. Good Night."

After a bit of clomping around and banging drawers, we

heard the front door shut. The doctor clapped his hands together and laughed.

"Boys, that felt great and I've been wanting to say something like that to her for a while now. She's been especially peckish, as of late! Have a seat, gentlemen."

"Know what you mean," I said as I settled myself in, "I never keep a secretary more than a year. After that, they get too wifely."

He laughed and offered me a drink from the bottle on his desk, which William turned down and I accepted. I didn't really want it, but one of us had to show a little comradery.

"Please don't think ill of me, gentlemen." he said as he raised his glass, "I'm really not in the habit of liquor before dark, if and when I do imbibe, but today has been a trying day. That poor boy, Nickolas, had more damage to his body than I have ever witnessed on one human being. Nickolas was more damaged than all the separate cases I have seen since I've been in practice."

I could believe that. It was bottom shelf gin and a better drinker would have something smoother. I just tossed it back before I could taste it. The doctor went to pour me another, but I declined. I laughed to myself at the look of relief on Will's face.

William went to speak, but Blum held up his hand and cut him off.

"I know why you're here gentlemen, but quite frankly, I haven't finished debating the morality of disclosing my findings to you. The Chief Inspector's bullying aside, you are neither kin to Nickolas, nor sworn in with the authorities. There is the doctor-patient confidentiality to consider."

"Hell Doc, the kid's family is in Russia and he was living on Gillette's property! Besides, William is paying for the autopsy and burial" I pointed out.

The Doc furrowed his eyebrows for a moment then

smiled. "I can live with that."

Then he took a good slug of his drink and shifted his bulk forward over his desk folding his hands around his glass.

"Yet there is Chief Luboff to contend with. He was very adamant about me keeping this matter out of the public, and you two were named in particular. Despite the spiel I gave my nurse, he could make life quite difficult for me if he put his mean little petty mind to it."

"Doctor," William said in his quiet way, "The last thing I want is for you to suffer in any way for my inquiries..."

"Ours," I chimed in.

The doctor beamed ear to ear, "Well, I would have told you anyways, just for spite, but I do feel a bit more reassured now."

He sat back in his chair and proceeded to give us a detailed report. I will spare you the more gory aspects of the doctor's findings. Suffice it to say, it was a repetitious macabre listing of every fractured bone, and there was plenty of those, beside various contusions and scrapes. Doctor Blum ended with, "So, all of that is clearly reinforced my first diagnosis that he was dead before he hit the ground. However there are two things that have me puzzled. Despite the horrific mutilation of the rest of the body, I cannot fathom how these injuries happened."

When he didn't go on, and William just staring off into space, I took the reins.

"Could a beating have caused them, Doc?"

"What do you mean Sir, as in a brawl?"

I shrugged. "It's been told to us that some men had vowed to warn Nickolas off the girl. So we were wondering if maybe he was beaten to death."

The doctor shook his head. "Oh, you mean Catty's brothers! I imagine he gave those boys a wide berth. No, I saw no evidence of multiple bruising that would be consistent with a brawl, if that's what you mean, though I stand by my conclusion that he was dead before he hit the sand. After lying there overnight, there is just no way to tell what damage killed him and what occurred when he impacted. The damage was just too major and we got there too late!"

He shrugged and poured himself another splash. "As I already mentioned, although there was one wound that may fit your scenario and possibly another, both are an enigma."

William snapped his head around to focus on the doctor, "And what might they be?" he asked.

The doctor sat back in his chair and took a pull of gin from his glass. "His left testicle was crushed."

"Ouch," I said, wincing as all men do whenever they hear of pain striking that part. "Could that have killed him?"

"No, no," he shook his head emphatically, "I believe it too, was post mortem."

William mulled it over for a moment, "Perhaps, Doctor," The smirk returning ever so slightly, "Though one that could have some small significance. And the other?"

"Twin shallow scrapes, not quite cuts, the skin was never broken, more like deep indentations that started perfectly parallel from the base of his neck and ran down his back and across his buttocks. Whatever made those tracks was blunt but under a lot of pressure."

"Where did you get that from?" I asked, trying to imagine how someone could get a wound like that.

"Because his clothes were not cut. There were marks on the jacket that matched the ones on Nickolas' skin, but whatever put them there didn't go through cloth.

"They were deeper at the top and grew shallower towards the buttocks," William stated, looking right at the doctor. He wasn't asking a question.

Blum looked a little stunned. "Yes, that's true! How did you know?

Will added, "And they were perfectly spaced the entire length. Exactly three and three-eighths inches."

The stunned look on the Doc's face told me that William was dead on, though I had no idea how he came to that conclusion.

"How could you possibly know that?" Blum asked. "We found him on his back and I didn't find the marks until I stripped him down for the examination!"

"Merely a passing thought, doctor," William replied blandly.

I believe the doctor was not going to let it lie at that, but Will went on as if his revelation meant little to nothing.

"But all said and done, have you formed a conclusion as to the cause of death?"

"My gut feeling? Blunt force trauma to the right frontal lobe. But I can't be a hundred percent sure. There was just too much damage to the corpse.

"Just what then, was your official verdict on the death certificate?"

"I had to go with the facts, Mr. Gillette. I could not honestly list it as a murder."

"What else could you call it?" I demanded. "He didn't throw himself up on William's courtyard!"

Blum shook his head and waggled his drink back and forth. "That was all post-mortem! It doesn't matter what happened to the body after death. The death certificate is to verify the cause of death!"

"Have you determined a time of death?" William asked

"Yes, I did." He riffled through some papers on his desk and squinted for the numbers. "Death occurred between seven p.m. and midnight last night, twelve to sixteen hours before you found him."

"Interesting, how did you classify your official verdict?"

"I called it a 'death by misadventure.' I know it's vague, but it's the best I could do with what I found."

William mulled it over for a moment, and then shrugged. "Be that as it may, I suppose it gave Luboff enough of an excuse to railroad some poor soul into a cell."

"For the murder of your first mate?" Blum asked. "Jumping the gun a little, isn't he?"

"Apparently so, Doctor."

Blum's eyebrows crested his forehead. "That was fast, I must say! Even for Luboff! I'm surprised he found the time, he's been up to his ears lately."

"Ah yes, the ferry mystery!" William said, as if the thought had just crossed his mind.

"Actually doctor, we have just spent the day with Inspector Rowan and he has filled us in on that crime as well. I was wondering what your thoughts on the two victims from the ferry were."

Blum's whole demeanor changed instantly and he eyed us both with suspicion. "Are you claiming to be working with the police?"

"Well, not working, per say," I replied easily, trying to put him back at ease. I helped myself to another splash of the gut rot gin. "More like consulting with the inspector."

He shrugged again and seemed to relax a bit. "What did Inspector Rowan tell you?"

I was impressed with the question. I had put him down for an old, soft country doctor, but he showed the shrewdness inherent in his Jewish heritage. He was going to make us prove we were in the know before he let on.

William gave him a brief but detailed synopsis of what we knew about the wounds to both men.

Satisfied, all Doctor Blum could say was, "There's not much I can add to that, Mr. Gillette. The corpse was never brought to me and I had just enough time to put a few stitches and a fresh bandage on the live one before they whisked him away. I was told he'd be cared for somewhere else." He brightened visibly. "They took him away in one of those new gasoline motorized ambulances. It was really a sight, though they never used their lights. I hear they all have a loud siren that lets people know they're coming!"

"I've seen those in the city now," I said, "and believe me, you can hear them coming from miles away! They look like big boxes on wheels and really stand out in their white paint and big red crosses!"

"What doctor, in your opinion, was the cause of Agent Rashleigh's head wound?"

Blum shrugged, "Hard to say with certainty. He was blessed with a thick Irish skull and a thick Irish mane. Any harder and I'd have been picking bone splinters out of his brain. It had to be a blunt object, with some considerable force behind it."

"Yet you told the inspector you were certain it was a kick from a horse."

"Now now, I never said I was certain. It was just the angle that gave me the impression. As I said, it was a solid blow and it came upwards before striking him behind the right ear."

"You are certain of that?"

"That I'm certain of. Rashleigh was just a bit over six feet tall. The way the skin was torn and scrapes on his scalp, the injuries could not have occurred if he was struck from above or even parallel to the back of his head."

William thought it over for a minute, and then seemingly decided we were finished.

"Thank you for your assistance, Doctor," Will said.

"Please have the undertaker inform me when you release the body and we shall make the arrangements."

He stuck out his hand and William and the doctor shook. "Thank you for your cooperation, Sir, I know it was given under duress. Please let me know if Luboff causes you any inconvenience."

"Bah!" The old sawbones waved the thought away, "Luboff doesn't scare me." Doctor Blum raised his glass in a toast, "And when this is gone, I suspect so will the duress!" pulling the word into two syllables.

Reckless Children

William darted out the doctor's door with me hot on his heels. Something had him full of piss and vinegar. The entire day so far was becoming a blur, but thank God William's brilliant mind was holding tons of details ready to be stitched together. I had seen these mannerisms before, on the stage and off, and knew he was close to a solution.

He started down the street with purpose, his long legs giving him a spirited stride. He was halfway down the street before my eyes adjusted to the bright afternoon sunlight.

"William!" I hollered, annoyed that he just left me standing there with no explanations. He stopped and turned back; seemingly surprised I wasn't right next to him. I shrugged and raised my hands, palms upward, "Just where the hell are we going?" as I started walking towards him.

"To the ferry, of course," he replied. "I gave the Rowan my word we would return home, and so we shall."

The docks, and the town's common area were just at the end of the street, and I could see the ferry lumbering along, about in the middle of the river.

"William, what's the rush?" I asked, "It looks like we have some time before it gets here."

He followed my gaze to the ferry and nodded, "I believe you are right. Excellent! This will afford me an opportunity to organize my thoughts!"

"You've had all day to organize your thoughts, pal! What gives? What are you onto? And what was that all about with those long scrape marks on Nickolas's back that got you riled up? And how on earth did you know..."

"Frohman! Please!" Will barked, holding up his hand up to silence me. "You will derail my train of thought with that prattle!"

I simply jammed my hands into my coat pockets with my head down and started walking towards the ferry without another word. My mind was spinning with everything I had witnessed since breakfast and I was tired of being slapped down every time I voiced a thought.

"Let me ask you a question, Charlie."

"Why?!" I snapped back, coming to a halt and turning to face him, "However I answer I will be wrong!"

William at least had the grace to look abashed, "Please Frohman, you know I have always valued your advice and opinions since we met so many years ago." He clapped a hand on my shoulder and gave a gentle squeeze. The man could play me like a violin and my resentment melted away. I nodded, "Go ahead, ask away."

"How tall would you say the Treasury agent, Rashleigh is?"

"Six one, maybe two." I answered before the absurdity of the question hit me. "Why did you ask?"

He shrugged and smirked a little. "Gathering data of course."

He put his hands behind his back and stared out into space. "What are your thoughts on the fact that both these mysteries came to us the same time?"

I mulled it over for a minute and replied.

"Coincidence, I guess. The only reason we met Rowan was because of Nickolas. Otherwise we wouldn't have gotten the inside scoop on the river mystery! I don't know why you're spending any time on this river mayhem when you have a perfectly good enigma, lying back there in Blum's office. Shouldn't we be trying to figure out who snuffed Nickolas and tossed his body in your courtyard? I thought that's why we skipped breakfast."

"Quaintly put, Charlie," William responded with a laugh, and started strolling for the docks again.

I stepped alongside of him and he asked, still staring straight ahead, "Yet, what if the perception of separation was all that was clouding the solution?"

I really didn't have a clue what that meant. I wanted to call him on it but the questions slipped right from my head as we passed the last building before the open lawn of the park and I looked across the river.

That's the first I saw the Seven Sisters from across the shimmering waters, majestically rising out of the crest of the cliffs below. It's soaring stone walls jutted up from a cleared patch of pristine forests, looking both romantic and formidable. From this view, we could have been in Bavaria, with William's small castle.

"Jesus Christ William, that is something! It looks even more impressive from a distance."

"Thank you," he replied stiffly, "But there is no need to take the Lord's name in vain."

I tried not to heave a sigh. It was just one of his quirks. Though it did make me wonder that he still retained that trait while in his Sherlock role. William had a mysterious deep faith which was his foundation to see hidden facts. At times like these it seemed like he was surrounded by ghostly spirits whispering leading questions that led to the facts.

There was an empty bench at the edge of the park by the river, so we took a seat to wait for the ferry to arrive. I was going to start up again, but he was just staring off into the sky, deep in thought. I decided to give him a minute and turned my attention to a commotion out on the water. You can't push William into his little revelations.

A little ways out, maybe twenty yards or so, two sets of boys, one in a derelict dinghy and the other in a well-worn canoe began to make a din as they paddled around each other in a circle, splashing each other with the paddles and tossing bailers full of water. They quickly managed to get each other soaking wet as their play escalated, trying to capsize each other. The advantage was going to the flat bottomed dinghy.

"It's amazing how kids can embrace the water, no matter how cold it is! We'd be frozen solid in no time if we tried that!" I observed.

"The water's warmer in that vicinity." he mumbled. Is it shallow and warmed from the sun."

"SoWilliam, what gives? I know you're onto something."

William's lips twitched and he replied, "You have been with me, every step of the way. What is your take on the situation?"

"Well," I confessed, "I think he was murdered, but as to the how and why, honestly, between your home, the *Aunt Polly*, lunch, and then Doctor Blum's-- I don't know what to think. There's so much floating around inside my head right now, I can't see the forest through the trees."

"Exactly!" he replied, "But where your thoughts are like trees, mine are like dominoes. I am putting them in order and when I have them all lined up, I'll push the first one over and let the cascade lead me to the solution."

When nothing more was forthcoming, I rolled my eyes, always the theatrics.

"So you're saying that you're not going to tell me who the killer is." I changed tactics, "What if Luboff already has the right man? Perhaps he beat you to the punch."

He just looked at me like I made a bad joke and pointed with his chin to my right, and then stood. I glanced over to see the ferry was just twenty yards or so away from docking. I got up and we slowly walked towards the dock.

I just stared at William until he spoke,

"What?" he asked, innocently.

"Not what," I replied sarcastically, "who... how... and why..."

"Frohman," he sighed. "The Who and The How are no longer a mystery. It's the why that has led me to suspect there is more to this death than we first believed. If I am correct..."

He never finished the sentence because a chorus of screams that came from the river. The kids in the dinghy had won their sea battle and the canoe was bobbing upside down in the water. At first, as a parent, I shuddered to think the boys from that craft were submerged in that filthy water, but then my feelings went from squeamish to concern. I did a slow count and I saw no one come up for air. I instinctively shucked off my coat and hat and was starting to kick off my shoes when William stopped me.

"Wait, Frohman! There will be a need for heroics today."

I stood on my tiptoes, trying to see over the drifting canoe. "Do you see them? Are they on the other side of the canoe?"

The two boys in the dinghy were paddling over to the capsized canoe, yelling their friend's names. Neither of the boys had yet surfaced.

"Watch," he said, then his eyes widened to the size of coffee saucers. Looking closer at the boats, I saw that the canoe was actually moving against the current until it bumped the dinghy.

As soon as they touched, the two boys popped out from under the canoe and tried to pull themselves on the dinghy, while trying to pull the other boys into the water.

The scamps had been hiding under the canoe, breathing the air trapped inside. They all grappled for a while, but it quickly degenerated into peals of laughter. When we

205

turned away, the four boys were working on righting the canoe. Wet, cold, and having the time of their lives.

When they had just about succeeded in righting the capsized canoe, I took a deep breath, picked up my coat, and fished around for the flask. Another pull got my heart beating regularly again, and I turned to notice William staring out at the boys with a look of wonder on his face.

"What is it?" I asked. He had that faraway look again like his guiding spirits just gave him another leading question.

"Grinning ear to ear, he clapped me on the shoulder, "Charlie, we need to get back across the river quickly." He looked past me to the docks, "Ah! The ferry is in! We have a few more dominoes to check out then perhaps we can put this affair to bed! But we should move quickly!"

"What?" I blurted out, "Why?"

"Because if I'm right," he paused dramatically, "Our man is surely planning a quick departure."

Before I could start demanding explanations again, he deftly changed the subject.

"I must say, I am quite impressed with you, Frohman. You were very brave when those lads didn't emerge from the water. Were you really going to jump in and save them?"

"Just one of them," I replied.

"ONE?"

I shot him a grin, "Oh yes, my friend! The other one was yours!"

Ferry Ride

We strolled over to docks and purchased two one ways just as the ferry was pulling in. A youngish, bearded fellow with longish hair made the leap from the ferry to the dock with a rope in his hand as the captain skillfully throttled back, bringing the ferry to a near dead stop.

The crewman swiftly tied off his line and turned to secure the port side. He did it all with a practiced ease and went to the opposite side, tied off then opened the gate.

There was a group of passengers lining the starboard side, waiting to get off and an automobile engine started behind them. As soon as the lad raised the wooden barrier, the crowd surged off onto the dock and a family in a Ford Model T followed them off in a cloud of thick exhaust smoke.

A tradesman, sitting atop a large tarp covered wagon, brought his horses up and turned them around to walk backwards onto the ferry before we could step on.

We were further delayed by a trio of young ladies disembarking, who took William's tipping of his hat as an invitation for further conversation. He was gracious, but aloof and kept the conversation from blooming. I gathered that the girls attended the same church as William, though I paid little attention and didn't speak at all. I have seen doe-eyed women of all ages flock to William for as long as I knew him.

He deftly cut the chitchat short and we made the short jump onto the deck of the ferry. Damned if he didn't jump right back into character the minute we had both feet on the deck.

He hailed the tradesman with the wagon by name and then went over to speak with him. After a minute or so, the man bobbed his head and pulled the horse forward and then pushed his head to one side while walking it backwards. The wagon shifted over a few feet and William was satisfied. After shaking the man's hand and clapping him on the shoulder, he came back over to me.

I was processing what I had just witnessed when it came to me. I looked at him and shook my head. He had the man put the wagon right where Rowan told us the carriage was positioned.

"Can't you even cross a river without having to set a stage? You sure you don't want to come back to work?"

He just looked down his nose, "It is all in the details, Frohman. Life and death, it is all in the details."

I just shook my head. "You need a nap."

He ignored me as he cast an eye about the deck. I could almost see his keen mind log every detail and file it away in its proper place. A talent I never acquired chasing the butterflies.

After a long moment he looked at me and grinned, "I do not have anything to 'sleep off' my friend." He quipped as he tapped my near empty flask with the head of his cane through my coat pocket. We both heard the sad hollow thump.

I looked at him with a squinty eye, "I hope you noted the hollow ring. That's a bad sign!"

He laughed. "Never fear, Frohman," he said with good cheer, "I shall have you back home in time for a refill! In the meantime, shall we have a stroll around the ferry?" He answered his own question by walking away, leaving me to catch up with him.

As it was just us and the tradesman on this trip, we were spared the usual staring and whispering that usually surrounded William when he was in public. I think my friend was thrilled to have the boat nearly to ourselves. He could do his sleuthing in peace.

His first stop was the passenger area. It was a simple eight by fifteen, low ceiling box with a tin roof and benches set on either end. Three quarters of the front was an open doorway, so it would keep you dry but not warm.

He made a meticulous circuit of the shelter, paying particular attention to the scupper, where excess water on the deck ran out and back into the river. It was dry today as there was no weather to speak of.

After trailing after him, then standing patiently behind him for a few minutes, I had to ask.

"Just what are you looking for?"

He straightened and looked at me. "I am not looking for anything, Frohman. I am looking at everything!"

He made his way over to the community bulletin board that hung on the wall between the opening and the seats on the aft end. I studied the board alongside him, but saw nothing but the usual church fliers and notices for one town committee or another, surrounded by the more interesting handwritten For Sale or Looking For notes. A child's stick figure drawing with an X on it dominated the right side, along with some other doodling, typical Americana.

After an interminable wait, I quipped, "Think the killer left a confession, between the skiff for sale and the puppies looking for a home?"

He ignored my wit once again and pointed towards the stick figure, drawn on the right side of the board, and the doodling that was actually on the wall of the bulkhead itself.

"What do you make of those, Frohman?" he asked. "Step closer and get a clear look."

Confused, but curious, I did as he asked and gave them a good once over. It looked like any other stick figure a child might draw, although it did have an unusual X mark just to the left of the stick figure's body. The scribble next to it was another stick figure in a box. Another X was on the inside of the square.

I stepped back and shrugged. "You have no opinion?" William asked, slightly exasperated.

"Sure," I replied flippantly. "I think mothers should watch their children closer so they don't deface public property."

He sighed. "You would attribute these hieroglyphics to a child's imagination?"

"What are you saying, Will? Those are kid's drawings! Stick people in houses! I've seen my children draw them thousands of time. Not exactly 'dancing men', you know!"

Will just gave me that smug, pitying look again. "And what do you make of the medium used by your rambunctious tyke?"

Still ready to challenge, I stepped back to the wall and put my face just inches from the drawings. I was surprised to see the black material the kid drew with had some depth to it. The drawings were actually raised on the surface of the board and the paint. I took off my glove and wet my forefinger so I could rub the feet of the stick figure. My index finger came away with a thick, dark, almost waxy substance I thought I knew. It only took a few seconds after rubbing my thumb over it to name it.

"Greasepaint!" I said bewildered by what came out of my own mouth.

I pulled out my hanky and started to try and get it off my fingers before it spread any further. Greasepaint, I knew from our heydays in musicals, was harder to get off the longer it sat.

William just nodded sagely. "I thought it was, but thank you for your practical analysis Frohman." Then he deadpanned. "You are aware of how difficult it is to get greasepaint off of anything."

I looked at my fingers that still had dark smudges on their tips, and jammed the handkerchief back in my pocket. I threw my hands in the air. "Why would a kid have greasepaint on a ferry?"

William tapped the side of his nose and turned to start walking towards the stern. "Why indeed?" he said over his shoulder.

I followed him, but his stride slowed as we reached halfway back on the starboard side. There was a magnificent view of his home from the middle of the river and we both stopped to admire it. I watched my friend carefully as he stared at his home on the cliffs. I could tell from the melancholy expression that he was himself for the moment and thinking of the day's events.

I hoped that he would find the strength to stay, despite the circumstances, and make himself a home. His transient lifestyle was beginning to take a toll on his health which had been great for most of his life, but he was no spring chicken. And Ozaki seemed happy here.

As if he was reading my unspoken thoughts, he said, "I almost wish I still lived aboard the *Aunt Polly*. I was truly free then. I could come and go as I wished and still had my bed no matter where I anchored. And trouble rarely finds a nomad. I built my home here to get away from it all." He smiled sadly.

I felt for him then, so I placed a hand on his shoulder and said, "True, that heap of stones will keep you grounded in one place, with little room to run. But remember, my friend, when the hurricanes come, and they always do in one's life, you'll be much better off under that pile of rocks than out at sea!"

Slowly a smile came to his face and he looked at me, eyebrows raised, as if he was surprised I said something profound.

"Quite right, Frohman," he said, snapping out of his funk and back into character, "Excellent point. Shall we have a look at the engines?" And off he went again, only too quickly to stop in midstride and examine the deck beneath our feet. We were still about ten feet from the stern, just outside the opening that led to the engines. William went to one knee for a better look at what I couldn't fathom, and then beckoned me to look.

"What do you see, Frohman?"

I bent slightly forward to humor him and examined the weathered decking. The wood was worn and pitted and a milky white stain faintly glowed in the bright sunlight.

"I see a floor, William."

He took a deep breath through his mouth and let it out slowly through his nose. "Has your advanced age taken so much of your sight, you do not see the faint staining?"

I straightened up and looked down my nose at him. "Of course I do," I replied testily. "It's just residue from the salt in the water. Every boat I've ever been on has them. This may be a river but the water is still brackish."

He came to his feet and beamed at me. "Thank you, Frohman, another excellent point!"

He walked away leaving me shaking my head as I followed. At the very stern, where the engines were situated, the back bulkheads of the ferry didn't meet, but veered off from their lines to create an opening about four feet wide. You couldn't see into the engine area unless you went around the port side bulkhead.

William took a few moments to stand at the opening and study the wagon he had exactly placed. He obviously was getting a feel for the setup of that frightful night and the movements of the boiler man that night.

He paced back and forth, muttering to himself as he crouched and shifted positions to get a view from all angles. I knew what he was doing, but the other crewman and the tradesman on his wagon both stared at him in utter fascination. This wasn't going to help the rumors of his eccentricities.

Thankfully, he straightened up and then ducked around the bulkhead into the engine area. It was a fairly large area, running almost the width of the stern, but it was crowded nonetheless. A huge bin of coal dominated one side and two immense steam engines sat under covers half sunk into the deck, connected to a fire box with a young man busily shoveling coal into its open door. A lonely stool sat along the other wall with a tackle box and the inevitable fishing pole next to it. A small peg jutted from the steel above it, holding, of all things, a slingshot.

The boiler man threw a last shovelful into the furnace and shut the door before he noticed us. He was startled but his expression grew more of a suspicious nature as he leaned his shovel against the wall and took out a dirty rag to wipe his hands.

"Can I help you? Passengers aren't supposed to be back here."

Will gave him his most winning smile and stuck out his hand. "Glenn, is it not? How are you? I am William Gillette."

The lad shook his hand and relaxed a tad. "Well, sure, I know who you are, Sir. I've seen you on the boat many times."

"Very nice to finally do a formal introduction. I thought it might be time we were introduced."

"Well, yes, uh, thank you." The boy was flummoxed. It was one thing to see a celebrity walk in your midst, it was quite another to have one address you by name and carry on a conversation. I had seen it a thousand times but I never failed to marvel at the common folk's need for celebrity worship.

213

His eyes flicked over to me and William said, "And this is my dear friend, Charles Frohman." He gave me a nod and respectfully didn't offer his coal laden hand.

"I was just giving my friend a tour of your fine vessel. Being he was a boiler man himself," he continued with a small smile played at the corners of his mouth, "back when he was a younger man, of course. I hope you do not mind. I do not wish to interfere with the ship's operation. I know you are busy with your duties."

"Oh, no Sir. I'm fine. Once the old girl gets up to steam, I just add a little coal every now and then. It's actually boring most of the time."

"Hence the fishing pole, I presume?"

"What do you catch, here in the river?" I asked.

"Not much now," he replied. "But the shad will be running soon and Jimmy over at the Inn will take everything I can catch. Folks love their shad and roe when it's in!"

"And this?" I said, as I plucked the slingshot off the peg. "I assume you use to keep the gulls away from your lunch."

"Oh yeah," he replied, "I also try to keep them from doing their business all over the engines. Their droppings smell awful when they hit hot metal!"

We all chuckled at that. Something caught William's eye and he took the sling shot from my hand and looked it over. He rubbed a finger over the patch that held the stone and I could see it was slightly burned.

I started to have my doubts about this person. It was one thing to scare away a few birds but even a seagull didn't deserve to be hit with red hot coal.

William handed the devise back to the lad. "Pity you didn't have it handy when the intruder came aboard the other night."

I was wondering when he was going to start pumping the

kid.

"Oh, I'd have pinged him good if I had laid eyes on him! I..." He stopped himself short.

"What's all this then?" said a voice from behind us. We all turned as one to see a tall, slightly graying man, with the weathered face of a seaman looking at us, his arms crossed over his chest.

"Ah! Captain Burke!" William exclaimed and stepped over to offer his hand.

"Mr. Gillette. I thought that was you who boarded." he replied as he shook William's hand.

I chuckled in my head, because he knew exactly who boarded his boat. There were only three of us. I knew his type also. He was the kind of local who would make a point of not being star struck.

"And what brings you back to the engine area?" He didn't seem happy we were in a restricted area.

"I was just showing my friend, Mr. Frohman here, the ferry. He comes from a long line of seamen himself. I hope we have not trespassed too grievously?"

He gave William a long look. I think he knew what William was up to but didn't want to call him on it. No need to piss off a rich and famous passenger if it wasn't necessary.

He shrugged, "No harm done. Perhaps you'd like to return to the passenger area. We're about to turn around to dock and Glenn needs to man his station."

"Of course, Captain." He nodded to Glenn, who looked a little abashed, and then led us out onto the open deck area.

The Captain stopped and gave William a stern look.

"As you know, I'm sure. We've had a bit of an ordeal and under strict orders from the authorities to stay silent on the matter. I'm sure you wouldn't want to get Glenn into any more trouble."

"Of course not," William replied. "I am sorry to hear of

your troubles, Captain. It must have been hard on you and your crew. And I know the town people were in a tissy."

Burke grunted. "I hear you've had some troubles of your own, Sir. Is it true young Nickolas is dead?"

"Dead?" Glenn almost shrieked behind us, "Nicky is dead?" His eyes were wide and fearful.

"I am afraid so, Glenn," William said. Then he added, in a rather cruel tone "Murdered a most gruesome fashion - heinous really."

Glenn looked as if he was going to faint. Hands shaking and lips quivering, he asked, "What happened? Do they know who did it?"

"The police are looking into the matter, son," William replied.

The captain cut the conversation short. "There's nothing to be done for it now and we're about to dock, so man your station, Glenn. We'll talk about it once we've tied up. Go on with you."

The lad looked like he was desperate to ask William some more questions, but he took one look at Captain Burke and mumbled, 'Aye Sir' and disappeared around the bulkhead.

"If you'll excuse me," Burke said, "I've got to get back to the wheelhouse. He gave William a level stare, "It looks like we've both had our share of troubles recently, sir."

"Quite a coincidence, would you say?" William asked. "Two deaths, or rather murders coming so close together."

Burke gave him a long level look. "I'll leave that to the police and I'll leave you to your troubles." he said by way of dismissal. "Good day gentlemen." He turned and walked towards the wheelhouse.

His meaning was clear. You worry about your problems and I'll worry about mine. William wasn't making any points with the populous today.

We continued walking while the ferry turned around to

dock and came to a stop near the railing on the bow. The other mate, Gordon if I remember correctly, walked past us a few times while getting ready to dock. He mumbled a greeting but thankfully didn't pause long enough for William to grill him.

I really didn't see the point. "I hope you weren't too disappointed." I teased. "Not much to see on this tub."

"Au Contraire!" he practically crowed, "I have learned four salient facts that are now nicely coalescing!"

I didn't have a clue as to what he was referring, but there was one thing I wanted to know.

"What the hell got into you anyways? Why did you needle that crewman about Nicky's death? It's not like you to try and upset people, Will!"

He simply shrugged. "The locals have a saying, Frohman, something about 'poking the bear'."

"I know that one William and it's a warning! Don't go poking the bear!"

"Unless you want the bear to show its true nature," he replied with a smirk.

Before I could ask him what he meant, we heard someone shouting for him from the dock that was still twenty yards away. When we saw who it was, we looked at each other, me in bewilderment, and him in consternation.

It was an officer of the law and behind him was a town police car.

Mike and Lena

William raised his cane in acknowledgment of the flatfoot's hectic waving, and made his way off the boat in a stately manner. He was walking a tad slower than his usual bustling gait and I knew he was mulling the possibilities of the copper's presence. He looked at me and rubbed his hands together.

"This could be some new developments, Frohman."

I shrugged; weary of the day's events. "At least he's not holding wrist cuffs."

William smiled and I added, "Let's hope he doesn't have a warrant in his pocket either."

By the time we had cleared the dock, the constable was waiting on the dock. Fidgeting from foot to foot, he clearly wasn't happy with this assignment and that made me weary. William simply walked up to the man and waited for him to speak.

"Inspector Rowan has been trying to reach you, Sir. He missed you at the doctor's office and he sent me to find you. I'll drive you up to the castle, so you can call the Inspector on your telephone. He's waiting word from you in his office."

"Oh well, very good then. We'd be happy for the ride and thank you for your courtesy. There is much I wish to discuss with the Inspector, as well."

The officer led us to the back seats and opened the door, "The Inspector will be happy to hear you're taking it so well, Sir. He was mighty afraid you would be mad."

I had already slid into the seat but, Will froze half in and half out, "Why would I be angry?"

"Well, er.. You know, about arresting your Japer man and

all."

William pulled himself out of the car, "Arrested? Ozaki? On what charge?"

The sergeant took a step back in the face of William's rage. "Why, for the murder of your Ruskie first mate!"

I could see William's whole body stiffen in anger, but he managed to keep his voice level, "Who? Who arrested Ozaki?"

"The Chief Inspector himself, Sir." he replied. "Perhaps you should talk to the Inspector. I'm just the messenger. Can we go now, please?"

"By all means, please hurry." With that, Will slid into the seat next to me.

His face was stone fury when he looked me straight in the eye. "GOD Damn that fool!" For once, I let it go.

With a hell of a lot of clamoring and bouncing up the rocky road, we quickly got dropped off at William's front door and he was out of the car and into the house. I thanked the copper for the ride, who acknowledged the sentiment and roared off.

Knowing what kind of state my friend would be in, I took the last pull off my flask and followed him through the doorway that was left open. I hadn't taken two steps in before the onslaught began.

William was listening intently to Mrs. Woods who was waving her arms about in an animated way. I wanted to get closer to hear her story when Catty came out of nowhere and latched onto me.

"Is it true, Sir? Did Ozaki really kill my Nicky? Why? Why would he do such a thing? I know he didn't like him much, but Nicky never did him any wrong! Why would he do that?" and her raving degenerated into a sob as she collapsed against my chest.

"CATHERINE ALEXANDER!" Will boomed in his

219

theatrical resonating voice, "Get ahold of yourself. Of course Ozaki didn't kill anyone!"

Mrs. Woods came to my rescue and took the hysterical girl from my arms. I hurried over to William who jerked his head in the direction of the telephone. Cranking up the contraption, we got through to the operator and after a few minutes of explaining who we wanted to talk to, William was connected to Rowan.

Holding the ear piece out so I could listen in, he barked without preamble, "What in the name of common sense are you people thinking? I demand you release Ozaki at once!"

"Please, Mr. Gillette, listen to me..." Was all Rowan got in before Will started up again.

"No! You listen to me! If Ozaki is not released immediately, I will hang up and call the Governor, the Senator, and the Police Commissioner in that order. I will bring down a landslide of misery on your department if this idiocy isn't corrected immediately! I will..."

"Now, just wait a minute Mr. Gillette," Rowan shot back, "I had nothing to do with this! Chief Inspector Luboff..."

Will interrupted, "That buffoon isn't fit to wear a badge and if I--"

That's when I took the ear piece from him and put my hand over the mouthpiece.

"That's enough!" I said firmly. "All this ranting and raving won't help. Let me see if I can get to the bottom of this and you- calm down! Take a breath." A little stunned, William took a step back and I took my hand off the mouthpiece and put the earpiece where it belonged.

"Hello? Hello? Inspector? It's me, Charles Frohman. Let's all just take a step back and a deep breath."

"I'm not the one making threats. Mr. Gillette has to understand that I had no part in this decision. Listen, I did manage to keep Luboff from actually charging Ozaki for the time being. I told Luboff that I just needed a little time to break him and get an air tight case. He caved in when I reminded him how stupid we would look if William's lawyers managed to spring him."

"That's all well and good, Inspector, but in the meantime, Ozaki is sitting in one of your cells, scared and wondering why the he was abducted from his home and imprisoned by a group of round-eyed thugs!"

"Actually, Ozaki is sitting here in my office, sipping tea."

"What?"

"Supposedly, I'm interrogating him, but," Rowan chuckled, "I don't speak Japanese and he seems to have forgotten most of his English, if you catch my drift, so I'm just softening him up."

"That's damn decent of you inspector." I remarked over the wire, "but how did he end up there in the first place?"

I could feel his sigh from across the river, "Luboff."

During his questioning of Ozaki he knew that Nickolas and Ozaki weren't too friendly to each other. Then he started spouting off about the growing tension between the Russians and the Japanese over some islands, God knows where, and that the Ruskies were hot-headed and the Japs devious. Apparently they may go to war over it, or so he read somewhere. So, he decided that the motive could have been political."

"And how does he explain where we found the body?"

"He says it must have been some kind of Asian trick. Please don't repeat this to William, but he says he'll have it figured out before they hang him."

That reasoning was too stupid to wrap my gin soaked mind around. It was time to give the young inspector the facts of life. "Do I have your word that Ozaki is comfortable as he can be for the moment and you will not allow any harm to come to him?"

"Of course," he replied indignantly. "I know he is innocent. Luboff put this wagon of manure in motion, I'm doing my best to slow it down!"

"Son," I said calmly in my best fatherly voice, "Since, you haven't made the mistake of charging him and he is relatively safe for the moment, I'm going to do you a favor by keeping William off the phone for a half hour or so to give you a chance to think things over carefully and to let William calm down. But if we don't see Ozaki released shortly, God help every one of you in that station, because William means it when he said he will make your lives a living hell."

I almost laughed when I saw William nod his head in cadence with my words. "And you better believe me when I tell you; he has the friends and influences to do it."

"I know, Charles. I'll see what I can do. Just keep Mr. Gillette calm. We can fix this."

"Best you make that happen. I'll have William ring you back in a short while, when everyone's a little more levelheaded. I believe he has a lot he wants to discuss with you. Now put Ozaki on."

Ozaki got on the line and I asked him if he was alright. William practically tore the phone from my hands when he heard Ozaki's voice and they talked for a few minutes. William profusely assured him that everything would be fine. After a moment, he said goodbye, then asked for the Inspector. I leaned in close to listen in.

"Inspector?"

"Yes, Mr. Gillette. But before you blow your top again, remember who I was with when Ozaki was picked up...."

"Quite right, Inspector," William cut him off, "and for that reason I wish to apologize for my hasty words earlier. Ozaki is family, and though my sentiments were sincere, they were ill said."

There was silence on the other end. The Inspector was bright enough to catch my friend's drift. The threats just became a promise.

"Mr. Gillette," Rowan said after a moment. "You must understand, there is little I can do about Luboff. I'll do my best to straighten this out, but I have little to work with. He's got no proof however this would not be the first person railroaded to the gallows. Luboff is a stubborn man and I'll need to prove he's wrong before he'll budge."

"We shall do more than budge him, Inspector. By this evening, you may be able to give him a well-deserved kick in the ass! I will get back to you shortly. Goodbye."

He disconnected the telephone before Rowan could sign off. I'm sure he did it to stave off any questions the Inspector still had. Yet, like mine, they would go unanswered for the time being. If I knew William, he was setting the stage for the final act. He then fished the ring that I remembered he took off of Nickolas's finger out of his vest pocket. The reason why he took it still escaped me, but I was too frazzled to ask. Turning to me, he said, "There is something I need to check before I telephone the inspector back. I'll be in the library."

"That's fine," I assured him. "Take as long as you need. I'm going to make myself a drink, gather my thoughts and go visit Mike and Lena in the conservatory – perhaps they got some useful advice."

I was on my second drink when William came to the conservatory. I had been bribing Mike and Lena with dead flies to get some advice, but they just croaked for more.

William spoke in a soft tone, "Thank you for making me take a step back. I let my emotions cloud my thinking for a moment. At least I know the full cast of characters now and who I was dealing with.

"Did you know what your next step is?" I asked.

"Actually, yes. I will be ready to bring this matter to

223

settlement in a short while. I just got off the phone with Rowan and we are ready to act. I'm sorry to have to leave you here alone, but there could be an element of danger to this next phase and I don't-"

"Skip you!" I said vehemently. "There was no way I would miss the ending! If you think you're going off to resolve this and leave me here, you can forget it!"

"Then you wouldn't mind playing a role in a small deception I have planned?" William asked.

"I'll take whatever part your offering. I'm in this until the last curtain call!"

He smiled ear to ear. "I knew I could count on you my friend! Grab your hat and coat, and don't forget your cane." He whirled and darted out of the room, calling back over his shoulder. "Your cane! Be sure to load it!"

I had one parting comment to make to Mike and Lena, my only amphibious friends, "The game's afoot!"

The Boat House

William took us out the side door and we retraced our steps of this morning until we were almost to the tramway. There we ran into Ollie.

"Ollie! Is the tramway working?" Will asked.

"Better than ever, Sir. The lads worked through lunch and got everything shipshape."

"Excellent! Mr. Frohman and I are going to take her to the bottom. When we have disembarked, please bring it back up and hold there. Ollie, can you figure out how much that load of mortar weighed and let me know later?"

"Understood, Sir." Ollie acknowledged. "I'll stay right here till you get off and get you the weight." He opened the gates for us and I stepped onto the platform. The gin smothering my phobias.

"What the hell was that all about?" I asked, as William stepped onto the platform.

He pulled a lever and said loudly, over the sound of the tramway engine. "It is time to turn over a few rocks, my friend!"

Ollie was true to his word and the trip down was much more pleasant than the one I took up just the day before. The pulleys were rotating smoothly and the floor beneath us seemed much more solid.

Still, I did better when I looked at William instead of the looking over the railing. As for him, he alternated scrutinizing the machinery and scanning the ground directly below us. As we neared the bottom, he took out a piece of paper and pencil and jotted down some math equations! I was too relieved to feel us touch down on solid ground to try and wring an explanation out of him.

"Ah!" He exclaimed as he lowered the gate and we stepped off. I was surprised to see him examine the machinery so closely. Then William handed me his cane so he could use both hands to grasp a thick metal rod that seemed to be woven into the steel cables of the pulley system. William was putting all his weight on the rod but it refused to budge.

"What is that thing?" I asked.

It's the bell striker I had fused on the cable. It's what strikes the bell at the bottom and the top of its loop. I told you about it yesterday.... Ah!" He took his cane back and fished around the recess of the pulley housing. He pulled what he was reaching for close, then straightened and held a piece of cloth up for me to see. With a smug look on his face he asked, "Recognize this, Charlie?" he asked.

"No", I kept it short because I wasn't in the mood for another riddle.

William turned and stuffed the scrap of cloth into his coat pocket and glanced at his watch, "We should move along if we're to stay on schedule." He set off at a brisk pace. "I need to take a peek in one more place, and if I'm right…" He let the thought trail away as he held one finger in the air.

"In retrospect, their budget should have been my first clue. As with most crimes, 'follow the money' is the golden rule."

I still wasn't sure of what the hell was going on about, but I knew what he said was true. In business, when the money gets funny, it's rarely a laughing matter.

William bee lined it over to his boat shed where he told me that Roy and Nickolas had been working on a motor launch for him.

"Though, despite the endless stream of noxious smoke

they generated in the past few months, I have yet to see it, in spite of the exuberant bills that the motor launch project has incurred."

"You paid for it and haven't seen it?" I asked, "That doesn't sound like you, William."

"I have not seen it since I first bought it. The Captain Roy and Nickolas wished to surprise me after she had been put in the water and did a few shakedown runs with her."

He shrugged, "It really was no inconvenience, leaving them to their work. I have been extremely busy with the house and don't get down to the docks very often. I've been on or around the *Aunt Polly* more in the last two days than I have in the last four or five months! They have always done such outstanding work, so I was content to leave them on their own."

"Why did you want a launch?" I asked as we reached the shed.

"In the future, I will need a faster and more maneuverable craft to ply the river with. Even more so when I begin the second phase of construction." He pulled a key ring from his pocket and after finding the right one, opened the door to the boathouse and we stepped in.

Dark and musky, we had to leave the door open until William found a lantern. He gestured at me to close the door before he lit it.

"Why all the cloak and dagger, Will? It's your property, for Pete's sake!"

"We don't want our presence here to undermine our timetable."

I didn't have a clue what he was referring to and I was getting more uncomfortable being kept in the dark.

"Damn it, William! Would you please tell me what we are doing here?"

He gave me a withering look. "Shall we discuss this later Frohman? We only have a few minutes to spend here. Let us concentrate on our surroundings!"

I found another lantern on the workbench and lit it for myself. The second lamp gave enough light for my poor eyes and I looked about. On the left was a long workbench piled with tools, parts, valves, clamps, and bits of tubing that overflowed tin buckets amongst scraps of wood and steel. Shavings and debris littered the floor between various spills of what looked to be oil. William pointed out some shiny filings on an old drill press, but I sloughed him off as something caught my eye. Next to the bench was a pile of folded material. I prodded it with my finger and everything fell into place for me!

"Will!" I said excitedly. "Do you know what this is?"

He walked over and looked down, "Of course I do Frohman, rubber coated canvas. It's used for caulking and waterproofing."

"Right," I said smugly, "And you can also use it to make a balloon! I saw them do this on a trip out west. There was this fellow that sewed together canvas and used melted rubber to make it airtight! Then he filled it with hot air and off he went!"

He just sighed, "Are you still trying to sell the balloon theory, Frohman?" He smirked and patted me on the shoulder. "Well, in any case, you may be closer to the right track than you know."

With that, he wandered off towards the back of the shed. I have no idea what he meant, but Lord, I hated that condescending tone.

In the dim light I could see the back wall was dedicated to building materials and various items I assumed were in need of repair. But my eyes were drawn elsewhere.

On the right side, running the entire length of the shed was a beautiful launch. I walked up and down her length, just taking in her form. She had an open cockpit that seated six, sported a long graceful bow, and the hull planks were tight and without blemish. A slightly elevated cockpit was protected by four panes of glass, angled and tilted back just enough to keep the wind out of the pilot's face and to cut down the wind resistance. She gave me the impression that she could easily run up and down the river at a good clip.

Even in the light of a lantern, I could see that she was in need of her final coat of varnish, along with a hard polish on the brass. My initial thoughts were confirmed when I walked around the back of the boat and found the twin propellers and their restraining bolts lying on a tarp.

"She's a beauty, William," I commented as I walked back to join him. "She'll be a lot of fun once she's finished. I don't know what kind of shape she was in when you got her, but it's really just the cosmetics as far as I can see. With a little elbow grease it looks like she could be ready in a few weeks unless there is a problem with the engines."

"She was quite seaworthy when I purchased her last October." he grunted, not taking his eyes off the debris piled against the wall.

It was obvious to me that the captain and his former mate had been slacking on their promise to William and hadn't put too much into making her ready. Probably why they told William they wanted to surprise him, so they could hide their laziness. Yet, something bothered me as you could see they haven't so much as wiped the dust off her glass.

William never even glanced at the craft. He was busy going through a pile of material stacked up against the back wall. There was wood, a lot of canvas scraps, and a smattering of dismantled equipment. He was focused on a pair of incomplete bicycles that were really no more than frames without pedal cranks. He rummaged through the empty pails for a few more moments then stepped out of the mess and dusted himself off.

"Well, well," William murmured absently as he tapped a finger against his lips, "This fits nicely into my theory."

"What are you talking about now?" I asked, looking the piles over. "Why would you have a theory about pine scraps, snippets of canvas and empty buckets of pitch and resin?"

"Not exactly unusual to find in a boat shed."

"Frohman!" he admonished, "it is all right here in front of your eyes! Look again. This time observe!"

Sighing inwardly, I did as he asked. The pine was fairly thin and longish, with a great pile of shavings swept off to the side. The canvas was waterproofed with pitch and resin. There were empty bucket after bucket of pitch and resin, piled around a mixing vat that was heated with a wood fire. Like I said to William, nothing you wouldn't be surprised to see in a boat shed.

I didn't need to look at the launch again to realize what he was getting at. The launch was primarily cedar, with a mahogany and teak. All the trash and scraps had nothing to do with the restoration of William's launch.

"What the hell were they doing in here?"

William waggled his eyebrows, he was enjoying himself far too much, "What the hell indeed?"

Rather than answer my questions, he turned and headed for the door, extinguishing the lanterns. We stepped out into the sunlight, and though my eyes had not adjusted to the daylight, I was looking in the direction of the *Aunt Polly* and I thought I saw movement on the bow.

When I could see clearly, the movement was gone and William was striding for the docks.

"Aren't you going to lock up?" I asked.

He said over his shoulder, "No need my friend. The proverbial horse is already out of the barn!"

A Dressing Down

"Now Frohman," he began to explain as I reached his side without breaking stride. "Your roll in this is relatively simple. Our ruse centers on the fact that you are going to purchase the *Aunt Polly* from me. I am going to tell Roy that ownership of the yacht is being transferred to you immediately and that he must go ashore tonight. Then we shall see what transpires!" He was almost chortling.

"You think you have all this figured out, don't you?" I knew in my heart that he did and wasn't about to share it until he was ready, or until he had a larger audience!

"You probably already know how Nickolas ended up where he did!"

"Oh Frohman! I had strong suspicions of that before we left my property this morning. And I knew his killer before we crossed the river. Those were relatively simple problems. My old friend, the question I have been wrestling with all day is, why? Why was he murdered the night he was to leave and begin a new life?"

"Maybe someone caught wind and stopped him in his tracks."

"Certainly, but an elopement hardly seems like a motive for murder."

"Unless you're the father or brothers!" I said.

"No, the Inspector has cleared them and even if he was mistaken, he was right that the family would not have left the body for Catherine to discover."

I shrugged, "Maybe it was the booze. If they were drinking, maybe they had an argument that led to a fight. We both know that anything can happen if enough booze is poured."

He shook his head, "Do not base any conclusions on the good captain's narrative this morning. It was nearly all lies. I think the Inspector Rowan put us on the right course today. A course that led us to even deeper waters." He checked his watch again, "Which is why we need--"

I never let him finish. I had had it. I reached my saturation point. To think he had known since this morning and I had no doubt he was right, and that we spent the entire day flitting about like birds. My Irish was up!

I snarled at him as I grabbed his arm and jerked him to a halt, "What we need, is to stop and think about what you're doing - what we're doing! No more talking in riddles and theories before we're in over our heads!"

William looked completely aghast at my outburst, so I took a deep breath and moderated my tone before going on,

"Look, the boat rides, the doctor's office, lunch, even for whatever reason our jaunt through the boat shed was harmless enough. I was happy to be your shadow. I still don't have a clue as to what's going on, but I was willing to see it through to the end. You have one employee who is dead, Will! Another who is incarcerated and now you want to flimflam the man you believe is the murderer! I just think that this is going to end badly!"

His eyes grew wider as I ranted on and his face softened until I could see my old friend beneath the Sherlock persona. Looking abashed, he hung his head and spoke softly.

"Oh, Charlie. I am so sorry. You are absolutely right. I've been arrogant and obtuse all day. Worse yet, I have been rude. It was never my wish to put you in harm's way."

He was so contrite, I had to let him off the hook a little. "Well, you haven't been all that bad. A bit too caught up in the chase perhaps, but I have to admit you seem like you've been on top of it. I'm just worried that this may be a bit more than we can handle safely. Your riddle solving abilities are impressive, on stage and off. But murder and mayhem are in another class altogether!"

It was time for my haymaker. "Remember what's important. Ozaki could be home by dinner time. You can make one phone call and make that happen."

He nodded slowly, looking like a school boy caught in a prank. "You're right, of course. I'll understand if you want to step away from it now. I...I can manage."

I gave him a stern look and was about to let him have another blast but he held up his hands, "Alright, yes, there is some danger. And if you insist, we'll both go back to the house and let the police handle it."

He glanced out to the river then back to me, "I didn't mean to be such a sod, Charlie. It is hard for me to explain, but when I saw Nickolas lying there this morning something snapped inside me. This is my home Charlie, and I liked all the people that worked for me, and trusted them! Then that idiot Luboff comes into my home, when I am absent no less, and practically kidnaps Ozaki!" He shook his head. "I just wanted to set things straight. But you're right! If you think it's too much for us, we'll just walk away and let the authorities flounder through!"

Even as he espoused his heartfelt sentiments, his hangdog expression nearly made me laugh. William was so dramatic and I couldn't help but love him all the more at that moment. I knew he wanted to see this through from the bottom of his soul, so instead of listening to my own good advice, I found myself saying, "Oh, skip the crocodile tears. What the hell, William. Let's show the world what a retired actor and an overweight producer can do!" I lifted my hand in the air, waving my loaded cane about, "Besides, we have our canes! Let's serve some justice!"

William beamed ear to ear and clapped me on the shoulders, "Excellent, Frohman! That's the spirit!" He checked his watch, "Now come along, Frohman. We're in danger of falling behind schedule!"

And, once again, we hustled away, only one of us knowing the schedule.

We stepped onto the stern of the *Aunt Polly*, but instead of going into the saloon, I followed William along the port rail towards the bridge. The door was open and we could hear movement from within, but the captain did not come out to greet us. He lifted his cane and waggled the tip out towards the pylons, trying to bring my attention to something. It took a moment then I noticed the lines that moored the *Aunt Polly*. I was familiar with the slack rigging, having grown up around boats and docks and there was definitely a strange configuration to them.

Then he did the strangest thing and dropped to the deck on his belly and stuck his arm out over the side of the ship. Using his cane, he wiggled it under the water line for a moment then got back up on his feet. He had that smug smile on his face again.

I was about to comment but William shook his head quickly and gestured towards the open door. He continued on, gesturing for me to follow him.

William stopped and let himself into the saloon through the side door. The captain was still out of sight, yet I knew he must be aware of our presence. Without a glance at his surroundings, William kept moving and I followed him as he made his way over to the door that accessed the engine room and slipped down the stairs.

Though the engines were silent, the warmth told us that they had been running, and not too long ago. All the gauges read up to pressure.

"Looks like the captain got everything put back together," I observed. "You think maybe he's planning a little jaunt?"

William didn't reply, just walked around me to study the tanks on the captain's over-engineered bilge system. He was tapping the gauges when I came up behind him.

"What are you thinking?" I asked him.

He bent over to read the specification plate on the pump machinery and then stood straight. "I have been thinking, what a fool I have been! I have let my passion for building my home turn into an obsession that has blinded me to nefarious activity happening in my own back yard! And to salt the wound liberally, it was my money and my materials that funded this evil!"

His eyes blazed in righteous anger and he said in a low menacing voice, "But now the guilty will pay!"

Without waiting to see my reaction, he turned and headed for the hatchway that led to the bridge.

Bad Opening

The Captain came in from the side door to the bridge as we entered from below. Before we could greet him, he stepped over to us in two great strides.

"Have ye learned any more about what happened to Nicky? What did the doctor say?" he asked without preamble.

"The doctor has ruled it an accidental death," William lied smoothly.

"As to how it happened and how he ended up in the courtyard, I'm sure that will remain unresolved if left in the hands of our local constabulary. In any case, it's out of our hands."

"Might be it don't matter much, I suppose," Roy replied, "Don't change the fact that he's gone." His breath hitched and I almost thought I saw a tear in his eye.

"Is that it then? Can we lay him to rest now?"

"Yes, I suppose we can." Will answered. "I shall make the arrangements tomorrow."

"If I may, sir?" Roy asked, "Could I take the *Aunt Polly* out and bury Nickolas at sea? I'm sure that's what he would have wanted."

If William was surprised at the question, he didn't show it. "I am not sure that will be possible. For the moment, there is another matter we must discuss. Will you join Mr. Frohman and me in the saloon? We may as well be comfortable."

He turned and headed to the saloon without waiting for a reply. Captain Roy gestured for me to pass through before him and I did so, heading straight for the liquor cabinet.

"Care for a drink, Captain?" I asked, uncapping the sherry decanter. I kept my voice jovial, but I hung my derringer cane on my forearm to assure easy access. I had never knowingly offered a drink to a suspected murderer before. It was unnerving to say the least.

"Please, have a seat," William suggested.

"I believe I'll pass on spirits for the time being, Sir," he replied to me. Then he addressed William, standing ramrod straight with his hands clutching his hat behind him. "And I'm thinking I'll keep my feet on the deck, Mr. Gillette."

Stone-faced, he went on, "I always thought you to be a decent man, Mr. Gillette. Nicky was a good mate and done right by you in his berth here. What's more important than giving poor Nicky's spirit some peace?"

"I personally would be honored to use the *Aunt Polly* to lay Nickolas to his final rest Captain Roy, but you see, I no longer have the principal say in matters." William said.

The Captain's eyes narrow and suspicion clouded his face, but he said nothing. He just stared at William, waiting for an explanation.

"As I am sure you are aware, building my home takes the lion's share of my time and it will still be years before I have completed every phase of this estate. Though I am extremely fond of the *Aunt Polly* and the waters we have traversed, I simply no longer have the time to give her the attention and maintenance she needs. As your contract expires this month, I have decided after much consideration, to sell the *Aunt Polly* to Mr. Frohman."

The captain and William looked over to me. I took my cue and made up my lines as I went.

"It's the reason I made the trip up this week. I've always been fond of the *Aunt Polly*, ever since I took my first trip on her. She'll make me a comfortable diversion from the busy city and fit in fine at the marina on the Hudson."

Roy seemed to tense up, but relaxed a little as a thought came to him. "Will you need a crew, Mr. Frohman?"

I looked to William, "Um, no, I don't believe so Captain. William and Ozaki have put me to work many a times on this boat. I think I can handle her to New Haven, where I plan to have her refitted to my liking. From there she'll be delivered to her new home. Most likely, I'll use her more for entertaining clients and friends, than travel."

"Just a thought, sir." He turned to William, "Then I guess I've been given notice. Can't say I mind too much, truth be told. I can't see me self staying on without my first mate, Nickolas. Memories would be too painful, as you know." He paused and ran the back of his hand across his nose, then squared his shoulders.

"I'll be needing but a week to wrap up my affairs and ready the ship for her new master. Then I'll be on my way to the next port. Fair enough, Mr. Gillette?"

"Actually," William said with a grim face, "I've made other arrangements. Unfortunately, Mr. Frohman has been called back to the city. He'll be taking possession immediately. He plans on staying the night and leaving first thing in the morning for New Haven."

Then my oldest and best friend really laid it on with a shovel. "I must ask you to collect your personal belonging and be ready to disembark within the hour. Ollie will be along to collect you and your baggage. He will be here shortly. He will take you to the ferry or the train station, whatever you prefer. He will also have an envelope for you that has your last pay plus some severance and a generous bonus. I wish you..."

William STOPPED talking as a large caliber hand gun appeared just six inches from his face. Roy must have been hiding it behind the hat in his hands. He must have seen me twitch and try to slide my hand to my cane because Roy looked me in the eye and cocked the pistol, which was still pointed at my friend's forehead.

I froze. Keeping me in his peripheral vision, he turned back to William.

"Just shut up, Gillette. I'm tired of this little game. It's past time to put things in perspective."

I was never so in awe of my friend. A gleaming tube of death inches from his face and he didn't bat an eyelash. William merely raised his eyebrows and replied. "Yes. Let us. Surely you can see by now that you can't get away with any of this. I suggest you put down your weapon and surrender to the police."

I remember thinking, 'What are you talking about? He's got the gun!' and I realized Roy had swung the pistol over to point it at me.

"Or," he retorted, raising his eyebrows, "I can put a bullet in your friend's head and then yours. Unless you'd rather take the wheel and we'll all take a little ride." His finger tightened ever so slightly on the trigger. "Decide now."

"Then I suppose we'll take being kidnapped over being shot." William assured him quickly. He had lost some of his composure when Roy threatened me.

"Hostages or corpses," Roy said grimly, "This boat leaves as soon as the engines are hot enough!"

William said nothing in reply, but I could see his hand sliding down to grip the head of his cane, ready to draw its three feet of steel.

My mind racing with fear, I knew what he was thinking. That no matter what, there would actually be a burial at sea if we left these docks. Two, in fact.

William was coiled like a spring and I feared for his safety. A cane sword is no match for a pistol. All I feared had seemingly come to pass, and yet, I did not despair at that moment.

A spark of anger turned into a fiery rage as the day's

events and frustrations crashed over me like an ocean's wave. I was in motion before I could stop myself.

When Roy turned his eyes toward William, I swung my cane at his wrist in a vicious two handed arc in an attempt to disarm him.

Unfortunately, I underestimated the captain's speed.

My cane whistled through the air between us, missing its mark by an inch, as he dropped his hand under my swing. I just started to look up at him when the barrel of the pistol caught me square above my left eye.

Blood spurting everywhere, my knees buckled and I fell sideways into William who dropped his cane to catch me. We both stumbled back a few steps, knocking over a chair. William fell to one knee as I sagged into a sitting position.

William had an arm around my chest to keep me from keeling over, as he fumbled for a handkerchief to press against my forehead. The vision in my right eye cleared enough for me to see Roy step forward and lower his gun at us. His face was set in stone as he cocked the weapon.

I knew he was about to shoot us both.

Goose Egg

Suddenly, out of the corner of my remaining good eye, I saw a foot come up from the floor, out of nowhere, and connect with the wrist holding the gun. It flew out of Roy's hand and across the room, well out of his reach. Hands clenched in fists, he turned to face our savior with unbridled rage.

I was shocked to consciousness and focused on my surroundings once again. Ozaki, all five foot two inches, one hundred and three pounds dripping wet, was facing off with Captian Roy in rage.

Like a lumberjack, using his feet instead of axes, Ozaki went on the attack. He kicked Roy's left knee, then his right thigh. Two quit kicks to the left hip and then he pile drove a heel into Roy's right knee.

Roy's hands dropped, his face a collage of surprise and agony. As he began to sag at the knees, Roy marshaled his brute strength to launch an overhand right that would surely crush Ozaki's skull. The fist coming at him was at least half the size of Ozaki's head.

Ozaki merely shifted his weight and let the punch pass in front of his nose. Reaching out, he grabbed the giant's wrist with his right hand applied some unseen pressure that brought Roy to his knees in pain.

Ozaki proceeded to strike him in the temple with his left, over and over. None were exceedingly hard but they came so fast and furious that the collective effect quickly eroded the fight from Roy's hulking frame and he slowly sagged to both knees, dazed and near collapse. Ozaki, not breathing hard, stepped back but stayed ready on the balls of his feet.

Just as suddenly as Ozaki's miraculous arrival, a couple of coppers appeared to seize the hulking brute and wrestled him into submission, while he feebly tried to resist. The rest was obscured as the face of Inspector Rowan filled my vision. I remember him saying my name as I blacked out.

When the lights came back on, William and Rowan were hovering over me. William looked almost panicked.

"Charlie! Can you hear me? Are you all right?" He put his hand in front of my face, "How many fingers am I holding up?"

Rowan was acting just as stupid, kneeling next to me and patting my thigh as if I were a child. The two were so annoying that I did not realize the extent of my injuries until I tried to sit up and tell them both to shut up. A pain shot through my head that I could only describe as an ice pick being plunged into my left eye. Gentle hands held me down and I could feel pressure on my wound.

"Prease lay still, Mr. Frohman." Good old Ozaki! Even as I felt the blood run down my face and drip off my ear, I felt relief. He was a rock in any crisis.

"Good Lord!" William exclaimed. "He's still bleeding! Inspector, send one of your men for the doctor!"

"The hell with that! We'll take him in the launch now!" Rowan declared.

William agreed as he started to rise, "I'll find something to use as a stretcher."

"STOP!" Ozaki barked and they both, to my great relief, fell silent. "Calm yourserfs. Mr. Frohman does not need a boat ride now, nor is a doctor necessary. Scawp wounds bleed a great deal. It is messy, but not deadry."
Ozaki turned to William and asked, "Prease get the

242

medical kit from the bridge."

Ozaki pulled me into a sitting position and propped me up with a cushion from the divan. I was still a little woozy, but my vision was clearing despite the pain. I gingerly put two fingers to my face and felt a bump over my left eye the size of a goose egg beneath the linen over my forehead. When my fingers brushed it, it felt like ice water was poured on my exposed brain. I began to breathe a little fast and heavy.

Moving around to my field of vision, Ozaki knelt next to me and said gently, "Do not worry, Mr. Frohman. You be fine very soon."

"You sure, Ozaki?" I asked, "Feels like it's pretty bad."

He shrugged, "I sure it feels very bad and it rooks very bad," He smiled and shook his head, "but not to serious."

As I let that soak in, my breathing slowed and the throbbing subsided a hair. "I must look like hell."

Ozaki shrugged again, "Cut not so big. Stop bleeding now. Bump should go away in a few days. Black eye another week. Then you look the same again. Give all the women week off from having to swoon at your beauty!" Ozaki grinned like the cat that ate the canary at his sally.

"Think I'll have a scar?" I asked, wondering how I would explain it to my wife!

"No scar," he said solemnly, as he reached up to pat my face with affection, "It is a Badge of Honor."

I loved that old yellow bugger right then and I realized how much he'd been part of my life through my friendship with William.

"Thank you, Ozaki. But you're the hero. You saved us all." He started to protest, but I held a finger to his lips and said, "As you always have."

Luckily, William came barreling back with the medical kit or I might have even hugged my little Japanese friend.

After Ozaki sorted through the box of medical supplies, I ended up with a long linen bandage wrapped around my head like a turban, holding an iodine soaked patch over my left eye. I felt ridiculous, yet the bandage felt like it was keeping my head together and the pain slowly subsided to an irritating headache. He denied me a cocktail, but did give me a dose of opiate.

With a little effort, we managed to get both me and the cushion back on the divan, me trading the iodine for a cloth with ice on my wound and everyone in the room turned their attention to the captain, who sat in the chair, flanked by two burly constables. I noticed William and the Inspector exchanging nods and I wondered what the two had planned. It was obvious they were in cahoots.

Roy looked as if he had shaken off the dusting Ozaki gave him and sat stiffed back, his face a thunder cloud but his head held high. His eyes roamed around the room, taking in every detail until they finally fell on us with intense scrutiny.

It took everything I had not to cringe under that glare. He reminded me of a great python I once saw at the London Zoo once, all muscle and menace!

Rowan saw the look too and stepped in, "Hear now! What's this all about Captain Roy? Why'd you attack this man?" He jerked a thumb in my direction.

"Me attack him?" Roy asked, in all wide eyed innocence, "It was he that struck at me first, Inspector!"

I wanted to laugh at that absurdity but it only sent a jolt of pain through my head when I tried. William smirked and Rowan took out his little note book.

"Then perhaps you'd like to give me your side of the story," he suggested to the captain, "But! Remember anything you say may be used as evidence against you?"

"Against me... how? A half hour ago, I was just going about my business and in that short time, I've been beached, beaten, and now treated like a criminal. Sure I'll tell my side. First off, you gentlemen wake me and tell me my friend Nicky is dead. Even so, shocked as I was, I did what I was ordered to do by Mr. Gillette and put the engines back together." Captain Roy continued while holding his knees.

"No sooner that I had finished, these two show up and next thing I know I'm dismissed! Beached! The *Aunt Polly* has been my home for the last nine months and I was told to pick up my sea bag and put the dock beneath my feet! I felt threatened Inspector, and not a little shocked at the turn of events. So I suppose I became a bit irrational and pulled my pistol. But you already know I never fired it! Then the city slicker tried to hit me with his stick and I whacked him one back. Next thing I know, I was under attack again by the little monkey over there, using his heathen tricks to maim me!" Captain Roy took a deep breath, "I'm grateful your men rescued me when they did."

William did bark a short laugh at that and said, "Excellent, Captain! Everything you stated was essentially correct, yet so much was omitted, it hardly resembles the truth."

Rowan held up a hand to restrain my friend and addressed Roy, "I doubt you'll be grateful by the end of the day. Captain Roy, you are under arrest!"

Roy stiffened but held his seat, "On what charges?"

"Assault, threatening, and attempted kidnapping... you see, Captain, we boarded the *Aunt Polly* just before Mr. Gillette brought you in here to talk to you. We heard every word, witnessed every action."

"You had this all planned?" I blurted out, "you and Rowan?"

"Why, of course. We needed to draw the captain out before he could flee."

"Flee from what?" Roy scoffed. "I'll find a lawyer

who'll have me out on bond by this evening. In fact, Inspector, if you insist on arresting me over this misunderstanding, let us begin the process."

"He's right," Rowan said as he closed his notebook. "None of the charges will warrant us holding him, if he posts bail."

"Oh, I believe you can charge him with much more than simple assault, Inspector... much, much more!"

Roy jumped to his feet and would have been at him if the coppers hadn't grabbed him by both arms. The man that stood before us was deadly serious. His eyes bore into my friend with an intensity of a hunting lion. Here was the python.

"I say this once and then we shan't speak again, Gillette. 'Remove yourself from my ken!'"

The Inspector and the constables looked confused by the statement delivered with so much passion, but I knew what a dire threat it was. As William did also, because he wrote the line!

It was from one of William's most successful plays titled 'The Secret Service', in the play, one of the characters delivered that line to another and when it went unheeded, that character was slowly broken down until he died a horrible death. I'll admit I was impressed that Roy knew the reference, albeit a bit unnerved at the threat.

William, on the other hand, showed nothing resembling fear. He just nodded, as if to acknowledge the eloquence of the veiled warning, and replied, "You should save your threats for when you stand beneath the gallows' pole and now I'll add plagiarism to your list of crimes. "

"Gallows!" Roy scoffed, "You're going to send me to the gallows? You're nothing but a flop in show business with delusions-"

"That's enough," Rowan roared. "Captain Roy, sit down and shut up! You are still under arrest." Clearly, he was angry at losing control of the situation.

He took a deep breath and addressed Will, "Mr. Gillette, if you have something to add to this investigation, please do it now." He was clearly becoming exasperated because of his frustration of not knowing what was going on. I knew exactly how he felt.

"Inspector, if you can bear with me for just a bit longer, I believe I can help resolve several issues that are now plaguing you." William said, warming up to the final act.

William Takes Center Stage

"Are you alright Charlie?" William whispered to me as he and Ozaki got me propped up in place. "Are you sure you wouldn't want to see the doctor? We won't stay a moment longer if you feel you need immediate attention!"

Ozaki stiffened at the remark, but I just smiled. The genuine concern on his face touched me to my soul. It was like seeing my friend for the first time since we had coffee this morning. "I'm fine Will. Ozaki here is all the physician I need."

I could tell by his hesitation that he wanted more. He wanted his producer.

"Break a leg William!"

With a bit of a struggle, the constables managed to get Roy seated in a chair that sat between the ends of the divans, one of which I occupied. All four officers flanked Roy, two on each side and Inspector Rowan took up a position standing near the end of the bench I sat on, notebook at the ready. Ozaki stood behind me and we all turned our attention to William waiting for him to begin.

"All settled then?" he asked and without waiting for an answer he added, "Excellent! It is time to put an end to this very busy day!"

Even I, who saw this act many times, was impressed at his transformation into character. He seemed to change with every measured step he took then turned with a flourish of his coat tails. Every eye was on him and they were enthralled. He had the room in the palm of his hand.

"For the benefit of those who were not among us this morning, I will start with the discovery of Nickolas's body, brought to our attention by the screams of my maid, Catherine. The most striking enigma of the situation was the position we found the corpse in. He lay in the near center of a wide courtyard area on the riverfront side of my home. Yesterday, in anticipation of laying the stone work, my crew had graded the area with sand. The flat even surface highlighted the broken, mangled corpse as it lay upon the pristine surface.

There were no drag marks or footprints to be seen around the gristly heap. After some deliberation, we determined that Nickolas could not have jumped or fallen from my home, nor could the body have been dropped or thrown from the wall that surrounded the area. The distances were simply too great. How we ascertained all this, I will not delve into for the sake of expediency. If you are curious, I am certain the Inspector has it all in his notebook, for your review." He gestured to Rowan, who was scribbling away, with a glint of amusement in his eye. The uniforms all snickered, and William quickly pressed on.

"The authorities were called and your illustrious Chief Inspector Luboff quickly took the situation in hand. In no time he had reduced poor Catherine to near hysterics, yet, he did manage to uncover an elopement plan that Nickolas and Catherine were to put into motion the evening before."

The three younger cops were obviously startled by that news. William had them, lock, stock, and barrel.

"But the singularly important point she raised was the existence of an engagement ring. Bear that ring in mind, gentlemen. It has great meaning later on! The esteemed Chief Luboff once satisfied the elopement was off, quickly wrapped up his investigation and left.

The medical examiner arrived shortly afterwards and

with Frohman and I in tow, the Inspector and he examined the body. I'm sure you have all heard of the gristly state that we found the body in, so I will not delve into the mutilation and gore we encountered. The only significant fact of the examination was that Nickolas was dead before he ended up where he did. He did not place himself there!

As the cause of death could not be determined on site, it was decided the doctor would take the body back to his office for an official autopsy. Before they departed, we searched the body and revealed two more key points. The first being that Nickolas had all his papers, passports, and savings in a money belt strapped beneath his shirt. This of course, confirmed the story Catherine told us, though not why he was on my property. Their plan was to meet at the Chester rail station and take a train to New York City."

I happened to be watching Roy as he revealed that fact and I saw something in his eye, a malevolent recognition that made me nervous enough to start looking around for my cane, which I dropped when Roy clobbered me. I saw it sticking out from under my couch so I reached down for it and nearly passed out for my efforts. Ozaki caught my shoulder just before I tumbled to the floor and pulled me backwards. When I could focus again, he handed me the cane, which I laid across my knees.

William had stopped talking and everyone was looking my way. I flapped my hand and made a 'get on with it' gesture. He gave me a quick look of concern and jumped right back into his soliloquy without missing a beat.

"The second point has to do with what we did not find, an engagement ring."

"Again with the ring," Rowan said, "What makes that stick on your craw?"

William smiled his little cat grin, "Why would he not have it, Inspector?"

Rowan looked like he might get irked, still unsure of

what William was getting at, but a sudden thought made me speak.

"I see it now! Nickolas should have had the ring on him! He wouldn't have eloped without it!"

"Excellent, Frohman! I found it extremely curious that a man who had taken the trouble to collect everything important to him, in preparation to leave the *Aunt Polly* and my employ, would have left the very symbol of this life-changing event behind. So, indeed, where was the ring? What happened to it?" He let the question hang in the air.

"Well, what did happen to it?" the youngest constable blurted out. "What does it mean?"

The lad looked embarrassed to have spoken up, but he need not be. Even the Inspector, who was absently patting the pocket he had put the ring in when William gave it to him earlier, could not answer both those questions.

"Soon Constable. Let us press on for the moment. After the good doctor departed, we made our way to the *Aunt Polly* to interview Captain Roy and to search Nickolas's room for some indication of what might have happened. All in all, it was quite illuminating. First, we found the room to be a red herring."

"A red what, Sir.?" Another of the constables asked.

"Herring, Officer. It was a ruse. Someone was trying to make us believe he had not packed his belongings. That he had not planned on leaving."

"I'll admit the clothes bothered me some," Rowan observed.

"I was there too," I said, "but I don't see where sloppy housekeeping constitutes a conspiracy! Bachelors aren't known to be as neat as pins, you know. Hell, I used to have to look under my bed for a clean set of drawers!"

"Washed and neatly folded, Mr. Frohman?" Rowan asked skeptically, "a person who takes the time to wash,

251

press, and neatly fold their clothes usually doesn't end the job by scattering them willie-nillie about the room."

I had to give him that, so I nodded and sat back as Wiliam continued on.

"Yet, perhaps the key point in our discoveries was the fabled engagement ring." William turned his head to address the young constable. "The ring is singularly important because it establishes a timeline. We can be fairly certain now that Nickolas had made all his plans for the rendezvous. He washed and packed his clothes, gathered his necessary items and placed them in a pouch strapped to his chest, and yet failed to retrieve the ring from its hiding place before he left. From this we can surmise that he was interrupted between his preparations and his departure.

This now brings us to Captain Roy. The only man, besides myself that had a key to that cabin. The type of door to that cabin can only be locked with a key."

You could see the wheels click in the Inspector's head as he flipped backwards in his little book. He raised his head with a triumphant look, "Nickolas left his keys inside the room. The door was locked when we arrived!"

"Bravo, Inspector. Your notes serve you well!"

Rowan looked at Roy, who sat glaring at all of us, "What do you have to say to that, Roy?"

"You're talking nonsense! I told you what happened last night!"

"Yes Captain!" Will barked as he rose from his seat. He did not get up so much as he flowed upwards with a grace learned over thirty years. All eyes were drawn to him as he slowly began to pace in front of the prisoner.

"Yes. Let us talk of that pack of lies you spewed out this morning."

"Lies? What lies? Prove it!"

William stopped and turned towards him, well out of

arms reach and held up a finger.

"First, you told us the engines were disabled because Nickolas was working on them all day, but we found the ship to be quite warm and comfortable. We both know that the heat only works when the engines are operating! This was just to disguise the fact that Nickolas spent his time making ready to leave."

Another finger joined the first. "Second, you claimed that Nickolas had drunk himself into insensibility with his homemade potato vodka, yet the doctor found no traces of alcohol in his stomach. And in fact, his clothes reeked of--"

"Scotch!" I cried out. I nearly slapped my forehead, "How could I have missed that! He reeked of Scotch!"

Rowan turned to stare at Roy. "As if someone wanted us to think he was dead drunk when he died. Pouring Scotch all over his clothes might do that."

"Quite so, inspector," William acknowledged. Another digit popped up next to the other two.

"Third, you testified that you staggered off to your bunk, drunk, and you never awoke until I roused you this morning. Yet there were clumps of mud on the gangway when we arrived this morning."

"I noticed them too," I blurted out.

He looked sideways at me for the interruption of his performance. "Thank you Frohman. Confirmation is always reassuring." William continued.

"As the doctor determined that Nickolas died between the late afternoon and early evening, he was already dead before it rained. It rained briefly last night between eight-thirty and ten o'clock. So only one person could have ventured out after the rain, Captain Roy - You! The wet ground you stepped in as you disposed of Nickolas's corpse!"

At that point, I'm loath to admit, the audience seemed on

253

the verge of slipping away. The coppers and the Inspector gave each other skeptical looks. Even Ozaki gave his master a puzzled look. I could see their point. It made no sense. But when I saw a little smirk grow on Roy's mouth as he gauged the reactions around him, I desperately sought a way to back my friend up. Nothing had come to mind when Rowan spoke up.

"You kind of lost me there, Mr. Gillette. If, as you claim, the captain took the body off the ship, how do you explain how he managed to drop it on your front door? I thought we had already proved it was impossible for one man or even several."

William seemed almost amused by our disbelief. "You gentlemen need to open your minds a bit more. You are confined by your assumptions. You are only considering the positioning of the body from the point of view that it was a deliberate act."

"Well, he didn't put himself there! He was already dead, for Pete's sake!" I blurted out. "How else could he have gotten there?"

"Why, by accident, Frohman."

Unexpected Results

The constables were looking at my friend like he had three heads and I just wanted to knock the smug look off of Roy's face. I groaned inwardly. I was afraid to hear his explanation for such an absurd idea. I half convinced myself that William was over his head and about to flounder badly. His theories were sound up to this point but I feared his last act was about to flop.

The only one in the room, besides the top suspect who didn't look bewildered was Rowan and was starting to look a little perplexed.

"Accident, Mr. Gillette, an accident?" He jammed his pencil under his hat and over his ear. He used the free hand to slowly massage his forehead. "You walk us through a solid case against this man for murder, and then tell us he 'accidentally' disposed of the body in your courtyard?"

"Inspector," William said with all dignity, "we have already established that Nickolas could not have jumped, fallen, or been tossed where we discovered him. When all other possibilities are eliminated, whatever remains, no matter how improbable..."

"Must be the solution!" We finished together and laughed. It was our favorite Doyleism and a private joke of ours.

"Inspector!" Roy snarled from his chair, straightening in his seat, "Are you going to let these two clowns..."

"Sit back and shut up!" Rowan barked. "You'll get your chance to explain." Roy did as he was ordered but I could see he was about to snap.

Rowan inquired, "For the life of me, I can't understand why he would bother to haul the body out into the rain when he has the river to dump it in right outside that door!"

"Exactly Inspector!" William replied. "And yet he did." He paused and looked pensive for a moment. Everyone leaned forward to hear his next words. "I'm sure you will all see the explanation for that in a few moments."

Rowan was obviously not pleased with another cryptic reply. A sudden thought came to him and he flipped through his notes. "Besides, wasn't the tramway broken that night?"

"Of course, common knowledge. The question before us, is who broke it and when?!"

You could see the steam coming out from under the inspector's hat, but he kept his voice civil, though extremely sarcastic. "Shall I add the charge of vandalism to his list?"

Will's eyebrows narrowed and his face became frosty. I know him and he was expecting applause, not adversity.

"I do not think you could make that charge stick, Inspector. I'm quite sure he broke it by accident."

The two glared at each other for a moment and while everyone else was watching to see which way the tension was going to snap, I noticed Ozaki edging himself into a position between Roy and his master.

I looked over to Roy, who sat in his chair, legs crossed like he was waiting for a train. His face was outwardly calm, almost bored, but his knuckles were white as he grasped the armrest. I thought the rails were going to snap off in his gorilla like hands.

Thankfully, William, the consummate showman, had judged his audience correctly and saw they had reached their breaking point.

"As I have already shown the facts that support my

synopsis of the events which led up to the murder, allow me now to reveal the details of what happened afterwards."

Almost all of us had a look of relief on our faces as we gave him our full attention again.

"Captain Roy was faced with a dilemma. He needed to dispose of the corpse before his misdeed was uncovered, yet he did not want the body to be found anywhere near the dock area, nor did he want a search to even begin in this vicinity. Nickolas had to be found somewhere else, with a plausible explanation for his whereabouts."

"He missed that mark by a mile, I'd say, or else we'd all be having a drink at the Inn right now!"

"He did indeed Frohman," William replied, "yet his original plan was quite sound, ingenious, actually. You see, he doused the body with cheap scotch then planned on taking the body on a ride up the tram..."

"I see where you're going with this, Mr. Gillette!" Rowan blurted out. "The plan was to make Nickolas smell like a boozehound and then toss him from the top of the tram! When found in the morning, everyone would assume he was drunk and had fallen from the platform."

I mulled over the possibility for a moment and nodded, "Personally, I think it's a damn good theory myself, but there are still two problems. It doesn't explain how he ended up where he did."

William rummaged around in his coat pocket and produced the swath of cloth we found in the pulley system of the tram. He handed it over to the inspector and asked, "Do you recognize this?"

"I do," Rowan replied, "It looks like a piece of the coat we found Nickolas wearing this morning."

"You have a keen eye, Inspector. So will you agree that Nickolas was at least at the tramway last night?"

"I'll have to match it with the coat, but yes, I'll go along with that. But it doesn't give us a motive and it's still a long way from the bottom of the tram- especially a broken one- to your courtyard, Sir."

"It is shorter than it appears," William replied with a twinkle in his eye. Again, Rowan clenched his teeth at the teaser. It was time to bring the suspense to a head and William was a pro at this.

He sauntered over to the table and picked up a cigarette. He lit it and struck a pose in the center of our group, near my left side. His right leg planted forward and his left hand on his hip. When he was sure all ears were perked and eyes were on him, he started his soliloquy.

William smiled, "I shall let you ponder the first question for a bit, though I assure you that all will be revealed in due course."

He went on quickly before Rowan could object, "I shall answer the second question now. This is what I believed happened. Having decided to elope, Nickolas gathered his possessions and packed his things during the day yesterday. By early evening, he had but one thing left to do, remove the ring from its hiding place in his cabin and take it to Catherine.

Now, either the captain came across Nickolas making his preparations to leave and surprised him, or, what I think is the more likely, Nickolas told the captain of his plans and the captain objected fiercely.

Enough to kill him!"

Looking directly at Rowan, he went on, "Not wanting any attention drawn to the *Aunt Polly*, he decided to take the body ashore."

I think most of us in the room wanted to call him on that assumption, but William just held up a finger to stop us and we held our questions for the moment.

"Roy's well thought out plan was to douse Nickolas' clothes with liquor, then take the body up on the tram and push him off. When the body was found, we'd all assume that he was drunk and fell from the tram on his way to meet Catty. Once he disposed of the body, he could make his was back to the *Aunt Polly* down the path and go to his bed. Then he only had to act surprised when we came to tell him of his first mate's demise!"

As I pictured William's narrative in my head, an idea began to tickle in the back of my mind, but the sergeant of the constables who was with us this morning when we examined the corpse, asked a question and threw me off track.

"Beggin' your pardon, Mr. Gillette," he said, "it may be that the captain did indeed try to dispose of the body in that manner, but I was there this morning when your man told you the lift was broken. Wouldn't that have spoiled his plans?"

"That is true, Sergeant!" William answered the man. "The tramway was broken because the Captain, in a manner of speaking, broke it! You see, I believe Captain Roy, after carrying the body to the tram, set it down against the pulley cables, where it would be somewhat hidden until he could bring the tram down and load Nickolas onto it. As the tram was in the up position, he had to first release the locking brake mech..."

At that instant, it all became clear to me. It was as if someone handed me the piece I needed to finish a jigsaw puzzle.

"Oh, my Lord!" I cried out as I used my cane to raise myself into a standing position, "I see it now!" I looked at my friend. "It really was an accident!"

Rowan looked skeptical and two of the coppers rolled their eyes. But then, before I could stop myself, I turned to taunt Roy, a small payback for the goose egg he gave me.

"You thought you were so clever. Thought you had the perfect plan, didn't you?" I managed to laugh without

259

splitting my head wide open. "I would have paid any amount of money to see your face when you pulled the brake release and that platform came down at you like an out of control locomotive!"

Roy didn't answer me, but I could see the rage building.

"Outstanding, Frohman," William cried out, "the veil is lifted and the blind can see!" He was having the time of his life.

Rowan put his hands on his hips, "Well, perhaps you gentlemen would like to share with us, or would you prefer to continue baiting the prisoner?"

William wiped the smile from his face and cleared his throat. "Of course, Inspector. You see, when the captain set Nickolas's body on the ground next to the cables, he must have leaned him on the steel rod bell striker fused to the cable. What the captain was unaware of, that we learned this morning as we attempted to take the tram down, is that a couple of my workers had carelessly left a load of mortar sitting on the platform."

Rowan nodded his head, "I remember that."

"So!" William paused for effect, "When the brake was released, the weight, close to half a ton, caused the gears to strip and the platform became a free falling mass. Freed from restraint, the cables spun on their pulleys and Nickolas was flying upwards."

I remembered something from the doctor's report then, "That's how he got his jewels crushed!" That caused everyone to look up, but I plowed on, "That bell ringing doodad!" I snapped my fingers. "that iron bar bell striker must have caught him right in the seat of his pants. I'd lay even odds that his overcoat got caught up in the cables keeping him upright. Remember the doctor said his coat was shredded from the shoulders down!"

"There are no less than six points, in the doctor's report, to support my explanation, Frohman," William replied.

"Including one you mentioned already, and also the parallel scrapes on his back that match the gauge of my pulley system, three and three-eight's inches. And with the weight of the mortar that was falling, he must have shot up the cliff like he came out of a cannon! When the platform struck the ground, his body must have been at the apex of the pulley's cable and he was catapulted into the air with enough force to land in the middle of the courtyard. There were no foot prints, no drag marks, or any other signs of passage."

There was a stunned silence, everyone tore their eyes off William and stared at the captain. To my surprise, Roy just smiled.

"I suppose you think I should clap now, eh Gillette? Looking for a little adoration for your performance? Well, don't be holding your breath; your little attempt at reviving your career didn't impress me much."

"Save your glib remarks for when they put the noose around your neck, Roy! You will hang for your crimes!"

"Hang?" Roy laughed, "dirty laundry and mud on the docks after a rain aren't be sending me to the gallows!"

I was looking for utter condemnation of the captain's remarks, but I was sorely disappointed. The constables seemed reluctant to accept this bizarre scenario, and the inspector wasn't that amenable either.

"Still seems like a long way for the body to travel." Rowan said. "It must have been thirty feet from the tram to where we found him."

"Closer to fifty," William replied reaching into his jacket. He pulled out the papers he was scribbling on during our ride down the tram and thrust them at Rowan who took them.

"I've done the math, Inspector. The weight difference between the large mass of the mortar going down and Nickolas going up, placed him in the middle of my courtyard - simple physics."

When he stepped back to me, I asked in a hushed tone, "Physics? How did you come up with that?"

He gave me a withering look, "Granted, it was some time ago that I did attend a university."

Rowan looked the figures over, but you could tell he might as well have been reading Greek. He shrugged, "I'll take your word for it." He stepped over in front of Roy. "And what might you have to say about all this, Captain. This gentleman makes a strong case."

Roy stood, squared his shoulders and answered, "My dear Inspector, whatever yarn this playwright wishes to spin, it is no concern of mine."

"So you deny having anything to do with Nickolas's death?"

"As I told you before, I was passed out in a drunken stupor when this story supposedly happened. So, even if it happened like he's guessing, it happened to someone else. Now Inspector, I would like to ask you a question."

Rowan shrugged, "Please do."

"Why, for all the finger pointing, the posturing, and the fairy tales which any decent attorney would shred in a courtroom, I haven't heard a single testament as to WHY?"

That very question had also been nagging me. From what little I knew, the two had worked well together for a long time. Killing Nickolas on the night he was going to elope, no matter what Roy's feelings on the matter might have been, seemed a bit over the top. Rowan must have been thinking along the same lines, but I think he knew William's explanation was the right one.

"Perhaps you felt strongly against his running off with Catty. It would have certainly hurt your standing with Mr. Gillette and you might have even lost your position. We all saw what happened when you were dismissed, after all."

Then the young Inspector tried a different tactic. "It's possible you may not have to face a murder charge, Captain. Is that what happened? Did you lose your temper when Nickolas told you what he was planning? Did you fight? You know, if it was an accident and you come clean, things will go a lot easier for you?"

To my shock before Roy could even respond, William stepped forward and boomed.

"There is no need to lessen the severity of the charges that will be laid upon his head, Inspector. I believe I can supply you with a solid motive!"

Once again, the main spotlight was on William as he stepped over to Ozaki and whispered in his ear. Ozaki whispered back and William sent him off. We all watched in rapt attention as the little man went through the door that led to the engine room.

Almost immediately, the soft hum of machinery starting was heard as William led everyone's attention to the windows. Everyone was wondering what the boat was going to do.

As soon as the inspector turned away, an enraged Captain Roy sprang out of his seat and lunged for William, his massive hands reaching to seize him! With no conscious thought, I brought my cane up with my left hand and my right hand deftly hit the release button. The derringer slid out smoothly and in one fluid motion, I planted my right foot forward and brought the weapon up at the end of my outstretched arm.

The captain realized he was staring down a double barrel and he skidded to a halt. Captain Roy's arms flew back and my pistol ended up jammed right between his eyes.

No one spoke as the four coppers, already in motion, leaped on the brute and dragged him back in handcuffs.

William looked at me intensely for a moment and smiled

as he clasped me on the shoulder.

"Now gentlemen, if you will join me on the portside railing, the answers to all your questions will be revealed!"

The Truth Rises

William led the way, with me and the inspector right behind him. The four coppers surrounded Roy and filed out behind us. Since I thwarted his attack, he seemed resigned to his arrest and remained staunchly silent. I don't believe I heard him utter another word.

William directed us to stand at the railing about mid ship. Our position was between the piers. Ozaki reappeared on deck and William had him man the stern ropes that tied us to the pilings as he walked up front and took the bow line. In unison, they pulled their lines and the *Aunt Polly* drifted away from the dock. They stopped after a few yards and tied off again. William returned to us, rubbing his hands in excitement.

"Gentlemen, keep your attention on the water. It should not take much longer."

Nothing happened at first, and then a few air bubbles started bursting on the waters surface. When the extra lines started to go slack, a dark shape was slowly coming into view as it rose from the depths. We all gasped and took a step back as a single gigantic eyeball broke the surface, perched upon what struck me as a giant black fluke.

Our reactions were varied. My heart skipped a beat or two at first, and then as the craft became visible. William wore a slight smirk and his eyes twinkled with delight. Rowan was shocked at first, but his expression changed as he realized what he was looking at. He had a look of profound disbelief. The rest of the flatfoots had a bird.

Two grabbed hold of Roy and the sergeant went to the rail, hand on his gun. The youngest of the constables, went as far as to pull his revolver.

"Mary, mother of god!" he shouted, as he held his revolver in both hands and pointed it down, over the rail, "Should we shoot? What is it?"

"Put that gun away!" Rowan shouted, "It some kind of underwater vessel! A submarine!"

Though this craft was nothing like the tubular behemoth I had seen or read about, I was shocked to see it here, in this river. It seemed flatter from our angle and much smaller, only eight or nine feet at most. It was black with brass fittings. Shaped more like a parallelogram with one end more closed than the other. Two large metal cylinders with fins welded on them ran from front to back on either side and there was a visible seam for a hatchway with a thick glass view port located near the bow. A series of wing bolts obviously kept the hatchway sealed. The view port is what I mistook at first, for a giant eyeball.

It was sleek, dark, and mysterious. I had a feeling William was going to want one. Ozaki was the only one with the where-with-all to grab a gaff hook and he pulled the slack lines attached to it until it bumped the side of the *Aunt Polly*.

"That's incredible," Rowan said to my friend, "and you had no idea it was here?"

"I must admit, in all honesty until today I was ignorant of it. But a series of deductions led me to believe in its existence, or something along these lines. You see Inspector, if you follow the pulley system, you will note the extra lines that..."

"Forget the lines William," I interrupted, "even I can see that there are far too many now! How the hell did you raise it?"

"By way of the new bilge pumping system the captain

and Nickolas installed! That is why I checked the bleed off valve when we boarded Frohman. As I suspected there would be, I discovered a hose attached that led to the bottom of the river."

"Another point you neglected to share," I groused. Then I realized something. "Are you telling me that they modified the *Aunt Polly* to service that little black submarine?"

"Oh yes, Frohman. This was no fly by night affair. This was the work of a master criminal who planned it for a year or more."

"Planning what?" I asked stupidly, still not seeing the big picture.

William cocked his head. "You really do not know Frohman?"

He was damn lucky right then that my head was still spinning and whatever Ozaki gave me kept me fairly lethargic, otherwise I'd have choked the life out of him right on the spot! He chose to ignore my crossed eyes and flared nostrils.

"Ah! Well, perhaps I should show you!"

I just hung my head in desperation. Here we were again, another rung to climb on the ladder of resolution and deduction.

"Ozaki," William called. He pointed to the hatchway on top of the craft, and then stretched out his hands, placing one palm over the other and slowly lifting one away gesturing to Ozaki to open the vessel's hatch.

Ozaki nodded and kicked off his shoes, then grabbed the rails as he swung himself over the side and carefully lowered himself onto the submarine. It was riding high enough to keep the little man's feet dry but he needed all his balance to stay up right as it bobbed on the water.

After he had his footing, he quickly went from bolt to bolt and twisted the wing nuts. With his small but strong fingers, he slowly pried the hatch open. He looked up to William, awaiting further instruction. Such was their bond that William didn't even have to speak. He just pointed to pointed down and Ozaki nodded then dropped through the opening.

William, Rowan, and I all leaned over the railing to get a glimpse of the inside of this mysterious craft. What little I could see looked like a set of bicycle pedals and a few levers and ropes, but that's all I could glean before Ozaki popped back into view.

In his hand he held aloft a solid metal case with a pair of hand cuffs dangling from its handle.

An Open Case

There was another solid minute of gawking and then Rowan exploded.

"Jesus H. Christ! Bring that over here!" he commanded, and then turned to us, looking like a man who just found salvation. "Is that what I think it is?"

"I believe it is, Inspector," William said in a sly tone, "The very heart of this matter."

Ozaki climbed out of the hatchway and stepped over to the side of the *Aunt Polly* just below us. Rowan leaned far over the railing and took the metal case from his hand. He turned to Roy,

"Is this a figment of Mr. Gillette's imagination also?"

There was a bit of a ruckus as Captain Roy began to struggle between his guards. He settled down when two of the men drew their weapons and the sergeant lifted a nightstick over his head. Captain Roy looked directly into William's eyes with a promised of revenge at his earliest opportunity.

Inspector Rowan clutched the case to his chest and bellowed out an order to the coppers guarding Roy. "Take the captain and shackle him on the launch immediately!" His order was followed roughly as the four coppers dragged him away.

Wasting no time, Rowan set the case at his feet and knelt down in front of it like it was some kind of make shift alter. He slowly reached for the clasps that braced the front of the case, which were heavily scratched and dented. Obviously someone had broken them at an earlier time.

269

Rowan leaned forward and down to peer at the catches.

"Uh oh! I think the locks have been removed!"

The fear that the case would be empty was etched upon his features.

"Merely drilled out," William amended, "unfortunately in my boat shed."

Gingerly, he raised the lid. Gleaming brightly and set into their own padded slots were two rows of metal bars. Rowan picked one from the middle and turned it face up.

We were looking at the new five dollar bill, etched into a gleaming block of shiny metal, the newest U.S. Treasury's printing plates.

Rowan looked at the plate like he was holding the Holy Grail and then quickly put it back in its place and gently shut the case.

He looked to William, "So it was Roy who was behind the robbery! In the submarine! Of course, that makes perfect sense. How else could you slip on and off a moving ferry! It's ingenious!"

"I would have said diabolical," I put in.

"That too, Charlie," he replied, "But what about Nickolas? Why did Roy kill him? Do you think Nickolas got onto him and Roy had to silence him?"

William sighed and shook his head, "That is a bit naive, Inspector. Do not shed any tears for the former first mate of the *Aunt Polly*. Observe the cockpit of the craft."

We all looked over and I saw what he meant after a moment. "Too small and short. There's no way Roy could have fit in there, much less maneuver."

Rowan's eyes widened even farther, "Nickolas pulled off the caper? He was the one who carved up that agent and took the case?"

"I am afraid so, Inspector. There was a dark side to that lad he hid very well from all us."

A dark cloud fell across the Inspector's visage as a thought struck him.

"Including Catty? I'd hate to think she was mixed up in all this!"

"You may need to interview her and ascertain that for yourself, but I have given the matter some small attention and I believe she was as ignorant as the rest of us... more so perhaps. She was, after all, blinded by love."

"That dirty Russian! I liked him!"

"I know how you feel, Inspector. I was quite fond of the brilliant lad myself. Now I only wish that he was here to hang next to Roy, his ringleader."

"Ringleader?" Rowan exclaimed, "You make it sound like it was a gang or something."

"Inspector, a crime of this magnitude could not have been planned and executed so flawlessly with only two men," William offered in return, "Oh! By the way, you may also have to arrest that Perkin's boy Glenn, from the ferry."

"Glenn?" Rowan returned, "You think he was involved? This time, I'm sure we have to disagree, Sir. Glenn was under intense scrutiny!

"Then answer me this," William said, like a teacher to a student. "Where did he get the water?"

"Beg your pardon, water, did you say?"

"Exactly, Water, Perkin's claimed that he was taking two buckets of water to the horses when he discovered the first agent. He then dropped both buckets on the deck." William looked to me, "Is that how it was told to us Frohman?"

"Yeah," I replied, growing weary of yet another quandary, "So what?"

"So where did he get the water? There were no fresh water barrels on the ferry, nor any indication there ever was, and a man who grew up on a farm and worked on a ferry would surely know the water was far too brackish in that part of the river to be potable, even for horses."

I nearly slapped my head, when I remembered the salt stains on the deck where Glenn dropped the buckets. I knew where my friend was going with this.

"Therefore, I ask again, where did he get the water? The only water he had in those buckets was salt water. The white salt stains on the deck clearly indicated that. No, Inspector. It was simply another ruse."

"My word, Mr. Gillette, that's unbelievable! How did we all miss that?" Rowan said, trying to comprehend.

"Don't beat yourself up Inspector," I said, feeling a bit of a dolt myself. "It was an exotic crime and you were all looking for exotic explanations!"

"Nonsense Frohman!" William said. "It is a lack of logical, deductive reasoning and keen observation. Plain and simple."

Rowan mulled a thought over for a moment and spoke, "So, maybe Glenn needed the water for something other than the horses. I wonder if he meant to use them to cover up Nickolas's tracks. He probably got wet climbing aboard and would have left marks on the deck. Two buckets of water would have covered them nicely. Makes sense. But I hardly think I could arrest him on that slim evidence."

"Actually there are two more bits of evidence, though both circumstantial, but it may be enough to leverage the truth from him." William smirked again. "Failing that, perhaps you could offer him accommodations with the wretched captain."

When William didn't speak up right away, I knew he was looking for his cue, "Go ahead, you show off. What two pieces of evidence?"

"The burnt slingshot and the greasepaint stick men."

Now, I was on the ferry with William every step of the way and I was still in the fog. Rowan was completely lost.

"Say again?"

William just smiled and looked up at the sky. "Perhaps we should save that for later, Inspector. We are rapidly losing daylight if you wish to get those plates to safety and tow the submersible across the river before dark. There will be plenty of time to put the fear of God in Glenn after you have picked him up."

"So that's why you were needling him about Nickolas's death," I interjected. "You were trying to scare the wits out of him, letting him think Roy might be killing off his accomplishes!"

He shrugged, "I am not a sadist by nature, as you well know, but the man aided and abetted a brutal murder and helped to hold our economy for ransom."

Rowan snorted, "It's you he should have feared."

I was beginning to feel a little overwhelmed by all the revelations I had heard in the last hour. It was too much to grasp all at once.

"Could we please just finish what we started this morning, before you two go and lock up half the county? If Roy and Nickolas were in cahoots," I asked, "Why'd he murder him?"

William chuckled and clapped me on the shoulder, "You will have to ask the Captain, though, taking into account the timing, I suspect it had to do with Nickolas's impending nuptials and his desire to relocate with his new bride.

Nickolas may have demanded his share of the ill-gotten gains, or perhaps Roy just couldn't take the chance that he may let something slip down the road or something carelessly whispered between the newlywed's pillows. Whatever the reason, the nexus is tucked under the Inspector Rowan's arm at the moment."

"Yes, and the sooner it's gone from there and in the hands of the Treasury department agents, the better I'll feel!" Rowan exclaimed.

"Well, Inspector, you have your man. You have the printing plates and two crimes solved. Go and reap your rewards," William said magnanimously. "Frohman and I shall look forward to reading about your accolades in the papers."

But, unfortunately for us, that was not the way it was going to happen. Rowan's eyebrows nearly touched and his lips thinned until they nearly disappeared.

"If you think for one minute that I am going back into that hornet's nest with these plates... Captain Roy, no Ozaki, and half a story, you better think again! Not to mention that contraption!" as he pointed at the submersible! "I'll be lucky if Luboff doesn't throw me in a cell for disobeying his orders and taking his prisoner for an afternoon jaunt! I'll need all the luck I can muster just to keep my job! Besides, at the very least, you are both material witnesses. But we all know, in all honesty, you were the lead detective Mr. Gillette. Even without any official standing."

"Our clout, as you put it, is exactly why we should not involve ourselves any further." William argued. "In the end game, our involvement will end up being more of a hindrance than the boon you suppose it to be. I think it best you go on without us."

Once again, Rowan said with exasperation, "You'll have to explain that reasoning to me."

"Inspector, the simple truth is that if William's name is associated with this affair in the least way it will stir up a hornet's nest, the likes of which you have never seen.

And if they need a scapegoat for any negative publicity, you know where the blame will settle." I let my voice trail away, and thinking to myself, Lord help us when the press gets wind of this.

But Rowan could not be swayed.

"This is no longer a discussion, gentlemen. The fact is, I've never taken credit for another man's accomplishment and I don't wish to start now. What you did Mr. Gillette was amazing and there is no way I could pretend to fill those shoes. The launch will leave shortly and the two of you will be on it! So, with that in mind, please meet me on the launch in five minutes with Ozaki too please."

With no further chance to dissuade him, he turned and headed up the bow of *Aunt Polly* towards the police boat.

Dire Aftermaths

As Rowan made his way with the case of currency plates under his arm, I turned to look at my friend, and was shocked. He seemed frozen solid, his body ridged. Only a widening of his eyes and a nervous lip bite. I knew what had him in a tizzy, so I gave him a moment.

About half the time Rowan had given us passed before he turned to me with an almost panicked look on his face.

"Charlie! What are we going to do? When the press gets ahold of this I'll never have a moment's peace! I don't want this kind of attention anymore!"

AAAHH! So it was 'Charlie' again, my true friend was back. I was happy to see him, but I wasn't about to cut him any slack.

"Well? What did you think was going to happen? You think you're going to finger several murderers and save the U.S. economy in one afternoon and then just walk back to obscurity? You're a major part of this riddle William," I scolded. "I warned you! I told you it was going to end badly! Good for everyone else but BAD for you! You can kiss your retirement goodbye, my friend. They're going to be on you like ants," I gestured towards the castle, "and there's no missing that anthill!"

"Oh, don't say that, Charlie!" He almost wailed. "There must be some way to avoid all the hoopla! Think, Charlie! Use that devious mind of yours!"

Truth be told, if his involvement was made public, he would almost have to bow to public pressure and come out of retirement. The public would go ape if he were to write, direct, and star in a production of today's events. Simply because he would never allow anyone else to even attempt to bring this personal experience to the stage. Bottom line, we could make a lot of money, however its money we don't need. In the end, I already had a lot of money and not a lot of friends... and none so fine as William Gillette.

So, before Rowan came back down the walkway to fetch us, I made a plan.

"Now you follow my lead," I whispered out of the corner of my mouth.

"Gentlemen, we must be going," Rowan said brusquely

"Inspector," I said, "We were just thinking..."

Rowan pointed a finger at us, "And you can tell me all about it on the boat."

"That's the thing," I started, then rushed on before he could object. "Now, the sooner Captain Roy is in a cell the safer I'll feel, but I have to tell you, I'm more than a little nervous about riding over on the same tiny boat. Not to mention transporting the plates with the same man who masterminded the theft! Lord only knows if he has any more accomplices lurking about! We would have all our eggs in a basket, or rather launch. Not the smartest idea."

"My word, do you think there are more involved?" He looked about and clutched the case tighter.

"I'm just saying it's a possibility." William looked skeptical but thankfully kept his trap shut.

"So what did you have in mind?" Rowan asked me.

"How about you send Captain Roy over with the constables and the rest of us can follow on the *Aunt Polly,* with the printing plates. In addition to being more comfortable, I'm sure it's a bit too choppy for my head." I touched my bandage and winced. "We could also tow the submarine. Having it with us would surely make the explanations a little easier."

Rowan drummed his fingers on the case, "I didn't think

of that. You may have a point."

"Of course!" I agreed, gesturing at the case in his arms.

"What you say makes sense Charlie. I guess we could do it your way. I'll go tell the launch to make way. How long until we can follow?"

"I'm sure we can be on our way in no more than ten minutes." William replied.

I looked about for Ozaki, who would pilot us across the river and damned if the little bugger wasn't tying the two submersible lines onto the stern cleats already. He finished quickly and hopped on the deck and disappeared from my line of vision.

"We'll cast off while you give your men their instructions," William was saying. "Of course, bring along one or two of your men if you feel the need for extra security."

"I don't think so, Mr. Gillette." He smiled with relief. "I believe the river has gotten much safer as of late. Besides, I want as many men with Roy as possible. He's the dangerous one." He grinned at us, "You two I can handle for a trip across the river."

"That's where you may have made your fatal mistake, my boy." The *Aunt Polly*'s engines roared to life, and I raised my voice slightly, "You forgot about Ozaki!" We all smiled.

Just a Sherry

True to our word, we had the lines cast off and the *Aunt Polly* began to slide away from the dock in a little over ten minutes.

Ozaki went very slowly until the slack from our tow lines was taken up and then William signaled him to throttle up. The three of us watched the black little submarine bob on the water in our wake. Its sleek design easily handled the river's light chop.

"I can't help feeling like we're towing a gigantic black flounder," I observed.

Rowan laughed, "Well, Charlie, you'll be able to top any fish stories back in old Amagansett after today!"

"Wouldn't bother telling it," I replied, "No one would believe this one!" We watched a moment longer, and then I set my plan in motion. I turned to William, "Before we go in, you might want to tell Ozaki to throttle back some," as if I knew what I was talking about. "If that nose goes under, she'll dive for the bottom."

"Of course Charlie. Good thinking. We wouldn't want to lose her at this stage of the game."

"In that case," Rowan said, "I had better use the head. There's no way I'm going to hold it until we get back to the station."

"Certainly Inspector. You know where it is? Through the saloon and left down the hall. Charlie and I will meet you in the saloon."

Rowan headed in and I laughed to myself, wondering if he would put that case down to relieve himself. As soon as he was out of earshot, William looked at me suspiciously.

"There is no way, with those tanks full of air, that the submarine can possibly nose dive for the bottom. Why do you want to slow down? What are you planning?"

"I'm playing for time, William! All we can get! Now, listen to me carefully. When we go inside, you have to tell us the whole story. Everything, every detail, every nuance that led you to your conclusions. Leave nothing out! Hold nothing back! And, for Pete's sake, skip the embellishments. No drama... just the facts, and most importantly, how you arrived at them! Accurate, not verbose is what I need from you! By the time we get across this river, Rowan must know everything you do."

"I don't see how this is going to keep us out of the papers, Charlie!"

"I'm still working on that, but this is important if we're going to have the slightest chance. Do what I tell you!"

He sighed and relented. "I'll tell Ozaki and meet you in the saloon."

William turned and headed up the railing towards the bridge. He hesitated and said, back over his shoulder, "And no Gin! Ozaki says you're not to drink until your swelling goes down!"

"You tell him to drive the boat slowly," I retorted. "I'll decide how to continue my rehabilitation."

William chuckled and turned toward me with a somber expression on his face. "I should have listened to you, Charlie. I'm sorry I dragged you into this whole affair. Had I listened to you, we could have been enjoying a nice relaxing afternoon rather than getting pistol whipped!"

I thought about that for a moment, "Yes, and some killers would have gone free and our economy could have been jeopardized! All in all, a fair trade for such a memorable vacation, I'd say."

"But!" I added, because it needed to be said, "You could

have told me of your plan with the Inspector! If I had known, we could of had help on the way and maybe I wouldn't have this goose egg right now!"

He hung his head in shame, "Your right, Charlie. That was a horrible mistake on my part. I don't know what I was thinking. I..."

"I knew what you were thinking," I stopped him short. "You wanted to see the look on my face when all was revealed! I know you William and dramatics are like air for you. But this isn't just another dinner cruise or party! I trust you with my life, I owe you that much! But from now on, keep me in the know!"

William's eyes widened and he shook his head. "There won't be a next time, Charlie. I am done with it! William Gillette the detective will join Mr. Holmes in retirement."

I had my doubts, but as he seemed near to tears with sincerity, I relented. "Then all is forgiven, William."

I gave him a soft jab on the chin and added. "It wasn't your fault, William. It just happened. To be perfectly honest, it was worth every bit of this goose egg." When he smiled, I added, "Besides, every heroic deed needs a battle scar as a reminder."

He chuckled at that, then got serious. "The last thing I wanted, or want now, is to be a hero Charlie.

I shrugged, "We'll just have to see it through, William. The die is cast as they say."

He nodded and sighed. His sad puppy eyes almost made me laugh but I kept my face straight. He clapped me on the shoulder and spoke. "You are truly a wonderful friend and I can't imagine my life without you in it."

He turned and headed to the bridge to fetch Ozaki.

I was so touched by his words. I think it may have been the most personal thing he had ever said to me in our thirty years of friendship. So touched, I almost called to him and spilled my guts. I knew there was a more than good chance

William and I would walk away from this unscathed. I think he would have seen it himself if he was still in his role.

But there were a few reasons why I didn't spill my guts. One, call me petty, but keeping him in the dark was a little revenge for the way he kept me informed in dribs and drabs all day!

Two, if I even tried to explain the facts to our young Inspector Rowan, I knew he wouldn't relent and we'd have to make a trip to town anyway.

And third, I needed to hear the story from the top to bottom myself! There was still a lot of things I didn't understand and I was damned if I was going to wait any longer for explanations!

So, in a few short moments, Ozaki had cut our speed by half and when William joined us in the saloon, I had a glass in my hand and was pouring another for Rowan, who, to my delight, accepted a victory sherry.

"You know you're not supposed to be drinking, Charlie." he admonished me.

"I'm not," I deadpanned. "It's just sherry."

The Two Rings

I settled into a comfortable chair next to the coffee table and smiled up at William.

"Oh, my mistake, old boy," Will replied sarcastically and motioned Rowan to take a seat on a matching couch across from where he stood. He did so, tucking the case between his feet. After another look around, he downed half his sherry in one gulp. He almost seemed to relax.

When William was sure of our comfort, he gracefully sank into the sister couch to Rowan's and crossed his legs. Throwing an arm across the back, he looked the very picture of the cat that got the cream.

I wanted to point at the still oozing cricket ball on my forehead and wipe the smug look off his face, but I guess he deserved to bask in his success.

"Mr. Gillette," Rowan began, "There are a few points I'd..."

"Just a few, Inspector?" William cut him off. "I would say there were more than a few."

Rowan took a deep breath and his face pinched up. I wanted to scream with frustration! Now was not the time to play the haughty Englishman. Not if he wanted to sneak away from the publicity! My whole plan hinged on Rowan being up to snuff when we reached the other side of the river and in an amenable mood.

Fortunately, William was astute enough to read the young man's face and quickly covered his tracks. "Of course, there is no fault to be laid on your shoulders, Inspector! Your work has been nothing short of solid and professional! If you had not been recalled before the doctor's report, I am sure I would have been nothing more than a bystander in this investigation. Every deduction needs some observation!"

Rowan squinted at us. "I doubt that very much, Mr. Gillette. You have an eye for details that I've never seen the likes of! I'm not sure I would have made half the conclusions you already told me about."

"Hell, Inspector," I said, "I don't get any of it. And I was there! Perhaps William should walk us through it, step by step. I'd like to know just what he deduced and what was a lucky guess before we dock."

I was proud of that little stroke of genius. Not only did I steer the conversation in the direction I wanted, I threw the gauntlet in Will's face. He was sure to get fired up and explain everything.

"Lucky guess, indeed!" William barked, uncrossing his legs and leaning forward to put his elbows on knees. "Focus, Frohman, and try to follow me now." He looked to the Inspector and added, "Perhaps your notebook, Inspector. You may want to refer to your notes and fill in any details you might have missed."

Rowan had it out in a jiff and pencil ready to scribe as William began.

"Earlier today, in Chief Inspector Luboff's crass attempt at humor, he referred to this affair as 'The Case of the Flying Corpse', yet it may have been better named 'A Tale of Two Rings'. For you see gentlemen, it was two rings that really broke this case wide open for us."

"Hold on a minute," Rowan said, looking perplexed, "The engagement ring I know about but what's this all about a second ring. What ring would that be?"

"It was one I removed from Nickolas's hand when we first examined him in my courtyard." William replied. At least he had the sense to look contrite when he said it.

284

Rowan sat back, staring at him hard. "You stole evidence in a murder investigation and then withheld information about it?"

William put up his hands placatingly, "Now Inspector, that was never my intention, and I would remind you, at the time it was not a murder investigation."

"Still--," Rowan began angrily, "You --"

"In light of how things turned out, perhaps we could table this point for now," I said, talking loudly over the both of them. "Inspector, you can toss him in the hoosegow when we get to the station, but the river is only so wide and I really want to hear this before we dock. I'm sure we won't get a moments peace after that!"

Rowan looked undecided for a moment, but then smiled at me. "You're right. I can arrest him anytime." He winked at me, "I know where he lives!"

"And it ain't hard to find!" I replied. Then I gave William the same gesture he gave us all day long and said, "Come on, let's hear it."

William looked back and forth at us, unsure of how serious either one of us was, but when he opened his mouth, a lot of the smugness was gone.

"Frohman and I were enjoying our morning coffee and paper, when Catherine's screaming brought Nickolas's corpse to our attention."

'Good!' I thought to myself, we're back to Frohman. At least I knew he was on track.

"As you know," he went on, "due to the odd positioning of the body, we did not make a closer examination, opting instead to contact the police immediately. When you and the Chief Inspector arrived, Luboff -"

"Pompous Ass!" I interjected.

"Perhaps so, Frohman," he allowed, "but by insisting we forego the examination of the scene and instead question the staff, he laid the first strand of the rope that would go around Roy's neck. Had he not badgered the truth from Catherine, we would have perhaps wasted untold amounts of time and energy chasing false leads. Seeing what Nickolas wore and what he had on him, we might still be speculating on what his plans were."

"So the Chief was right, in his own way," Rowan observed, sounding like a man who wanted it to be true, yet not really believing it himself.

"Nonsense Inspector!" William barked. "Foregoing the examination was a gross negligence! No matter what the cause, any death in which the authorities are summoned, foul play or fate, needs to be reconstructed for the daily police reports if nothing else. That was some of the shoddiest thinking I have ever-"

"Will!" I snapped, tapping my watch.

He hesitated no more than a hiccup and he was off again and back on course.

"There is no need for us to go over our examination at the scene, nor the doctor's observations, except for the singular fact that Nickolas was dead before he mysteriously ended up where he did. Which became obvious when we tried to take the tram down to the *Aunt Polly*."

"Whoa! Are you trying to tell us you already knew how Nickolas flew into your courtyard before we even left the house?" I asked, a bit skeptical.

"I knew as soon as Ollie told us what happened to the tramway."

"How? We hadn't been to the doctor's yet, nor found the strip of cloth. Why did you think it was connected?"

"Because I was already thinking it! Only a catapult or some other devise could have sent a one hundred and eighty pound body such a distance. When Ollie told us of the repairs…" He winked at me "Elementary, my dear Frohman."

I glanced at Rowan who looked like a school boy who just had his knuckles rapped by the headmaster. "Sounds so simple when he says it, eh?"

"The next major fact was the missing engagement ring. I could not pair the way Nickolas was dressed and what he carried on his person, all confirming what Catherine claimed was to be the night of their elopement, yet he had no ring to give her, although she confirmed that he had one for her."

"Not so fast, Mr. Gillette. I'd like to hear a little more about the ring you absconded with!" Rowan put in.

"Patience, Inspector! I will get to that point shortly! But know this, a school ring- on the hand of my lowly boat hand- from the University of Vladinosk nudged at my mind. I only took the ring with the thought of contacting the University for more information about the lad. When Catherine told us he had a degree in Marine Engineering, I wondered why he would work as a deckhand. Especially, someone as proud to wear his class ring on the night of his elopement."

His voice lowered and he seemed to shrink a little, "Ironic that I know more about him in death than I did in life."

Rowan bobbed his head, "I can understand that, Mr. Gillette. But if things had turned out different, you could have been in some serious hot water. Tampering with evidence and hindering an investigation are near capital crimes here in Luboff's little fiefdom! I wonder if even your wealth and prestige would have protected you!"

'You'd be surprised', I thought to myself, but left it unspoken and another argument avoided. We needed to move on.

Rowan broke the ice, "Well, I think we all know what happened to Nickolas and the events on the *Aunt Polly*. What I don't know is what you think transpired on the

ferry the night of the crime and how you made the
connection between it and Nickolas's death or how you
came to suspect Glenn! Not to mention how you came up
with the submarine we're towing behind us!"

Some Apologies

Will slowly took out his cigarette case and lit one before he answered.

"There is no one fact that tied it all together but a series of clues, like dominoes. When the last tile was in place, I merely tipped it over and it led us right to the solution! Had Nickolas not been destined for such an unusual final resting place, we may have never reached the solution to both the crimes!"

"That's so true," Rowan conceded. "If we had found Nickolas at the bottom of the tramway smelling like a sot, I wouldn't have given his death a second thought.

But never did I think there was a connection between Nickolas's death and the theft of the printing plates?"

"At that time, I had not. Though I was pondering what Captain Roy might have been trying to hide as I had not yet tied the two crimes together. Even as we ate lunch at the Inn and you gave us the details of the river robbery, I failed to see a connection. Afterwards, when you were called away, the doctor confirmed my suspicions, basically with the facts that there was no alcohol in Nickolas's system and that he had twin grooves from his shoulder to buttock that would match the gauge on my tram pulley system."

"Not to mention the crushed testicle," I muttered.

"I haven't forgotten that, Frohman," he replied blandly. "I just choose not to dwell on it. The doctor was also of an opinion that it was a blow to Nickolas's skull that was the cause of death, though he could not be absolutely sure."

"So do you think they quarreled and it came to blows?" Rowan mused.

"I'd put my money on a sneak attack, rather than a fight." I claimed.

"Why's that?"

"Hey, Roy might be a big boy," I replied "but we know Nickolas put a trained agent to the deck and killed another by slitting his throat and cutting off his hand to get the case of plates! He was a vicious when he needed to be, have no doubt." I knew I was wasting precious time and led on. "It was when you saw those boys playing in the river and those little scamps snuck up on their friends under that overturned canoe. That's where you came up with the idea of a submarine!"

"I suppose that is right Frohman, although I had no facts at the time to substantiate the theory. That came later after I checked my reference books, as you shall hear. To answer your questions Inspector, we will proceed with my tour of the ferry on my way back home Dr. Blums. My first clue was found on the community bulletin board in the passenger area."

"Oh, William," I said. "You're not going to tell us about those doodles and a code again? Even you can't make 'dancing men' out of those child's scribbling!"

"Oh, but I can." He reached out for Rowan's notebook and pencil which he readily gave over.

William drew for less time than it took me to light a smoke. He turned the book as he set it on the coffee table between Rowan and I, so we could read it right side up.

Not that I was entirely sure, it was a pretty good representation of the doodling we saw on the ferry... a stick figure with a star on the chest and a box with another figure inside and an X marked halfway up on the left side.

The young inspector stared at it for a moment. He gave it some real thought before he spoke. "My daughter is quite the little artist whenever she gets her hands on anything to draw with, so I'll admit that it seems to be a bit, well, a bit symbolic for a child's drawing."

"Symbolic? Where do you see symbolism in that?" I asked, wondering what I was missing.

He shrugged, "One figure inside a house and one on the outside. Also, I can't help but feel there is a connection between the two X's." He looked surprised at himself. "Silly, but there it is."

"Bravo Inspector!" William's face lit up and he clapped his hands vigorously. "I'm sure, in time, you would have broken the code, but to recognize the pattern is an accomplishment in itself."

"Code?" I asked. "Now it's a code?"

The pompous ass just looked at me like I couldn't spell cat. "Let me walk you through it, Frohman. It will speed things along."

He leaned forward and tapped the areas corresponding with his explanation.

"First, as you pointed out Inspector, one figure is inside the 'house' and one outside. Only the house was really the carriage."

Understanding crept across Rowan's face and even I had to admit it was a possibility, but I was stubborn in my role of devil's advocate.

"And second?"

"The key!" Rowan cried out, tapping the X on the figure's chest then the one in the box. "The key that unlocked the carriage! That's how Nickolas opened the door!" He looked at me. "Don't you see, Charles? That's how he knew where to find the key to open the carriage door! It explains how he managed to surprise the agent inside without anyone noticing. He took it after he knocked Rashleigh unconscious!" Rowan sat back and ran a hand through his hair. "That one had us stumped."

I capitulated, "So you think Glenn drew it as a prearranged signal to Nickolas. Why write it in greasepaint though. It's not something I would think you'd find laying around a ferry!"

"Yes Frohman, but it will not wash off or run in the damp air of the river.   And of course, he could leave the can for Nickolas to blacken his exposed skin and thus aid him in his stealth."

"Why did you suspect Glenn? Why not the other man, Gordon, or the captain himself?" Rowan asked. "They all saw Rashleigh put the key in his pocket."

William pursed his lips and shook his head a little. "That should be apparent. As a professional-" he began to admonish Rowan.

"William!" I cut him off, tapping the watch at my waist. "Let's cut to the chase. I want to know as well."

He sat back in a little huff, "Very well! Yes, they all saw where the key ended up, but you will remember that it was Glenn who was assigned the starboard side for the pre-check of that run. He had ample time and opportunity to leave a message in greasepaint, out of sight from the rest of the crew and passengers. The burnt patch on the pouch of his slingshot and fact that the key was returned to Agent Rashleigh's pocket, confirmed everything I needed to know of his involvement."

Rowan began to sputter a dozen questions at his cryptic responses, demanding to know how a sling shot could fit into any scenario with William responding with more lecturing about observation and domino tiles. I only listened with half an ear as I stood to look out the windows. The looming lights of the ferry landing told me we were just about out of time.

"William!" I barked causing them both to quiet and look at me as I sat back down, wincing at the pain the movement caused.

"No more emoting! No more theatrics! Just tell us what you think happened and fill in the details as you go. We are almost to the other side and we'll have to go up and help Ozaki dock in a few minutes!"

He heeded the urgency in my voice and gave his conclusions in a straight forward narrative.

"I believe, on the night of the crime, Captain Roy and Nickolas readied the submersible at my dock and then Nickolas went out onto the river to lie in wait for the ferry. Mostly submerged, it would be near impossible to see him in the twilight. When the ferry passed, Nickolas came alongside and then, his craft hidden by the side of the ferry, gained access by the scupper hole in the passenger area. There he read Glenn's code and perhaps put on the greasepaint. Then he must have sneaked across the deck and rendered Agent Rashleigh unconscious."

"Seems a bit too coincidental that the horses started to act up and Rashleigh had to get down, just in time for Nickolas to wallop him!" Rowan interjected. "He could have never snuck up on him while he was atop the rig!"

"Excellent! Your senses are honing even as we speak! That brings us to the burnt patch on the sling shot, Inspector. I believe that Glenn saw the same problem. So, as Nickolas was coming aboard, he took a small ember from the boiler and used the sling shot to shoot an ember into one of the horse's flank. As you can imagine, when the horse jumped, it set off a reaction from the rest of the team and Rashleigh had to get down to quiet them, and allowing Nickolas the chance to strike. It was then, as he lay there, that Nickolas took the key and proceeded to slaughter the other agent and steal the plates. He then locked the door and stole back to his escape vessel. At that point, he most likely dove beneath the surface and made his way back to the *Aunt Polly* completely unseen."

"So how did the key get back in Rashleigh's pocket?" I

blurted out before I realized I was just further delaying the conclusion.

"By Glenn's last act...I believe, and this is conjecture, though I think you will find it sound. As Nickolas crossed the deck, he put the key down. From the spray of gore you witnessed at the crime scene Inspector, I could not imagine that Nickolas could have returned the key without leaving some blood or stain of some sort on Rashleigh's clothes.

As soon as he was away, Glenn gathered up two buckets of water from the river and carried them out onto the deck. I believe at that point he picked up the key and perhaps he even cleaned it. Then he knocked the buckets over and gave a great cry and hue. As Glenn was the first to reach the body, he could have easily slipped the key back into the vest pocket before bringing Rashleigh around."

Rowan was nodding his head slowly, clearly a believer. "Jesu-" He stopped himself as William's eyes narrowed, "I mean- that's incredible! Quite a bit of neat work there, Mr. Gillette. But how did you discover there was a submersible?"

"That was simplicity itself, really. First off, there was Doyle's maxim that always holds true. So I reasoned that if the ferry was not broached by another craft on the water, or one above it, I was forced to consider an approach from beneath the waves as a strong possibility. I shall admit though, it was the children and the up-side-down canoe that triggered a memory so I could connect to the ring I took off Nickolas's hand. I remembered another aspect the city of Vladinosk was famous for Submarines! Vladinosk, Russia, is the largest submarine base in the world at this time. Nickolas was a bright minded submarine engineer. "

"And that's why we took a look around the boat shed before we confronted Roy, where we found signs of some type of construction." I finished for him. "That was the only place where they could have built something like that, away from prying eyes."

Rowan just looked further awed and William beamed and gave us a gracious nod of his head.

Suddenly I was very tired. I had no desire to hear any more from the pompous ass he was portraying. My head was beginning to throb again and I didn't want to hear the words 'Elementary', 'Observation and reason', or anything else of a condescending nature.

So I slowly got to my feet and reached for my coat. "Now that we're all up to speed, I guess we'd better get up on deck so that contraption we're towing doesn't smash into us when Ozaki slows Polly down."

Rowan closed his notebook and stood quickly, putting out a hand to steady me as I almost lost my balance when I took the weight of the coat off the chair.

"Do sit back down, Charlie! The Inspector and I can handle the submarine." He chortled and rubbed his hands together. "I can't wait to try her out!"

We both turned to look at William and were stunned. William's transformation made us feel like we were kicked in the head by a mule. My true friend stood before us once again. Gone was the haughty expression. The creases in his forehead and lines around his eyes had miraculously smoothed out. His face seemed to flesh out and his ears flatten against his head. I could have sworn his lips swelled half again their size. He stood, back straight but not stiff, his hands folded at his waist and a humble noble expression on his face.

"There is one more thing that needs to be said." William stepped forward and put a hand on Rowan's shoulder. "Inspector… Kevin, I want to offer you my deepest apology for my harsh words and threats this afternoon. My only excuse is that I was distraught when I heard Ozaki had been arrested. We have been together a long time and I was afraid of how he might react."

Rowan laughed, "I can see why!"

He nodded to Will, "And I can see why you're so fond of him. He is quite an interesting character."

William smiled back, "I know you did your best to keep him safe and comfortable, and I'm grateful for that. Again, I'm sorry and I thank you."

"Apology accepted, but you don't have to thank me. It was the right thing to do. In turn, I'm sorry I have to bring your role in this to light, against your wishes. But this is bigger than all of us. It's a federal case and we need to present the solution without any dithering or covering up."

"That too, is the right thing."

Though he looked ill over it, William replied graciously. "I understand Kevin."

Just then a horn sounded from the bridge. Ozaki was letting us know it was time to dock.

"Well if we're all in good standing now, I suggest we get on deck before Ozaki runs into the dock!" I barked.

"Never you mind, Charlie," William admonished, "We can handle what needs to be done!"

"He's right Mr. Frohman," Rowan chimed in, "you are still shaky. Why don't you just have a seat and finish your sherry. We'll collect you once we're tied up. I'm sure there are men on the dock who can help!"

I started to protest, but William held up his hand and spoke sharply. "You are not helping us, Charlie. Do sit down!"

When I saw I was going to lose this argument, I threw my coat over my shoulder, "Fine!"

I started walking towards the door that led to the pilot house and growled "I'll go make sure Ozaki doesn't run us aground."

Bumpy Ride

Ozaki needed no supervision docking the *Aunt Polly* as he had done this a thousand times before. Ozaki did assist me with a little more of his magic potion which I drank down, and shortly thereafter the throbbing dulled.

Ozaki fussed a bit more over my wound and changed the dressing, and soon we were ready to join William and the Inspector on the dock. The *Aunt Polly* was secured and a group of coppers had managed to pull the submersible up onto the end of the dock.

I joined Rowan who held the case of plates closely. William was peering into the submarine, looking like the kid who got a new sled for Christmas and anxious to find a snowy hill. When he saw me out of the corner of his eye, he straightened and hustled over to us.

"Ah! There you are Charlie! You really should look inside her! I could use your help."

"That is going have to wait Mr. Gillette." Rowan said firmly. "Our first priority is to get the plates to the station. My men tell me a senior official from the Treasury department that showed up this evening and he's raising holy hell around the department."

"Well, imagine the look on his face when you drop these in his lap," I said, tapping the case with my cane. "You'll be quite the hero."

He grunted, "I'll be happy enough just to get them out of my possession. Dang things are heavy! I've sent for a wagon and the four of us can wait by the road. We'll go right to the station and close this case!"

"I'll have to make two amendments to that plan, Inspector," William spoke up, "Ozaki stays on the *Aunt*

297

Polly."

"I think not!" Rowan said indignant. "He is a part of this and there is no way I'm going to release this prisoner without authorization. Luboff would have an apoplexy!"

William was adamant, "Nevertheless, Ozaki stays on the ship. I will not subject him to any more interrogations! He won't respond to them anyway and quite frankly, I do not trust Chief Inspector Luboff with his safety. You have Charlie and I, and if that is not enough, I will just cast off and we shall sail home! You can have the full cooperation of just Charlie and I, or you can get a warrant for the three of us."

"And while you're doing that, we'll get our lawyers and turn this into a real three ring circus," I spoke in support of my friend. I was so pleased to hear him call me Charlie again! The only thing that could pull my plan apart was more of his showing off.

Rowan glared at us for a moment and slowly came to realize what he might be up against and he relented.

"Fine then," he said with little grace, "but he stays here. On the Yacht! In case someone needs to talk to him. And if I were you, I'd let him know." Rowan went on, warning, "If someone does come to fetch him we will have none of that spinning and kicking! If he starts that, someone might plug him for sure!"

"You needn't worry, Inspector," William replied with a touch of exasperation. "It's not in his nature to resist. In all the years I've known him, he has only used that fighting style twice. Both were in defense of me."

Rowan nodded, "If you say so, but even empty-handed, I consider him to be armed and dangerous and I'm sure the men do too after what they saw earlier! Now, what's your second condition?"

"Just that we make a stop along the way and have the doctor take a look at Charlie here. If you feel the need to press on, we can join you later."

Rowan snorted, "As if I'm going to let you two out of my sight before I turn these plates over and the grilling begins!"

I could see that William was going to get all huffy, and we won the Ozaki round, so I stepped in. "I'm fine, William. Ozaki fixed me up good." I pulled my hat onto my head, tilting it so the brim didn't touch my goose egg. My reflection in the window had a rakish look to it that I liked.

"Let's just get this over with. Besides, I'm sure the good doctor is three sheets to the wind by now. I wouldn't let him near me after swilling that rot gut he served this afternoon."

William sighed, "I suppose you're right Charlie. I just worry."

"If Mr. Frohman needs anything, I'm sure we can provide it at the station." He tilted his head, listening, "I think I hear the wagon now."

The wagon, to my dismay, turned out to be a noisy bouncing metal monster. I was already wincing at the pain I thought the ride would bring. I was even more uncomfortable when it pulled up alongside us and I discovered it was what the cops in New York City called a 'Paddy Wagon'. The windows had bars and the single door on the back had a massive lock.

Not only did the three of us get in the back, but four of the constables climbed in. Two sat on either side of William and I on one bench and the Inspector was flanked by a pair on the other.

At first I thought that Rowan was just being a bit paranoid, but when we didn't start moving after a few minutes, I grew weary.

"Before we go to the station, Mr. Gillette, there's just

one more point I'd like to clean up."

On his guard, William replied, "Whatever I can do, Inspector. I am at your disposal." He looked pointedly at the two flatfeet next to us, "Or am I in your custody?"

Rowan didn't answer the question and I could swear his hand was edging towards his revolver.

"You said that you had never laid eyes on the submersible before today, did you not?"

I was growing nervous by the second, but William just seemed amused. "That is correct, Inspector."

Rowan's eyes narrowed, "Then explain how you had a working knowledge of it. You sent Ozaki down to the engines to do whatever it was that raised the submarine."

William clapped his hands, absolutely delighted.

"Excellent Inspector! I thought you might have missed that point, although it did take you a little long to see its implications."

I just stared at him, aghast. Could he really be admitting to complicity?

Rowan did not share my friend's delight, "Just answer the question Mr. Gillette. It's far too late for games!" This time, I'm sure his hand was on his pistol behind the case in his lap.

William just held up his hands in a placating gesture. "Forgive me, inspector. I would not play games, it's just my nature to be theatrical. To be truthful, I really had no working knowledge of the submarine. When Charlie and I looked the boatshed over, and I realized that some type of submersible could have been built. It made me think of some overages in Captain Roy and Nickolas's expenditures."

"I remember you mentioning that yesterday," I put in. I winked at Rowan, "He's a bit Scottish that way."

William shot me a look. "In turn, that made me think of the money the two had spent on the *Aunt Polly* and the new bilge pumping system they installed. This system had air pumps built into it, which I figured could be used to service a submarine. When we first boarded the *Aunt Polly*, I checked the bleeder valve below the water line and found a tube was attached to it, longer than my cane could reach."

"That's true!" I spoke out. "I was wondering what he was doing lying on the engine room deck groping for God knows what!"

"Ergo, I deduced that the tube most likely ran to the submersible. Just logical steps Inspector. No prior experience."

Rowan didn't look quite convinced, "So you sent Ozaki down to turn on the pumps in the hopes the submarine would rise like you wanted?"

William shrugged and smiled, "I assumed if the air was pumped into it, it would rise."

"And what if it didn't?" I asked.

He shrugged again. "Then we would have had to pull it up by hand." He looked around at all of us, as we just stared at him in amazement. "Wouldn't that have been mundane!"

Rowan and the coppers relaxed and we continued to bounce and sway our way across town. William fidgeted and bit his lip. He was dreading the pandemonium that he feared was soon to ensue. I suppose I could have allayed his anxiety, but somehow I found the fortitude to let him stew.

Giggling to myself, I noticed a similar look on the Inspector's face and asked, "Why the long face? This is your moment of triumph!"

"Not till I get past Luboff," he said remorsefully. "I can't help but think he'll find an excuse to dismiss me out of jealousy or spite when all this is said and done."

"I wouldn't worry about that fool," William said sternly. "If I am to be in the spotlight, once again, I promise you I shall turn it on him and expose him for the narrow-minded ninny he is!"

"There you go, Inspector," I said and added as casually as I could, "Besides, even if you were to be dismissed, you'd have a job as soon as you wanted one. That much I can promise you."

He was startled. "How's that?"

I shrugged, "I'll take you on, of course. I could always find a use for a man of your talents and pay you better than this town to boot!"

"But I don't know anything about the theater business."

"I don't need you for that. I need your real talent... detective work."

"There is a rather slimy underside to the theater business, Inspector." William backed me up. The arts have always had a fringe of criminal elements and it has grown in recent years along with the business aspect."

"I hire Pinkies all the time," I explained, "I have to battle the skimmers, wreckers, thieves, con men and the worst of them all, the union organizers. Damn unions are trying to put me out of business! Believe me, son, there is plenty to do for a man with your experience.

It's the same work you're doing now, except bodies don't usually turn up unexpectedly first thing in the morning, and there is less paperwork."

He laughed but then looked at me seriously as the two cars came into view, "Thank you, Mr. Frohman. I appreciate the offer, but I'd rather stay close to home. At least till the babe's born."

"The offer is open-ended, Inspector," I assured him, "In the meantime, stand your ground!"

He squared his shoulders and patted the case in his arms, "You're right! It's time I stood up to that windbag!"

The Deal

There was a constable on the front steps of the station when we pulled up and when we got out, he darted inside. Apparently our arrival was awaited with some anticipation. Rowan stepped in front of us to face his men.

"Remember, not a word about this until I turn this case over to the Chief. If that lot inside the station catch wind of it, we'll find ourselves in a rugby match!"

"Lord help us," William whined in a whisper. "You know Charlie, once we go inside it's all going to blow up in my face."

"Just do what you do best, William." I whispered back.

"And that's what?" he countered.

"Smile and look good," I grabbed his arm for emphasis, "and, for God's sake, stay yourself! Anything to do with either murder, let me do the talking!"

That was all we had time for before we were through the doors and entered into chaos. It seemed like the muckety-muck from the Treasury department brought the entire force with him. Thank God Rowan had the foresight to swear his men to secrecy. As it was, it looked like everyone associated with law enforcement within ten miles was buzzing around the inside of a modest sized room like bees in a hive.

Groups of men huddled around tables or pointed at maps, all of them shouting questions or shouting answers. At the far end of the room we saw Roy, shackled hands and feet, being lifted off a chair and escorted towards a thick oak door with bars that led to the holding cells.

He didn't speak, but he gave us a smug smile and a slight

nod just before he passed through the door.

"I wonder if he'll be that cocky when they put a rope around his neck," I commented.

We were mostly ignored by the men in plain clothes, but the uniformed officers seemed to know what we were about. As we made our way across the room, we could hear them question and comment to each other and the four coppers that came in with us. Several men commented on the strange metal case in Rowan's white knuckled hand.

"Are they in that case then?"

"Where did they turn up?"

"Who's that with Rowan? I don't recognize them. What department are they in?"

"Jumping Jehoshaphat! That's William Gillette!"

"Of course it is! You think he knows something about Nickolas ending up dead on his doorstep this morning?"

"Which one's Gillette?"

That one made William and I smile.

The clamor was reaching a crescendo, when the roar of one word silenced the entire station.

"ROWAN!"

Everyone stopped talking at once and looked in the direction that the scream came from. Filling his doorway with his bulk stood Chief Inspector Luboff, his face beet red and his pig eyes crossed with rage.

"In my office. NOW!" He bellowed in the silence and stuck two fingers, like a claw, at William and I, "And bring those two with you!"

With that, he wheeled and disappeared inside.

I'll hand it to Rowan, while the rest of the room looked at us like we were being sent to the principal's office; Rowan just tucked the case high in his arm and gave one of our escorts instructions, who darted off. After checking to see if we were still behind him, Rowan marched right through the doorway Luboff just cleared. I had barely shut the door behind us when Luboff started bellowing like a wounded bull.

"Where's the little Japper?" he snarled. Luboff was so angry he didn't even notice the case Rowan held in front of him. William took a deep breath and I knew he was about to blast into Luboff, but I stepped on his foot. I didn't want the chief any more riled up if my plan was going to work.

But that didn't seem too likely at the time. The Chief just kept ranting.

"What has gotten into you? First, you take my prisoner without permission and it looks like you even managed to lose him somewhere! Then you commandeer the launch and pull six men from their assigned duties, all without authorization! Of all the stupid, idiotic-"

I drowned the rest out as I was fascinated by Rowan's reaction to the chewing out. As a boss myself, I was sure that Luboff was going to can him as soon as he finished chewing him out, but Rowan just looked at his chief like he was seeing the wall behind him.

Calmly, with insults washing over him like waves at the beach, he set the case on the edge of Luboff's desk. Luboff's rant slowed, puzzled by his subordinate's actions. The list of Rowan's faults died off completely as he popped the lid open, lifted it, and spun the case in Luboff's direction, all in one fluid motion.

He stepped back and clasped his hands behind his back with a wry look on his face. Luboff's reaction was priceless, worth almost everything we went through. The words he was shouting stuck in his throat, his eyes bulged like a stepped-on frog and the color drained from his face. He pushed his glasses up his nose and peered closely at the gleaming printing plates. Then he collapsed into his chair looking like a gaffed fish.

After a moment of his eyes rolling in his head, he looked up at Rowan in a much more subdued tone and asked, "Did the Japper have them?"

Being the last thing we expected to hear, William and I just looked to one another and shook our heads sadly in unison. Rowan, his ears still burning from Luboff's tirade, just shook his head in disgust and said through gritted teeth, "With all due respect, Sir... you are ignorant about these murder cases, and did more harm than good in our quest to find these printing plates!"

Both William and I were delighted and nodded our approvals. Chief Luboff did not find it amusing. He was not a man used to being insulted by the men under him and, plates or no plates, he was about to take umbrage as he sprang to his feet.

Before he could go on the attack, the door to his office burst open and two men in dark suits barged in. The lead man focused his sight on the case and his face lit up.

"Good lord! You have them!" he cried out and rushed forward. I had to step to the side, pulling William along with me or we'd have been bowled over. By the time he reached the case another dozen or so men had crowded in after him.

I maneuvered William and myself to the back of the office. As the back slapping and congratulations started to fly, I bade William to stay put, pull his collar up, and his hat down, and to keep his mouth shut. I then pushed my way to the center of the melee.

As I squeezed my way through the celebrants, Rowan saw me and with obvious relief, introduced me to the man who first entered the office, Assistant Director of the Treasury, Rippel.

"He's the liaison for the Treasury Department in this matter," Rowan explained.

"Actually, I'm the the Undersecretary," the man clarified, "I was sent here to oversee the recovery of the plates and also taking the opportunity to visit my father who lives in Chester, his name also Charlie. Rowan here tells me you and Mr. Gillette were instrumental in the return of the printing plates. The nation owes you both a debt of gratitude."

"Perhaps you could assist us in a pressing matter.," I said with my most winning smile. "Could we have a few words in private?"

We stepped away from the crowd that was still trying to get a glimpse of the plates, and I quickly made my proposal. He knew he had no choice but to accept, but the politician in him made him barter.

"You do realize that the two incidents are separate and we have no real control over the murder investigation."

"I assured him that his influence in this matter carried ample weight with the town officials and added, "If we're in for a penny, we're in for the new five dollar plate," I assured him.

He considered for a moment, and then nodded, "I think we have an arrangement, Mr. Frohman." He held out his hand and I shook it.

"Outstanding," I replied, then added, "You may have to coax Inspector Rowan a little. He has a sense of right and wrong that may be a bit naive under these circumstances."

"Mr. Frohman, President Wilson himself instructed me to settle this matter quickly and discreetly." He caught Rowan's eye and beckoned him to join us. He leaned in close to me and said in a low voice, "Perhaps you'd like to take a trip to Washington. I'm sure the President would be happy to express his thanks in private of course."

I shook my head, chortling inside. "Not necessary, already met the man." I leaned even closer to him and added in a conspirator voice, "William doesn't like him much."

I winked and turned away to fetch William as Rowan
stepped over to the Undersecretary. Rippel had already put
us out of his mind and didn't even glance at us as he began
talking the young Inspector intently in a low voice. I took
my shocked friend by the arm to make our escape.

William and I had just reached the door when Luboff
called out, over the chaos in the room.

"Where do you two think you're going? I'm not through
with you."

"Chief Luboff!" Rippel barked and in the ensuing
silence said in a threatening tone, "Sit down and stay quiet
until I get to you!"

As I opened the door for William and I to slip out, Rippel
told everyone to clear the room except for the Chief and
Rowan. "Now, Inspector Rowan, let's hear your report."

Curious, we stepped to the side as everyone filed out. I
left the door slightly ajar and we waited to listen as Rowan
cleared his throat and started to speak.

"Well gentlemen, you see, oddly enough a missing
engagement ring was the key to my investigation."

The Curtain Falls

With the excitement over and our escape secured, the rest of my stamina drained from my body. By the time we made the walk to the *Aunt Polly*, my head was throbbing again and my stomach was doing flips.

Ozaki took one look at me and started fussing all over again. He gave me another dose of his magic potion and William settled me on the bed of his stateroom, taking a chair for himself. Ozaki gathered a quick bite for us from the galley then got us underway.

The sky was just turning color, muted reds and yellows as the sun set across the valley. With William's castle as a backdrop, I felt like Arthur riding his bier to his final resting place on the Isle of Skye.

"Feeling any better, Charlie?" he asked.

"Much," I replied. Whatever Ozaki was giving me, it was doing the trick. Just a little tired."

"Then you have to tell me, Charlie. How did you talk our way out of Luboff's office so quickly?"

"Easy as pie, my friend," I said. "Just good timing and a little fast talking. Lucky for us, someone with more power than Luboff showed up. And he was a politician!"

"I thought he was with the Treasury Department?"

"Yes he was William, and a reasonable politician. Politicians I can deal with. They know how to give and take and are more concerned with image. It's the do-gooders like Rowan you can't sway. I just pointed out to Undersecratary Rippel that if our involvement became public knowledge, there was no way they could keep the theft of the plates quiet and that would make quite a stink from coast to coast."

Then I added, "The fact that the nation's confidence in the Treasury Department would surely suffer if it was known that a retired actor solved the mystery that had them stumped! Furthermore, in case news of the robbery did get out, I suggested that it would be a far better thing that the bright young Inspector Rowan, working with his department of course, made the arrests and recovered the plates. Believe me, it didn't take much convincing. In fact, he was the one who suggested we 'detach ourselves from the situation' as quickly as possible. That's when I grabbed you and made a beeline for the door."

He reached over and squeezed my shoulder, "You are a sly old fox, Charlie. It never occurred to me that our involvement would be such bad publicity."

"That's because you don't look at the big picture, William!! You're more a detail man, which is why you're so good at your craft."

"I suppose," he agreed reluctantly, with sadness in his eyes I could see through.

"What's bothering you now?" I asked him point blank.

He stood up and walked over to gaze out the window. He sighed and said softly, "All of it I guess, Charlie. I've been so wrapped up with building my home and planning my retirement that I failed to see what was under my very nose.

I should have been able to prevent this whole affair! Now, two men are dead and another two will hang for it. Not to mention that Rashleigh's career is ruined and the pain it has caused a great many others."

"You're worried about Catherine, aren't you?" It was so like him to get caught up in a side bar.

"How could I have been so blind?"

"Don't be an ass!" I snapped at him. There was no way

you could have foreseen this quagmire." I struggled to get through his melancholy.

"Think about this. Captain Roy and Nickolas didn't just wake up one morning and decide to build a submarine! They must have had prior knowledge of the shipment, the route it was taking, and a general time frame to pull it off and they must have known about it months ago. So, everything that happened after he introduced himself to you must have been carefully planned and that it would take more organization and resources that anyone ever imagined. Your construction of the castle was the perfect cover for their operation. As farfetched as it sounds William, it was fate with a lot of evil genius to shape it."

He spun to face me and I was gratified that I finally had the chance to amaze him.

"Good lord! You're right, of course. Roy must have had a network working on his plan for the last year... perhaps even years!"

"And you bested him in a day." I said.

"Maybe, but I don't feel much like a winner. I don't think I'll be able to trust anyone new for quite some time to come. People only seem to bring me grief."

"Does that include me?" I asked, half teasing.

He shook his head sadly, "No, no, Charlie, never you. But I do think it's time for me to step out of the public eye. I just want to finish my home in peace and live a quiet life."

The sadness in his voice bothered me. I hated to hear him talk that way. I knew him well enough to know that he was best in social situations and I truly believe that it would be the world's loss if he took up the life of a hermit.

Yet, I know how sensitive he is, no matter how much the other persona relished the challenge, the real William would be grieving for the lost and shattered lives. I could only hope that when Roy was hung and Perkins locked

311

away, he would be able to put it behind him and move on.

"Tomorrow's another day, and I meant to tell you have a new obligation to take care of after I depart. Undersecretary Rippel's father lives here in Chester. We both enjoyed his bread pudding recipe during lunch at the Inn. As part of Rippel's bartering, he requested that you treat his father to lunch at the Inn. William, you will have the chance to make a few friends in town. Just don't slip into your Sherlock mode. Maybe he can recommend a few good men to replace your captain and first mate.

"Charlie, thank you. Really, thank you for this." William went silent for a long minute. "Tomorrow we shall sleep in, then we continue our breakfast. You can swill drinks all day while we relax!"

"Sounds perfect," I mumbled, "As long as we don't find any more bodies outside your front door," I joked, as the darkness gently folded over me.

Epilogue

It was a week later and I was back in my office, tidying up my affairs before my trip to Europe, when the phone on my desk rang. My secretary put down her pad and answered it, then held it out.

"It's Mr. Gillette. He says it's important."

I snatched the phone from her, "Well hello, William. Calling to announce your comeback already?"

"Not likely, Charlie. I'm afraid I have some rather serious news. Can you speak freely?

"Hang on a moment," I answered, and said to my girl, "Can you give me a moment please?" She nodded and left the office, closing the door after her. I put the piece back to my ear, "What can I do for you William?"

"Captain Roy has escaped."

"What?" I asked as chill went down my spine, "How?"

"It happened when they were transferring him to the federal prison at Fort Leavenworth by train. There was a stop in Maryland and a group of men boarded the train. They shot it out with the federal agents escorting Roy and most were killed and Roy vanished."

"Damn. He must have a bigger organization than we thought! Do you think he'll come after us?"

There was silence on the other end, then William said "I don't know Charlie. I would think it too risky for him to show his face around here for a good long while, but you saw how he looked at us."

"How concerned are you? Do you think I should hire Rowan to try and track him down?"

"I doubt Rowan would be interested. He got quite a promotion for his recovery of the plates and a new baby on the way. I won't fault him though, an expectant father should not be taking risks with a killer like Roy. Besides, I'm not sure he is the right choice to track down Roy."

"Yeah, I suppose you're right. How about some Pinkies then?"

"No, Undersecretary Rippel from the Treasury contacted me just to let me know and he assured me that there was a massive man hunt in progress and he feels confident Roy will be recaptured quickly."

"Sure thing," I scoffed, "But how confident are we in them?"

"Until they catch Roy I'll be looking over my shoulder. I'm glad you're heading across the pond for a while. I doubt Roy will chase you across the Atlantic."

"And what about you? We both know that Roy wants to get his hands on you a lot more than he cares about me. What are you going to do? I doubt Luboff is going to break his back to watch yours!"

William laughed, "That's a moot point, Charlie. Luboff decided to retire and now he's relocating to Florida."

"Florida is a good place for him, and the town of Chester will be a lot better off without him around."

"William, did they finally pick up Glenn Perkins?."

There was a long pause. "Of course, you haven't heard. Perkins is dead."

"No! Really! What happened?"

"A day after you left, Rowan sent two men to pick Perkins up for questioning. They found him at the ferry but Perkins saw them approach and ran to the back of the ferry and armed himself with a length of chain. The officers tried to reason with him, but he took a few swings at them with the grapple hook and they were forced to draw their revolvers."

"Shot him down, eh? I guess it saved the courts from having to hang him."

"They never fired, Charlie. He wrapped the chain around his neck a few times and before they could reach him, jumped overboard. Officer Steele dove in after him and made a heroic effort to bring him to the surface, but couldn't. His last words were, "I didn't know they were going to kill anyone.""

"My word!" I exclaimed, "The poor kid got himself in over his head. No pun intended." I added.

"William, I suggest you have Ozaki stock the *Aunt Polly* and you both should take an extended vacation until Roy is caught. Go to Greenport for the summer, or better yet, up the coast to Canada. Or even better, learn how to work your new submarine. It's a cinch he won't catch you in that!"

"Oh, don't joke about that, Charlie! That is a sore subject with me."

"Why?"

"Because when I called Rowan to see when I could get my submarine back, he told me that the Navy came and confiscated it. Under the pretense that it was 'evidence in a federal crime'. And when I pressed my claim directly with the Navy, they told me I would be duly compensated but the submarine was of 'interest to our national security.' Apparently, young Nickolas made some innovations for the balance of ballast and air pressure, or some such nonsense. Apparently, those tanks not only provided air for the operator but could regulate the ballast with water to allow it to change depths more readily…"

A thought occurred to me, "So the miniature submarine that was built by a Russian submarine engineer and paid for by a private U.S. citizen, and used to steal U.S. Treasury printing plates, is now the U.S. Navy's newest prototype submarine."

"Exactly!! Bravo! I could not have said it any better. I would have loved to examine it at my leisure."

I laughed, "Man o man, you wanted that new toy, didn't you? You're just a kid at heart, William. You're lucky they didn't take the *Aunt Polly* also."

He laughed, "I know, Charlie, but think how thrilling traveling under water would have been!"

"Then build your own, Man! You've got the coin and the brains and you have half the system on you yacht! If you make another with a few updates I bet you could sell it to the Navy."

He laughed, "It's a bit more complicated than that, my friend. Besides, I have another project on a grander scale in mind."

"If you say so," I replied, but he didn't bite. I guess I'll have to wait for that one too.

"Well, whether it is by land or sea or under the sea or over the land, you should take a trip until Roy is dead, or at least locked away!"

"Maybe, Charlie, but I think I'm safe enough for the moment. I fulfilled my obligation and took Charlie Rippel to the Inn for lunch. I even dressed in some old cloths to fit in with the town's people. We had a grand time and he introduced me to a half dozen new friends. They all pledged to keep their eyes and ears on alert for any new strangers in town. We have a regular weekly gathering planned at the Inn. Thank you again for the obligation. With your help, I made more progress fitting in with Chester's township in a week, than in the past five years."

I swallowed hard, knowing how much William wanted to fit in with the township. "William, sounds like you finally found your way around in that Yankee town. Better get your smaller launch out the boat shed and in the water. You don't want to scare your new friends away by taking the *Aunt Polly* over to Inn just for lunch. And keep wearing those old cloths!"

"Thanks for the advice Charlie. So, when are you leaving for London?"

"I sail next Friday."

"Excellent! Bon Voyage! What ship are you taking?"

"Why, William, my boy, the only one I ever take, the Lusitania!"

JMW
May, 2016

William Gillette Facts

William Hooker Gillette was born in Nook Farm, a small town near Hartford Connecticut on July 24, 1853. It was an intellectual and literary center where Mark Twain and Harriet Beecher Stowe resided. Mark Twain urged William Gillette to take to the theatrical stage.

Charles Frohman was William's theater business partner and they brought Sir Conan Doyle's Sherlock Holmes character to the stage for thirty years.

William Gillette hired Yukitaki Ozaki as his butler in 1890. Ozaki served as his butler for 30 years. Yukitaki came from a wealthy Japanese family, and when his family finally visited the castle, he was so embarrassed by his humble servant position, that it was agreed that William and him would switch roles. William faithfully served Ozaki throughout the visit.

The Aunt Polly was William Gillette's boat, a 144 foot luxury steamer. During the five years of constructing the castle (1914 to 1919), William lived comfortably aboard the Aunt Polly.

Gillette spent approximately 1 million dollars which is about 14.5 million dollars in 2016 to build his castle estate.

William Gillette called the castle, Seven Sisters. The castle is now a state park in Haddam Connecticut and is appropriately called Gillette's Castle and is open to the public. The castle has twenty-four rooms and forty-seven unique doors. Material for the castle was transported along the Connecticut River and moved up the hill by horse and wagon, and a tram which Gillette designed.

Biography

J.M. Walker is a professional chef by trade with over forty years experience.

His love of the New England coastline, local history, and mystery classics has inspired him to pen this mystery. He has been creating books set along the Connecticut shoreline since 1998.

He lives in Mystic, Connecticut with his wife Denise, his oldest son Gordon, and his son's many reptiles. His youngest son Collin is proudly serving in the military.

**New Collection of William Gillette
Mysteries Coming in 2017**

One Part Suicide

Murderous Musketeer

Beginnings on Broadway

JM Walker is on Facebook
Amazon.com
Kobo.com
Local Connecticut and Rhode Island Book Stores